AN EVANS NOVEL OF THE WEST

STOP

RICHARD S. WHEELER

M. EVANS & COMPANY, INC.   NEW YORK

Library of Congress Cataloging-in-Publication Data

Wheeler, Richard S.

  Stop. / Richard S. Wheeler,
  p.   cm.—(An Evans novel of the West)
  ISBN 0-87131-547-5
  I. Title.   II. Series.
PS3573.H4345S7 1988
813'.54—dc19   88-15732

M. Evans and Company, Inc.
216 East 49 Street
New York, New York 10017

Manufactured in the United States of America

9 8 7 6 5 4 3 2 1

For Dale and Alice Walker

Chapter One

Sam Stop didn't look like a banker. He was tall and lean and weathered brown and too young, maybe thirty. His chestnut hair showed no sign of gray. His black eyes smoldered and mocked and took the measure of men—and women. His tan lips neither compressed nor lay loose but usually settled into a knowing grin that suggested an intimate knowledge of man's sins and weaknesses. Those who regarded him shrewdly usually concluded he was much better banker material than the soft, pasty-white, officious, arrogant variety.

Sam Stop had shown up in Pony unknown. No one had ever heard of him, no one had ever seen him. That happened three years before, in the spring of 1879. He had ridden in on a tall bay gelding with a roached mane, engaged a room at the Goldstrike Hotel, the best in town, and then had set out on foot to survey the town. He was a whipcord figure wearing a black broadcloth suit, boiled white shirt, and string tie.

There were many in Pony who remembered that day well. The unnamed stranger was a striking man, pacing each street deliberately, pausing occasionally before homes and mercantiles, as if to fathom the character of their owners. The houses of Pony ranged from crude log cabins, scattered aimlessly, to white frame buildings with high peaks and gingerbread around the porches and eaves. All these he studied earnestly, and then walked on up to the mine above town, the shanties and hoist beams of the Pony Consolidated Mining Company, whose shafts pierced hard into the bowels of the Tobacco Root Mountains towering to the west. He said nothing to anyone. Eventually old Dudley, the white-haired constable, had waylaid the stranger.

"You're looking for something. Anything I can help you with?" Dudley had asked, half suspiciously, letting his star glint in the morning sun.

Sam Stop had smiled, revealing even, white teeth. "No, nothing, Constable," he had said, and wandered off.

Dudley had shrugged. To all appearances the stranger was unarmed, give or take a hideout gun in the folds of his black suit. The man didn't seem dangerous. Dudley had retreated in defeat to his wicker chair under the tin-roofed porch of Spade's Mercantile, from which vantage point he had a clear view of the entire business district sloping uphill and down. Pony was a town perched on a grade.

So they watched, Dudley in his squealing wicker and the duffers on the splintered wood bench, as the stranger paced the streets and measured Pony, stopping at empty lots now and then, and in one case pausing for a long time before a corner lot with a tent saloon, a holdover from the early days. They speculated about him. He didn't quite fit any pigeonhole. Wasn't a cowboy or a drover. Too well dressed for that. Not a teamster, either. Not an indoor man, because he was weathered nut-brown, and muscle rippled beneath the suit coat. They settled on gambler as the likeliest possibility, and indeed the stranger was dressed like one. But the hands were wrong. They were work-hardened, not soft and deft. And those black, piercing eyes didn't slide on and off a person the way a gambler's glance did.

By noon the gambler had, it seemed, paced every street in Pony, taken the measure of every building, and studied every man on the street: the Irish and the Cornish Cousin Jacks off-shift, the merchants, the duffers on Slade's porch, and even the

2

children. Nor had he stopped at the edges of town. He had probed outward in several directions, up along the creek where more mining shanties perched, and off to the south where there were a few log cabins with pasture and gardens around them. Whenever the giant gray-weathered ore wagons squealed and rumbled down the mountain, with teamsters wrestling the brakes, the stranger had paused thoughtfully, eyeing the glistening white quartz rock in their bellies, rock pierced with strings and dots of gold.

For a while Constable Dudley had imagined the stranger was planning a robbery. But it didn't fit. Who'd rob raw ore? Anyone set upon robbing would go for the gold bullion stored down below, on the river, where Pony Consolidated had its stamp mill and reduction works and an office with a safe in it where bullion was stored.

So that didn't figure, either, and that made Dudley cross. He was used to knowing everything that happened in Pony.

A little after noon the stranger headed for the hotel for lunch. The hotel was a whitewashed frame building with clapboard siding, unlike most of the buildings in Pony. The dining room there served pretty hoity-toity food, Dudley thought. Better, anyway, than Ma Bell's joint, or that foreigner Enrico's long, dark place that smelled of olive oil and pasty flour things. On impulse the old constable followed the stranger into the small, dark lobby, and when the man had vanished into the dining room, Dudley had gimped toward the front desk and hunted down a name in the registry. He found it soon enough. Sam Stop, written in a huge copperplate hand, twice as large as most men write. The room had been rented for one night.

Sam Stop. A made-up name. No one could be named Stop. Maybe an outlaw name, a hideout name. A no-good name. It wasn't a name on any of the dodgers in his office, he was sure of that. Not that an outlaw would use a name on dodgers. Dudley thought he'd go through the mess of dodgers, anyway, just to check. Not that dodgers ever did any good. The descriptions were poor, the drawings primitive, and not once in twenty years of lawing had he ever caught a man as a result of seeing a dodger.

Dudley didn't want to do it, not on a fifty-a-month constable's salary—when they bothered to pay, which was always an interesting question in his life—but he did it, anyway. He hunkered into a padded chair in the dining room, a little behind and to the right of the stranger, and settled in to watch. There was nothing to order. A patron there took whatever was set before him by Hannah Mills, the lumpy widow woman who served there. But Stop did order one thing, a cup of coffee. "Fresh," he added.

And another thing. This Stop ate well, held a knife and fork like a proper fellow, and not like a shovel the way the miners often did. A proper fellow with manners, using the napkin, respectable. Not a likely background for a robber, Dudley thought. Maybe a con man, swindler, mountebank, tinhorn. But not a rough customer. Stop ate swiftly, as if he were a man in a hurry, with large projects in mind and not enough time to do them, and when Stop rose, old Dudley was half into his beef and boiled potatoes and beans. Dudley usually had all the time in the world, and he liked to dawdle his way through a meal, savoring it all and killing an hour or even two in the process. But not now.

Hastily Dudley rose, too, cursing his luck but determined to keep a handle on this crook Stop, who was paying the waitress from a big roll of bills that he had extracted from his black suit coat. A lot of money, Dudley had thought. A lot. And then he dug in his own worn leather pouch for four bits he kept there and dropped it into Hannah's hand with a wan smile. She didn't return his smile.

The stranger, Stop, was just vanishing into Bonack's Livery as Dudley emerged from the hotel. Dudley lowered himself into the shade and watched. When Stop appeared once again, it was from the barn aisle, and he rode the big, leggy bay, sitting on a shining basket-weave saddle that showed no sign of dirt or scuffing; a proper, clean saddle for a man in a black broadcloth suit. Not once had Stop paid any attention to Dudley, even though it was obvious that Dudley was paying a lot of attention to him.

Stop rode easily, almost too easily for a slicker from a city, westward, upslope, along the creek, and then cut south along a tree-lined lane. Old Dudley didn't want him to go there, not out to the mansion that loomed red on a bench southwest and above the town. That was Ben Waldorf's place, and he had started construction the same year he'd struck gold there in Pony. That was in 1872. Waldorf was sixty-five that year, and Dudley figured the old fellow wanted to enjoy his treasure just as fast as he could, while there was time. So even when Pony was a sprawl of log huts, shanties, and canvas-over-frame buildings, heavy ox-drawn wagons were hauling stacked red brick down from Helena, and the walls of Waldorf's mansion were taking shape.

It wasn't Waldorf who had Dudley worried. The old man enjoyed and welcomed guests, although he preferred to meet strangers, salesmen, and job seekers, over at the mine office on the hill. It was that hellcat Jezebel and those two wild boys. Just recently Jezebel had drawn up her carriage at Spade's Mercantile and addressed him from her padded leather seat.

"It's your job to protect us. Your job to preserve our privacy. If you let bums and vagrants and snake-oil sharpers up that lane, I'll see that you're fired."

That's how she had put it, and she meant it. And now that snake-oil sharper, Stop, was riding out there, and all hell would break loose. Well, Dudley thought, it was too late to do anything about it. Maybe Ben would be more lenient. No way a constable could simply stop every stranger in town from heading out toward the mansion.

Even now he could see Stop riding down the lane, splashed by sun and shade from the cottonwoods along it, heading out toward the imposing redbrick building with the mansard roof. Ben wouldn't be there, of course. He'd be over at the mine, or maybe down at the stamping mill and leaching tanks below. There'd be no trouble from Ben, only the black-haired hellcat Ben had married the summer he'd struck gold, a woman ten years younger than Ben's sons.

But Stop didn't go to the door. He just sat his horse up there, taking it all in, the red manse with the gingerbread veranda clear around all four sides, the tall windows that let the mountains and the Big Sky into Ben's house, the brick carriage house and the log barn beyond, the fenced pastures. Even from where Dudley watched, in the shade of the hotel porch, he could see Stop up there on that bench just sitting and looking and studying. And then Stop touched heels to the bay and rode on to the south, having pestered no one there, and the stranger vanished from sight. Dudley, somehow disappointed, settled back into his wicker chair in front of Spade's.

Then, wouldn't you know, the stranger rode back in, coming uphill from the east, having made a big loop around town to the south, and just as mysterious now as he was when he'd arrived. It had driven Dudley plumb nuts and caused him to spring up out of the squealing wicker chair and hobble down over to Bonack's just to listen a bit. But by the time he had gotten to Bonack's, the bay was in a stall, the saddle on a wall rack, and the stranger had gone. Cussing his luck, Dudley had stomped back to Spade's— only to find the stranger there, sitting in his wicker chair. Unthinkable! It had never happened in all of Dudley's years in Pony. Steaming up, the constable gimped across the wide street, hell in his eyes, and the whole town, it seemed, watched.

Stop smiled at Dudley. His even white teeth seemed bright in the deep shade of the porch. "Mind answering some questions?" he asked in an even baritone.

"Now see here . . ." Dudley said, fuming. "We've got a respectable town here—"

"Who owns that lot on the corner with the tent saloon on it, old man?"

Dudley had turned crafty by then. "I ain't telling you nothing until you tell me your business, Stop."

"I'm going to open a bank."

"A bank?" Dudley was flabbergasted. "A bank?"

"Town needs a bank," the stranger said. "And where do I get the red brick? A bank needs to be solid, good brick. Is it made around here? And where do I find Ben Waldorf? I want to talk to him about the bank."

And that was how Sam Stop came to Pony. In the next days Sam Stop had talked to old Ben Waldorf at length about the long-term prospects of the mine. Sam didn't want to start a bank in a town where the mine was playing out. From Tim Christopher he bought the lot with the saloon tent on it and registered it over on the plat rolls in Virginia City. Red brick could be bought in Bozeman now, and Waldorf advised Stop to haul it from there, which is what Sam Stop did, after hiring some skilled craftsmen and masons who built Stop's bank from rough drawings. And by fall of that year, Pony had a redbrick bank on the southeast corner of its main cross streets, a solid place with golden oak counters and wainscoting inside, and a gilded sign over the beveled corner entrance that read BANK OF PONY, CAPITALIZED AT $25,000, SAMUEL P. STOP, PROPRIETOR.

The bank had prospered at once. Pony Consolidated shifted its accounts there and shut down its informal operations as the town's bank now that the town had a real one. Miners and tradesmen gradually opened accounts there and found their money to be safe, and interest payments on their savings prompt. Stop had hired Myrtle Phillips as a teller, and that had been unthinkable, a woman teller, but Stop had always heeded his own counsel and paid no attention to the mutterings. It had been like sitting in Dudley's wicker chair. Some of the merchants weren't sure women could add and subtract and divide. Women could multiply, everyone knew that, but the rest they weren't certain about, and they checked Myrtle's calculations with feverish eyes, and found that she actually had corrected their errors, and finally, grudgingly, agreed that Myrtle, at least, had overcome the natural disabilities of the inferior sex.

Pony was a small town, its population hovering below one thousand, and there wasn't a lot for Sam Stop to do, so he had taken to keeping morning hours and vanishing on afternoons. In the hands of the competent Myrtle, the bank functioned flawlessly, and all Sam Stop did, really, was examine loans. About these he was usually careful, cautious, and always shrewd. But on rare occasions he plunged on a project that pasty-faced white-jowled bankers would have rejected automatically. And usually he came out fine. Sam Stop could read character, and that influenced his judgment heavily.

Still, there remained a mystery about Sam Stop and his bank. No one knew where he came from, and when anyone probed, he gently turned inquiry aside with a smile and a joke. The man seemed to have no past. Likewise, no one had an inkling where Stop's capital had come from. Rumor had it that a few days after Stop had arrived in town, he had brought a packhorse heavily laden with gold in from the mountains someplace and had kept the gold in Ben Waldorf's safe until the bank was ready. But that was only a rumor. Some guessed he'd won it gambling; others said he'd gotten it in a previous strike, maybe out in Californy, or down in Colorado, or at Nevada's Comstock. But that was all just talk.

One thing that wasn't talk, though, was Madam Lou's account. Louella had the log place down on the northeast edge of town, where the miners came. Mostly miners, anyway. She had six girls, changing them often enough so that there always seemed to be a fresh face among them, and that was good for business. Louella frequently walked to Sam's bank. Lots of people had seen her go in and out, even by broad daylight. Louella always dressed in elegant tailored gabardine suits, with a ruff of cotton at the throat and a cameo on a choker. If anything, even more respectable-looking than any local wife, and in particular, the Waldorf woman, Jezebel, who always managed to dress a little like a soiled dove and enjoyed the sensation she caused doing it. At any rate, lots of people had seen Louella slip in and out of the bank, and lots of people thought that maybe she owned it and Sam Stop was a sort of front man. Dudley had finally asked Stop, and Stop had grinned and said he never discussed people's private accounts. But that didn't stop the whispering. Some people said Louella didn't trust banks or greenback money and simply kept her entire wealth in double eagles in the bank safe. But no one knew, and Sam Stop never said.

Plenty of people wondered about the bank's security and what would happen if it was robbed. This talk was mostly behind old Dudley's back, because everyone in Pony knew that the old hip-shot constable would be no match for serious bank robbers, and there was only Myrtle in the wicket most of the time. And that always raised another question whenever Stop and his bank were discussed in the saloons or in the merchant offices in town.

8

Where did Stop spend his afternoons? Outside, for sure, that's all anyone knew. Stop's tan, if anything, deepened into a deep nut-brown that seemed embedded there through winters as well as summers, so that Stop's even teeth and white eyeballs seemed brighter than other white men's teeth and eyes.

The first year Stop had boarded at the Goldstrike Hotel, but as soon as the bank was built, he started on his own house at the southern edge of town, discreetly below the red mansion. He built a clapboard house with high peaks and colored glass panes around the windows, and a porch trimmed with gingerbread. A medium-sized house made from milled lumber freighted up from Bozeman, not the whipsaw kind that came down from the mountains green and rough. The odd thing was, no one had ever been in that house, except maybe Ben Waldorf, who had dealings with Stop and seemed to like the young banker. But rumor had it that it was modestly furnished. Anyone expecting it to be decorated like a Persian seraglio would have been disappointed, indeed. Sometimes one or another had tried to worm something out of Ben Waldorf about Stop's life and his house, but Waldorf kept confidences and just smiled the way old men will. Whatever the case, Stop seemed to have no private life anyone could figure out, was gone for long periods, and seemed in pretty thick with the old mining magnate, and maybe Madam Louella too.

For all the rest of the town, Stop was courteous, amiable, courtly, and reserved. Several maidens set their caps for him, but he just smiled politely and didn't respond. Which made them petulant and inclined to say tart things about him, linking him to Louella and her girls. Things like that. In his three-year sojourn he had become a respected, if mysterious, citizen, a familiar sight on the streets, striding in his black suit from bank to mercantile to the hotel saloon, where he had a single drink on some evenings and was never known to show a weakness for that vice or any other.

Among those who eyed him with increasing disdain was Jezebel Waldorf, who was barely thirty herself, married to an amiable old man in his seventies, and looking around town with predatory eyes that kept returning over and over to Sam Stop.

Chapter Two

On the third day of June 1882, a special train chuffed into the Northern Pacific railhead at Livingston, Montana. That was as far west as the tracks had been laid, and it would be another year before the construction crews completed the grades and tunnels over Bozeman Pass. The engine, a diamond-stacked and green-enameled giant called Old Sentry Number One, hauled only two cars. One of them was a maroon private car gilded in gold, and the other was a boxcar.

In the lushly furnished coach, which had a parlor, a kitchen, sleeping chambers for four, and even a water closet, were two great and famous financiers, Jasper Kennedy and Drago Widen. Also a cook and a houseman. In the boxcar were an ornate barouche with twelve coats of black lacquer on it, shining brass trim, and two carbide lamps for night travel, a pair of matched dappled gray trotters from famous bloodlines, and identical twins, Paddo and Lethbridge Dowling. These two, bulging out of double-breasted suits and wearing black bowlers, were so alike that their employer, Jasper Kennedy, could barely tell them apart.

The trip from New York had progressed comfortably and with

speed, because both gents were major stockholders in the Northern Pacific, and their special had highball priority so that it slid down the new rails unhindered, while lesser freights and passenger trains steamed on the sidings. After a restful night on a siding at Livingston, the barouche was carefully unloaded from the boxcar, and the matched grays harnessed to it. All of this was done by the Dowling twins, who had cots in the boxcar and were not allowed inside the gilded coach, although meals cooked in the coach had been taken out to them.

Eventually, after a fine breakfast of oatmeal, bacon, and toast with a selection of six jams and jellies, and after-breakfast Havanas, Mr. Kennedy and Mr. Widen emerged into the morning sun; briefly admired the towering, snow-clad peaks looming in the south; and entered the waiting barouche behind the Dowling twins.

"Does thee enjoy the clean mountain air, Drago?" asked Jasper Kennedy, who grew up a Quaker but no longer was. He had retained all the pieties but believed only in himself.

"It has no effect on me," Drago replied. "The things of the spirit are more important," he added. Drago Widen was an earnest Baptist who prayed on his knees morning and night and never made a business move without first consulting God, who happened to approve of everything Drago proposed to do.

The velvety black barouche was an extraordinary sight in the shanty camp of Livingston as it rolled gracefully through the squalor, and if the motley gandy dancers, Chinese, and slatterns stared resentfully at the pristine carriage, its occupants did not deign to notice. In any case, Dowling A and Dowling B, as Jasper called them, were well equipped to deal with a rowdy mob. Both of those gents had mastered every martial art and armament known to modern man. The burly pair were superb boxers and wrestlers; handy with knout and stiletto; formidable with firearms such as the shining Stevens shotguns at their feet; and adepts of the cane. Indeed, the one way Jasper could tell them apart was by their sticks. Paddo had a gold-handled oaken walking stick with a spring dagger at its base. Lethbridge had a hooked cane and could use either end of it, or its middle, with devastating effect. Added to all this was a whole lore of maneuvers the twins had acquired from a Japanese seaman on the docks of New York. With such formidable guards, it was no wonder that the financiers felt no fear of road agents or stray Indians as they began their journey westward, up the long slope of Bozeman Pass.

At about ten o'clock they paused to rest the trotters, whose energies flagged because of the relentless uphill journey to the famous pass. At that time the Dowlings raised the hood of the barouche to protect the financiers from the relentless summer sun, and to permit them to peruse their business papers without having their eyes water from the alpine glare. The route they followed was the old Bozeman Trail, which once had poured miners into the gold camps of Montana in the early and middle 1860s. But now, here and there were railroad crews grading the steep incline, digging cuts, and tunneling through the rocky saddle at the pass itself, all of it a noble feat of modern engineering made possible by the capital these gents and others like them had raised back in New York.

At about two that afternoon they reached the summit and lunched there, enjoying capital sandwiches and other dainties in a wicker basket supplied by the cook. The Dowling twins sat discreetly to one side and a few feet lower on the gentle slope.

Mr. Drago Widen was a tall, skinny man with a ferret face heavily marked by smallpox scars, a man with quick, darting eyes that nevertheless occasionally focused in relentless observation upon anything that intrigued him. Mr. Jasper Kennedy looked rather the opposite—meaty, florid of face, and a little older, with gray at the temples starting to whiten his sandy hair. Years of voluptuous living showed upon him, although his sternly black suit, tight vest, maroon cravat, and gold watch fob tended to harden his appearance and render him formidable in the eyes of observers. Both men seemed to possess a keen intelligence and shrewd daring.

Mr. Widen amused himself during the nooning, not by soaking up the grandeur of the alpine land but by rereading the report from the Pony mine superintendent, Murray Eickles, whose fealty he had easily acquired for a pittance of two hundred dollars a year. For that length of time, about one year, Superintendent Eickles had dutifully supplied information about the mine's management, prospects, profits, reserves, grade of ore, as well as every imaginable idiosyncrasy and weakness of its owner, Mr. Ben Waldorf, and his peculiar spendthrift family.

"Does thee find anything new in it?" asked Jasper.

"He deserves what's coming," Drago replied. "God will have his revenge. God punishes the dissolute and the wastrel. We will merely be his instruments. Here, listen to this, Jasper."

In a clarinet voice with a trace of bassoon in it, Mr. Widen began quoting certain passages from Eickles's most recent report.

"Mr. W—this is Eickles writing now—continues to live at the limits of his income. I am sure he has nothing put by. He lacks a sense of decent providence for the future and mismanages his assets, paying labor too much, wasting timber on shoring, fraternizing with the help, all because, as he so often says, he was just a penniless stiff with a pickax and singlejack just a few years ago. And, of course, he indulges that wanton wife of his, Jezebel, in anything her wild fancy imagines, and no less does he indulge the young men of the family, the pair of them lost souls. While I am not privy to his accounts at the Bank of Pony, I should imagine his funds are limited and his way of living wholly dependent on continued production from the mine."

Mr. Widen laughed dryly. "That's where we want him."

The downhill run was easy, with the barouche pressing against the breeching of the dappled grays and hurrying them along. In Bozeman City, the brass-trimmed barouche flabbergasted denizens and dogs, and set a rowdy boy to howling. The Dowlings drew up before the town's best hostelry, which was none too good, it seemed. The Hotel Banco Republic was a clapboard affair with a sagging roof and a long line of rooms facing off a single center aisle. It was the best available, and the financiers resigned themselves to a night of mild discomfort, a necessary thing sometimes in the quest for profit. Mr. Widen took Room 12, and Mr. Kennedy Room 11 across the dark hall, and the twins slept in the livery barn after ordering the best feed and oats and care for the trotters, and wiping down the shining black barouche. In the night Mr. Kennedy was bitten twice by bedbugs, once in a most embarrassing and irritating place upon his heavy anatomy. But, as always, he had a solution for life's minor problems. He found the manager, Hiram Wincoop, at breakfast with his wife, whose hair had been tied up in a scarf of some sort and was lounging over bitter coffee in their quarters at the front of the hotel.

"Ah, my dear Mr. Wincoop," said Jasper. "Would thee sell this establishment? I shall make a splendid offer if I must."

Hiram Wincoop hemmed and hawed, then allowed that he might; that the hotel and all its goods and appurtenances therein might be worth well over three thousand; that the figure was modest, considering what its value would be next year when the railroad came through; that it earned a steady four-fifty a year, and that would increase dramatically for anyone eager to be in the hotel business in Bozeman City.

Mr. Kennedy peeled four thousand-dollar bills from a roll in his vest pocket. Hiram Wincoop stared at the bonanza bug-eyed, then hastened to his small safe, where he found the necessary papers and executed a deed to the real property, goods and appurtenances, goodwill and existing trade. In an hour it was done, and it was scarcely eight-thirty.

"Now, then, Mr. Wincoop, I shall be back in three or four days at the outside. Time enough for thee to move thy wife and chattel. I want that done by tomorrow. And when that is completed and the guests removed, burn it."

"Burn it?"

"Yes, Mr. Wincoop. Burn it. Or I shall rip up this paper and take the greenbacks back." He nodded in the general direction of the Dowling twins, who stood nearby menacingly.

And so it was done.

En route to Pony in the morning sun, Drago Widen grew perturbed. So much so that he failed even to notice the grand scenery, the great peaks and grassy parks and elk upon the foothill meadows.

"What will we do upon our return?" he asked. "We shall have

nary a place to lay our heads. That was the only spot in Bozeman City, save for a few dives for the common."

"I was bitten twice by bedbugs, and it is good riddance. I have done the world a favor, doesn't thee agree?"

"Of course I agree. And you have a valuable lot besides, which you'll be able to sell for a handsome profit when the railroad comes through. But where will we sleep, Jasper?"

The older magnate smiled. "Why, we shall seek out the local parlor house. There never was a good parlor house yet that suffered a bedbug."

Light illumined Drago's face. "Why, that is a stroke, Jasper. A fine stroke," he said, smiling beatifically.

The ride to Pony was long and hot, and by the time the sun sank low, powdery dun dust covered the shining barouche. It was well after the dinner hour when the tired trotters dragged the handsome barouche into Pony, fighting the last uphill miles right to the doorstep of the Goldstrike Hotel. People gaped. There had never been a rig like that black barouche in Montana Territory. Toward the end the Dowlings had lit the carbide lanterns, so that the carriage seemed to float along on twin beams of light piercing from the reflectors in the lamps. It became a source of wonder, even to the miners who used carbide lamps down in the shafts.

Dudley was making his evening rounds when the barouche rolled in, rattling doors, peering into the saloons, and letting his gaze rest dourly on the denizens of the Mint, where nine tenths of the town's night troubles arose. When the carriage, with its glowing lamps and sweated grays, rolled in carrying two gents in bowlers and two more in prim broadcloth suits and cravats, old Dudley was galvanized and hobbled his way toward the Goldstrike, as eager as any child to see the sights. Here was a sight never before witnessed in Pony.

Mr. Jasper Kennedy and Mr. Drago Widen registered, separate rooms, best available, while the two Dowlings wheeled the barouche off to Bonack's Livery to give the trotters a well-deserved bucket of oats. The Dowlings, of course, would find bedding there, perhaps in the hayloft if it was cool. Windham Pyle, proprietor of the Goldstrike, accompanied his distinguished guests to their quarters, hastily inquiring if the arrangements were suitable.

"Mr. Kennedy, sir, you have the Abraham Lincoln Suite, and Mr. Widen, sir, you have the General Sherman Suite," he said cheerily while Pony's citizens gawked.

"I never heard them names for plain old rooms before," said Cyrus Barteau, twelve-year-old son of a leading merchant.

"Hush your mouth," hissed Willie Graves, who was a saloon swamper and knew about such things.

After a brief respite in the necessary rooms behind the hotel, and some scrubbing with water from the vitreous white pitchers and basins on the commodes in the rooms, the financiers met in the Lincoln Suite and ordered dinner. No matter that it was past ten and the hotel dining room had long been closed. They summoned Windham Pyle himself and ordered a quart of Old Crow, a magnum of the best port, and whatever was best in the house by way of viands, plus the best Havanas available in Pony. They suspected it would take the quivering Pyle some time to reopen his kitchen and dragoon a cook or two, but that was of no consequence. They poured some Old Crow over ice straight from the town's icehouse, where it had lain buried under a mound of sawdust since last winter, and settled down to plot their strategy. It would take some doing to get old Waldorf to go along peaceably, like any reasonable gent would under the circumstances.

Among the things to do was meet sub rosa with their agent and confidant here, Murray Eickles, and take the measure of him. As any good financier knew, there was false information and good, and an informant would as lief take gold and supply the inventions of his imagination as he would take gold and supply hard fact and shrewd conclusions. So they wanted to take the measure of the man. A man of some substance, obviously, or he would not be the general superintendent of the Pony Consolidated Mining Company. For this purpose they summoned Paddo Dowling, who was faithfully awaiting the instruction of his masters at Bonack's Livery. After a hurried consultation Paddo Dowling disappeared into the night, jauntily rapping his stick along Pony's boardwalks. The mine super would be located and, if necessary, routed from slumber to meet with his sub-rosa employers. Failure to come at once, of course, would result in instant exposure and disgrace. Mr. Kennedy and Mr. Widen had made all that clear from the beginning.

"Well, Jasper," said Drago by way of a toast, "we are here at last, and within twenty-four hours, I imagine, we shall both be a quarter of a million richer, at the very least, and if the mine's reserves prove to be enduring, a half, or maybe a whole big one richer."

Jasper nodded, drank heartily, and rattled ice. He liked ice. This Pony had that civilized touch, at least. Probably a pretty good little business supplying the saloons with it. He was in the ice business himself and had a virtual monopoly on it in Gotham because he controlled the transport from the New England lake areas where ice was cut and stored, down to the city. The Yankee yokels who cut it all winter long up there hadn't the foggiest idea of its value in midsummer on the streets of New York and all but gave it away in gratitude for a customer.

"Now, then, Jasper, let's go over these papers," said Drago. "The call loan unequivocally gives old Waldorf thirty days to meet the call, and that would be an inconvenience, I'd say. We have better things to do than twiddle our toes in Pony. He'll object, of course. He's kept up with his semiannual payments quite flawlessly, and the place is far from bankrupt. But it doesn't matter, eh? It's here in black and white—the lender can call the loan at any time, any place, under any circumstance. And tomorrow we'll do just that."

Mr. Drago Widen's ferret face broke into a grin, lumping up the pox bumps along his cheeks and jowls. "The task is simple enough—to get it over with in twenty-four hours rather than thirty days, and I reckon the versatile Dowlings can manage that. From what Eickles says, the law consists of one gimpy old constable— Elmer Dudley is his name. And the sheriff is off in Virginia City, too far to help if we do this in one day. We have an army, though I'm sure no rube in this town has the faintest notion of it."

"I think thee should pray about it. If we are the Sword of God visited upon that old wastrel, then we should seek divine guidance, wouldn't thee say? I've given up that business myself. Hard on the knees."

"I will, before I lay me down to sleep," said Mr. Widen. "But now my spiritous instincts lean toward Old Crow."

They sipped contentedly, admiring the late lavender twilight and the looming hulk of the Tobacco Roots off to the west. Their second-story rooms fronted on the main street and afforded them a fine view of Pony and its miners and night people strolling from one lamplit saloon to another.

"What if Eickles is wrong and Waldorf has the money salted away in that bank? Or what if the company had enough reserves to pay off the loan? Or old Waldorf has a line a credit, a means of paying the called loan?"

"Thee worries too much."

"No, I'm not worrying at all, Jasper. At the very least we walk out of here with a paid-up loan, two hundred thousand in fresh capital. The trip was well worth it even if that is all it amounts to."

There came a knock, and Widen let in Pyle and three flunkies, each carrying trays of viands and linen and silver such as is rarely seen in a frontier village. And after setting a table, and with due bowing and scraping, the hotel staff backed out, and the financiers settled down to devour what was before them.

They were scarcely half done when Murray Eickles arrived, so they let the porky, sandy-haired manager languish in a chair while they ate silently.

Down below on the street, and in the gloom of an overhead porch above the boardwalk, an amiable man watched the lamplit window, caught glimpses of the great capitalists, saw Eickles among them. This observant gentleman, a man of some years, had spent the evening engrossed in poker with his cronies over in the Buffalo Hump Saloon. The arrival of so formidable a barouche, glistening blackly as it toiled up Pony's street, had drawn them all away from the green baize table. The old gent wondered, recognized, and knew. He had won fifteen dollars that evening, and perhaps lost a mine.

18

Chapter Three

Ben Waldorf hated to wake a man up, but this thing couldn't wait until morning. He jogged his white Arab horse down the lane to the south edge of town and tied it to Stop's hitching post. A big gibbous moon lit the way. Stop's house glowed pale in the night. But even as the old mining magnate clambered up the steps, the front door swung open and Waldorf caught a glimpse of blue steel and Stop in a nightshirt.

"Why, it's Ben," Stop said, the steel lowering in his hand. "I thought maybe—"

"You must sleep with an ear cocked," Ben said, his glance on the revolver.

"It's an old habit," Stop said. There was a questioning pause.

"I need to talk," Ben said. "It can't wait until morning. Sorry to bother you."

Stop waved him in, lit a kerosene lamp, and disappeared for a while. He was dressed when he returned, looking somehow fresh and trim, even after only an hour or two of early sleep.

Ben himself never bothered much with dress and was attired about the way he always was. He was sixty-five when he'd struck his bonanza, and set in his ways. The white beard and white hair worn long, to the nape of his neck, were the way they always were. His gray wool pants were baggy and nondescript, and his suit coat—the only insignia of success—hung limply on his old frame. His shirt lay open, stained, and rumpled. Since he'd hit gold, he'd become simply a rich prospector rather than a poor one. But his twilight-blue eyes winked brightly, and there was always the hint of humor on the chapped lips tucked under his beard.

All this Sam Stop took in, even as he waited patiently for the substance of this nocturnal visit. He did not offer his guest a drink but would have provided one instantly on request.

"I've lived too blasted long," Ben Waldorf began, crabbing toward what was on his mind. "I planned to kick off long before this. Hell, when I hit that quartz gold, I figured I had maybe five years to whoop it up before I kicked off. Well, I whooped, and I haven't kicked off yet, and now it looks like I ain't for a while. The harder I whooped, the healthier I got."

He eyed the quiet young banker with merry eyes. "I had it all figgered. Fast as I got rich, I married that hellcat Jezebel, figgering on some funnin' for an old man. And funnin' it was, too. She was plumb under thirty, raven-haired, lavender-eyed, and built—well, you've seen her, lad. Hasn't changed much. Well, what I figgered was, I'd kick off in her arms. See? I mean, if a rich old prospector has to kick off, he oughta be having fun doing it, see? I mean, move from one paradise to the next, with only a temporary inconvenience while my ticker quit. Onliest trouble was, my ticker stood it fine, and I never succeeded in kicking off, and all I did was excite that hellcat to amazing ah . . . well, hell, didn't mean to plumb you into the well of my wedlock. Only to explain things didn't go to plan and I didn't kick off yet."

Stop arched an eyebrow.

"Thing is, I didn't give a hoot and a holler what happened after I kicked off. The hellcat can find another rich prospector, and them two sons of mine . . . they don't know it but I call them Beelzebub—that's Willie—and Satan—that's Stanley—they can git out on their own, do 'em good to have to earn a buck. So I ain't got a will. If I couldn't spend it while I was alive, at least I could refuse to pass the boodle on to those two knuckleheads and that she-wolf. Let the courts and creditors fight it out, I thought. Pour me a whiskey if you got it, Sam. My throat's as cold as a prospector's pick."

Sam Stop nodded and pulled a bottle and a short glass from a shelf and poured. Waldorf watched him. The young feller was as peculiarly quiet about himself now as the day he rode into Pony and everyone thought he was a riverboat gambler. But a competent young fella, it seemed. Made some good loans, kept bank reserves high, one third of his assets in gold and greenbacks, he had told Ben once. Made the whole town hum. Funny how he didn't look like a banker at all. At the door, young Stop looked like he'd drill a night visitor without a second thought. Handled that revolver like a man who'd felt the grip on one often enough.

Sam Stop set the bourbon glass on the table. "You'll like it," he said. "It came down from Helena."

It was good sipping, Ben had to agree with that. Stop had not poured any for himself.

"Anyhow, this here telling you how come I'm making a night call upon you is taking some time, I see. Hope to finish up quick enough so you can get back in the hay."

He pushed the long white beard away from his lips so he could sip without straining that good Kentucky through it. Stop waited patiently.

"You know, Stop, getting a mining company started takes a lot more than just hitting a vein of ore. I hit it, and then what? That's not placer gold off a stream bottom, that's quartz gold dug out from the belly of the earth. And heading deep in, too, fifty-degree angle downward, that's how my glory-hole shaft went. That meant getting capital in. Hiring miners. Getting shoring timbers. Building a hoist. Getting rail in and ore cars. Buying up the claims around mine so's them other pirates didn't horn in. I was sixty-five, mind you, and not much time left. So I contacted some of them eastern financiers, the ones you read about all the time. Tried Morgan and Vanderbilt and Jay Gould and Bet-a-Million Gates and Jim Fiske and got nowheres. Tried old Daniel Drew, the bible reader, and he was interested all right, but wouldn't

21

finance the mine without his owning the majority. But then he did put me onto a pair of deuces, younger ones back there in New York, fellers named Jasper Kennedy and Drago Widen, young comers, maybe on their tenth million instead of their fiftieth. And they bit, all right. Wanted a piece of the mine, but I wouldn't give it, and they finally lent me four hundred thousand to get the Pony Consolidated rolling. Fifteen-year note, semiannual payments—I've met every one promptly—interest at eight percent, which is pirate rates, but I had to take it. And like all notes, a call loan. They can call most anytime they feel like it, and the debtor, that's me, has got to pay up within thirty days, whole amount owing."

Stop nodded. He was familiar with finance.

"Of course, it ain't normal for any creditor to call a loan unless the repayment has quit, or the company's going down the chutes, or trouble like that. But these horned toads had that look about 'em, and I figgered I would just as soon have my fun. Built that palace up there, just to live in a palace, and kept the hellcat in feathers and furs, and bought racehorses for Beelzebub and Satan, and kept them in enough pocket money so's they could blow their wad down to Louella's every night almost. I ain't saved anything—hell, you know that from my account in your Bank of Pony. The company ain't got reserves, either. Twenty thousand in bullion awaiting shipment down in the safe, and expenses pretty close to that for the month. I said let her rip, and I'd do the ripping and then kick off, and now I've lived too long."

"You're saying they're calling the loan," Stop said.

"It ain't happened yet, but it will tomorrow. A couple hundred grand still owing in principal and interest. They rolled in here tonight in a black carriage like I ain't never seen—it'd excite a year's envy from the hellcat, she saves up envy like other folks save corncobs—and took rooms. They got a pair of bullyboys with them, just to make life interestin' for me tomorrow. Solid meat under derbies. And a pair of gray trotters that'd make Beelzebub faint."

"The company owes two hundred thousand?"

"Approximately."

"And you got thirty days."

22

"I'd say I got one day, if I read old Kennedy and Widen right. It's a shame I didn't kick off, ain't it? I tried. God knows, the hellcat will testify to it."

Stop nodded. "The entire assets of the Bank of Pony, my initial capitalization, plus all deposits, runs to $150,000," he said quietly. "Of that, a third is reserved, and all but about seven or eight thousand is presently committed."

"That's what I figgered. Even a dumb old prospector can figger that much, Stop. But I want you with me tomorrow when them pirates measure me for some plank walking. I figger maybe you can sort of talk bankerish to them—maybe insist on the thirty days, at least. Maybe you got some ideas, declare bankruptcy, sic the hellcat on them, you know. You bankers is full of tricks."

Stop stared at the old man and smiled. "I don't have any tricks, Ben. But I'd be glad to side you and maybe talk 'em down a little. But why bother? You got assets. Sell that red brick pile. Sell Jezebel. Put Willie and Stanley in bonded servitude. Get your mule and pick and go off prospecting."

"Not a bad idea, Stop. Not bad. But even illiterate old prospectors get to enjoying luxury. Especially at age seventy-five. Best bet I got is to get on up there and wake the hellcat and try to kick off tonight. Maybe if I try hard enough . . ."

They sat silently in Stop's kitchen, watching the night breeze tickle the flame of the lamp.

"How'd they know you've no assets?" Stop asked quietly.

"They got a spy. They got that turd, Murray Eickles—he's the mine superintendent—for a little gold, I imagine. He's got less loyalty that Beelzebub and Satan put together. Eickles knows the score, all right. Access to the books and all that. Eickles been complaining, too, about costs all the time. Too much for wages, too much for shoring timber, and all that. Keeps telling me how I can make more, and he's right. I could make more. That's middlegrade ore, nothing fancy, but at least it shows no sign of pinching out. I could make more. But I'm an old pick-and-shovel boy meself, Stop. I been in pits. I been where there's no shoring. I seen widows and busted limbs. And I'm one of them, not one of the bankers . . . ah, financiers who see only profit and loss. So the place is pretty good for the Cousin Jacks to work. They get paid comparable to elsewhere but get a few extras: shorter shifts, plenty of timber overhead. So I ain't had labor trouble, anyway. Never had a closed-up day. Guess I'm drifting off your question. They got that rubber-spined Murray Eickles to tell them what's what."

"What happens if Kennedy and Widen take over? Among other things, it affects my bank."

"Hard times for Pony, I can tell you that. Cut wages and less timbering, which means less money going to suppliers. More cash going out. Maybe injuries. Your bank'd be out of it. They'd do their own banking. Issue checks from New York. Maybe more, too, but I can't hardly give it a name. If them hooligans stay here, this town will change. Old Elmer Dudley's no match for those boys. I've seen a few of those derby boys in my day, and I'll tell you, this would become a company town fast. All the merchants would sell out to the company—or be driven out. That sort of thing, if you get me."

"I do," said Stop.

"Hell, they'd even take over Louella's operation. Probably first thing, seeing as how she's the biggest business in town, after the mine. I figure Spade's is third."

"And you think I have some magic, that I can do something about it."

Ben Waldorf's old eyes gleamed. "I know you can do something about it, Stop. I don't know what you are, but you ain't just a banker. You're something more. Dudley tried to find out, wrote around, and no one ever heard of you. But you ain't just a banker. That's how come you don't worry about Myrtle there in the wicket alone. Whatever it is, you got something else in you."

Stop's gaze stiffened as he listened to that.

"When do you figure they'll open the ball?" he finally asked, softly.

"Late morning."

"I'll be at your office early. Maybe I'll think of something by then." Stop yawned.

"I'll git," Ben Waldorf said. "I'll git now. Knew you were the man to see."

Ben hopped into the Arab's saddle, as springy as he had been twenty years earlier. Inside, Stop's lamp blued out, and the house fell dark. Ben rode cross-country, upslope to his place, not bothering with the lanes. He unsaddled the Arab, put it out on the meadow, lumbered toward his study and lit a lamp. The study was a fine room with walnut wainscoting and bookshelves filled with leather-bound editions, most of which Ben could barely read. He had mastered the labels of airtights and knew how to do his name in a legible script, but he was no great shakes with all those lines of type in books. Still, he intended to have a look at the loan agreement if he could, and poked around in the rolltop desk until he found the right pigeonhole and the papers.

He fought the blasted words for a while—he needed specs, he knew, but since he hardly ever read, he hadn't bothered—but it wasn't as easy as he had hoped. All that stuff on the papers wasn't the same as a canned tomato label. Then, irritably, he shoved them back in the desk. He'd have Stop read them in the morning. What did he need reading for, anyway? He'd gotten rich with a pick and shovel, hadn't he? And hell, if those slickers got the mine, what difference would it make? He'd lived sixty-five years with little more than a mule and a rifle and a pickax, and he could do it again. This whole thing, this brick pile, the hellcat, the good horses, it was all just fun, and he'd as soon kiss it off with the spin of a roulette wheel as hang on to it. He laughed. The hellcat didn't think that way. She'd taken an instant fancy to rich living.

He wondered for a little whether he should go waken her and start a romp. Then he decided against it. She was like children and baths. You couldn't hardly get a little boy into a tin tub on a Saturday night. And once you did wrestle him into the tub, you couldn't hardly get him out of it. The hellcat was like that. You couldn't hardly fire her up, but once she got fired up, you couldn't hardly stop her. He had better things to do than wrestling with the hellcat. Tomorrow would be a big day, but at least he planned to get a little fun out of it. He didn't give a hoot and a holler what happened. Let the hellcat and the boys worry.

A tintype of her in a gilded oval frame perched on top of the desk. He stared at it, admiring the wild jet hair, the saucy stare into the lens, the soft pout of her lips, and the suggestive smile. Plainly she had been put on earth for carnal purposes, and that is what he'd bought her for. Not bought, exactly. Just a large wedding present for her, and a little gold for her old man in Virginia City, a skinny traveler in a green checked suit who sold ladies' shoes off the back of his pink wagon, and had his luscious daughter with him to model them and show some leg and draw in the customers. Respectable, more or less, but Ben had always figured less.

Ben remembered the first time he'd seen her, perched on the tailgate of her pappy's wagon, skirts hiked high, beautiful tanned legs showing as she wrestled on a high-topped shoe.

"Now, this here is my little girl, Jezebel," her pappy had said to the assembled rubes. "Yes, sir, I named this little sweetie puttin' on shoes for you Jezebel. That shock you some? Sure does! You'll know the Bible. How could I name this beautiful gal Jezebel, after the gal who worshiped idols, worshiped Baal? Condemned by the prophet Elijah, thrown out a window and et up by dogs. Yes, sir, I named her Jezebel so you dogs could taste a morsel."

Her pappy had laughed and promptly sold seven pairs of shoes.

They'd been married in twenty minutes on the second floor of the courthouse by Judge Ambrose Leary. So he had bought her and it had been fine, the best any old prospector could hope for, paradise. When she turned out to be a hellcat, that was all the more fun, and he had laughed every time she howled. But she wouldn't leave him. Not unless someone richer came along.

He turned down the lamp, and it blued down, then smoked a little, lifting the aroma of kerosene into the room. The silvery light of the moon pierced through the great high windows of the manse, illumining the rooms as Ben Waldorf lumbered through them. Grand piano shining dully. Settees, love seats, coatrack, oil portraits, doilies, Oriental rugs. High-backed dining chairs, Tiffany silver, Wedgwood china, teacups, demitasse. Marble-faced fireplace, cast-iron enameled stoves, corniced ceilings. The servants' quarters, carriage house, hay barns. And the Paris gowns, Arabian horses, thoroughbreds bloodlined from Equinox. Greener shotguns, Manton rifles, all in a case. He stood in the middle of it all and laughed. Old pickax prospector, old man, laughing in his mansion.

That evening he had won fifteen dollars, an eagle and some bills, now in his pocket, and that had been fun, too. He was a good poker player, liked to bluff, and sometimes did things for fun, just to be a little outrageous, and the more outrageous he got, the more he won, because it unnerved his cronies, Spade in particular, who had a good accountant's brain. Over there in the Buffalo Hump, a quiet saloon that didn't attract the Cousin Jacks. He always felt uneasy there, like he didn't belong, but that was where he had to play, because custom dictated it, and the other players— Pony's merchants—gathered there. Funny that Stop never played. Maybe a good thing, too. Maybe a banker shouldn't play poker, shouldn't wager.

Then the other mood came over him, and he thought about the little town of Pony, perched high on the slope, eking out its living from his mine alone. He thought about the solid wives of the Cousin Jack Cornishmen, raising their sprouts, depending on the weekly brown envelope with the cash in it, and the merchants, Spade and Bonack and the rest, making the place live, providing the necessities, contracting for goods and selling them. All because of the Pony Consolidated Mine Company. What would happen to them? If those vultures called the loan and took over, what would happen to Pyle and Spade and Bonack? They'd be driven out. Stop, too. Company bank. Company store, company hotel, company livery barn. And what about the men who went into the pit? Less shoring, old handcars, banged-up rail, no air vents. Lower pay, as low as the vultures could get away with and still keep them down in the bowels of the Tobacco Root Mountains.

It was worth a fight, he thought. Maybe he could raise the money in thirty days. Go up to Helena, down to Virginia City. Even Denver, if it came to that. There was time. Time was the thing. He'd need all of thirty days to do it. Maybe Stop could help him there.

He lumbered on up the curved hardwood stairs, his hand on the glossy banister, and off to his room. They had separate rooms, of course.

She was standing in the door of hers, in her fifty-dollar French peignoir, all ruffles and white and cottony.

"You're as quiet as a circus parade," she said.

"You're gorgeous, tootsie," he said. "Go to sleep."

"I don't want to go to sleep," she said.

"Then don't," he said, and closed his door on her pout.

Chapter Four

Promptly at ten the next morning the shining black barouche pulled up in front of the Goldstrike Hotel, with the Dowling twins aboard. Shafts of sunlight danced off the brass trim, awing the town duffers under Spade's porch and exciting children in the streets. The Dowlings stared lazily at the rude frontier folk, from small, watery blue eyes in the shade of their brushed black bowlers.

One minute later Mr. Jasper Kennedy and Mr. Drago Widen emerged from the Goldstrike in freshly brushed summer wool suits and newly shined black high-topped shoes. Mr. Widen carried a matching black carpetbag with fleurs-de-lis woven black on black into the velveteen. Neither financier deigned to notice the citizens of Pony who were gaping at them.

Pulled by the sleek trotters, the barouche rolled up the dusty road toward the mine, its elegance somehow shaming the crude buildings and wagons of the mining camp. The road twisted along North Willow Creek as it cut its way between mounding foothills, spring-green in early June. A half mile and numerous miner's shanties later, the road debouched at the mine, which hung starkly on a rocky grade and seemed chilly even in the June sun.

Drago Widen glanced casually at the mine works, the timbered winch and engine platform, the rails erupting from the mouth, the outlying shanties that husbanded blasting powder and other necessities. It held no interest to him, beyond registering that it was there and that it manifested something of his investment.

What interested him, rather, was the administrative building where the unfolding events would spin out; where he would soon become incalculably richer. It was a crude rectangle of board and batting, whitewashed once but grimy now, with dirty windows gaping carelessly from it, and all under a glinting metal roof. An appalling affair, actually.

The Dowlings swung the barouche around and drew to an adroit halt near the front door, but just shy of a mud puddle that would sully the financiers' high-tops. Gingerly Jasper Kennedy and Drago Widen stepped down and onto the raw earth, and then through the sagging door. The interior of the executive offices of Pony Consolidated Mining was no more assuring. There seemed to be private offices at either end of the rectangle, and a hollow grimy cubicle in between where two pale men—clerk and accountant, apparently—toiled over large books with nib pens. Mr. Widen took it that old Waldorf had the office at one end, and Murray Eickles the office at the other end. Eickles was nowhere in sight, but Ben Waldorf stood at his door, a young stranger behind him.

"Gents," he said in a booming voice, "come right in."

The office of the chief executive officer of Pony Consolidated was as dismaying to Drago Widen as the rest of the building. The whitewash here looked marginally cleaner, but that was all. Waldorf's desk was nothing but rough plank stretched over a cobbled-up frame of some sort. Not a paper lay on it. The sole concession to comfort was a vast padded chair behind Waldorf's desk, a comfortable throne now being occupied, after brief handshakes—Lord, the old miner brutalized a man's fingers in his iron grasp—by Waldorf. All that remained to sit upon was a wooden bench grimed with the dust and dirt of numerous miners who had perched on it over the years.

That annoyed Jasper Kennedy, who liked his comfort, and irritated Drago Widen, who realized that sitting on a hard bench put them at a disadvantage. They sat down gingerly on the cold, hard wood, the velveteen carpetbag between them. The Dowling twins bulled in and spread to either side, Paddo to the left and Lethbridge to the right, and neither blinked.

"Welcome, gents," rumbled old Waldorf. "This here is my banker, Sam Stop, and I don't believe I have the acquaintance of these other gents that just came in."

"They are our assistants, the Dowlings, Paddo and Lethbridge," said Jasper amiably. "Now, since you've brought your banker, I gather you've already discovered our business, Ben—" he began amiably.

Sam Stop had a faint grin on his face, and a rather intelligent look, Drago thought. The man looked like anything but a banker, with lean muscles, a deep tan, and brown eyes that gazed straight into a man. It made Drago faintly uneasy. He had heard that these frontier types tended toward wildness, and even though Stop seemed civil enough in his rude suit and cravat, some stark power seemed to emanate from him.

"I think," Drago said, interrupting Jasper, "that this meeting should be among principals only. Ben, you and Jasper and I, we'll just have a friendly little parley without outsiders."

It was Stop who replied, quietly. "I am negotiating for Ben Waldorf." There seemed something insolent about the way he said it.

"Ben? It's between us. We'll inform Stop about it later," Drago said.

Old Ben's twilight-blue eyes lit up mischievously, but he said nothing.

Stop answered. "Principals it will be. Send the Dowlings out, if you will, Mr. Kennedy." He smiled amiably. "I have purchased a small and junior share in the enterprise, so you may consider me a principal. Now, then, if the Dowlings will step out . . ."

It annoyed Jasper Kennedy famously, but he nodded, and the two derby-men filed out, at least as far as the outside of the door, where they resumed their vigil.

"We are at your service," said Sam Stop, who stood behind Waldorf, there being no seat for him.

Jasper Kennedy sighed, plucked something from the wool of his suit coat, and began. "Thee have been a fine debtor, Ben. Never missed a payment. We're fond of thee, and think the whole world of this fine mining enterprise thee have built here. We'd never think of calling a loan upon a strong debtor, except that hard times have hit us. Small panic back there. Why, I can tell thee in all earnestness, Drago's been on his knees seeking ways and means to avoid or delay this sad duty. But the good Lord has guided our hand to thee, but thee are to be the salvation of a lot of desperate widows and orphans back East who have suffered reverses in some of our other enterprises.

"So we must inform thee—we have done thee the courtesy of coming clear out here to do it—that we must call thy loan, Ben. Now, hear this. We want to make it easy for thee. We know thee has not the means to repay us, and so we've agreed to offer thee five thousand in gold for a quick settlement. Why, a man could live handsomely on it for a decade, as thee knows. We have transfer papers all prepared here. If thee will sign, why, it will be simple enough. Thee will forfeit the mine to meet the debt and be well comforted with gold."

"No," said Stop.

That was not a word Mr. Drago Widen or Mr. Jasper Kennedy were used to hearing.

"I believe," said Jasper carefully, "that we are negotiating with Ben Waldorf, here, and not thee, Mr. Stop."

"This here banker's doing the negotiating for me. I got it all proxied over to him this mornin'," said old Ben.

"Thee should reconsider. The young are impetuous and cause unnecessary pain, hardship, and delay."

"Now see here, Ben," interjected Drago. "We're making an outstanding offer. We have no desire to dally out here. We'd like to get on back to New York. You just turn it over now and be done with it."

"No," said Stop.

"I don't believe, sir, you have anything to say about it."

"I do," said Stop. "The terms in the contract are thirty days to repay after the loan is called."

"A frivolous delay, Stop. We know the company has no reserves. Surely your little country bank—"

"Thirty days," said Stop.

"But you have no means," protested Mr. Widen. "A waste of time. I tell you what. We shall add a thousand dollars—one thousand in gold—to whatever your equity is worth if we can complete these matters summarily."

"Thirty days," said Stop.

Drago felt choleric. The bumpkin banker's insolence was beyond suffering. But he contained himself. The hard bench bit at his tailbone.

"Now, now, gents, let us counsel," said Jasper Kennedy equably. "Perhaps thee would tell us where thee will raise the money to meet our call, Mr. Stop?"

"That's private company business, sir."

"I thought so. Thee has no prospects at all."

"You may think it if you will," said Stop.

"Perhaps you can tell us just when you will meet the call?" asked Drago Widen.

"We have thirty days," said Stop. "And after that, recourse to the courts. It's unusual to call a loan when a company is sound and its repayments are current, wouldn't you say? It might interest a judge."

Jasper enjoyed the visit less and less. They had thought to deal with amiable, semiliterate old Ben easily enough. The man was in his dotage and wanted only a high old time to finish out his life. But this Stop—a rude banker, a cowboy in a banker suit, really was unexpected. Still, he thought, there were measures.

"Thy bank is capitalized at twenty-five thousand. I saw thy sign as we passed it. What are thy assets now? Thy deposits and liabilities?"

"Private," said Stop.

Mr. Kennedy sorrowed. "I surely don't understand thee. I was preparing to make thee an offer, most generous, for thy bank. It would fit into the company here."

"Not for sale."

"We could start our own, thou knowest. Drive thee out swiftly enough. The miners, if they wish our employment, would be required to bank with us. We have the assets, thou knowest, thousands of times thy own. We could do the same with the merchants here: require our employees to buy in our company store. Then thee would have neither miners nor merchants as thy depositors."

"If you get the mine," added Stop.

Ben Waldorf guffawed, and his eyes glistened. The old man was enjoying himself.

"Not a laughing matter, Ben," snapped Drago. "Unless you agree, and immediately, to forfeit, the town will die."

"How's that?" asked Stop politely.

"Why, it is a matter of money. We have it, you don't. We can do things—amazing things—with it, Stop. There is nothing that cannot be hired or lacks a price."

"What is my price?" asked Stop.

Mr. Kennedy eyed him lazily. "That is for thee to determine, within reason."

Stop stared at him insolently.

Mr. Kennedy was finding the hard bench acutely uncomfortable. He shifted his heavy weight.

"Thee has met our two assistants, Paddo and Lethbridge. They have come to smooth the way for us and assist in the transfer of the assets. They are very knowledgeable."

"Familiar with high finance," said Stop. His lips were mocking again.

"I should say, yes, they are persuasive."

"What is their price?" asked Stop.

Jasper smiled. "They are very loyal."

"Didn't know the word was in your vocabulary," said Stop.

Drago stood suddenly. "You misunderstand us, Stop. We have given over our lives in the service of our fellows and the republic. Between us we have made tens of thousands of jobs. All because of an ideal, a vision, a stewardship."

Stop was staring insufferably. "And the Dowlings, too. They

pass the collection plate in their churches, do they? Rap the knuckles of those who doze during sermons?"

"I think you are mocking me, Stop, and I don't take it kindly. I would have expected more of you, the town banker."

"Come back in thirty days," said Stop. "I believe that would be the sixth of July."

Jasper Kennedy rose, too. "We shall return tomorrow. Give thee a day to think matters over before thee engage in folly and ruin the livelihoods of thy citizens here."

Old Ben stood. "Good to see ya, gents. You'll find Murray Eickles across the way if you want to visit. He's got himself a dandy office there."

Mr. Kennedy and Mr. Widen departed, both feeling Stop's relentless gaze on their backs. They did, out of curiosity, troop across the central room to Eickles's office and peered in. The man was absent. There were, at least, comfortable leather chairs in that one.

Outside, the weather had changed. Massive black-bellied thunderclouds had built up over the Tobacco Roots, plunging the area into a cold gloom. The Dowlings raised the hood of the barouche and rolled down the isinglass windows. At least the financiers would remain warm and dry within. And could talk privately, too. The gray trotters wheeled around toward the road down to town, even as the first spits of cold rain snapped against the hood and the isinglass, sounding like flying pebbles.

"A martyr. I've seen the type. Stop will resist, even as we roll over him, and probably enjoy it. They are always the most troublesome, never reasonable, always impeding progress," muttered Jasper.

"I will begin measures," said Drago. "After luncheon you can go visit the mansion."

That was how it had always been between them. Drago Widen handled the stick, Jasper Kennedy the carrot. Mr. Widen even looked like a stick, and Mr. Kennedy like a stout carrot.

Jasper smiled. "Obviously there should be a little visit to the bank. From what Eickles said, the place is scandalously unguarded, and with a woman teller, too. Stop is an oddly reckless man."

"Martyrs are reckless for a purpose," said Drago. "Odd that Eickles said so little about Stop. Scarcely mentioned the man, and here we were confronting the unexpected this morning."

"Eickles had his head in the mining business. A rather poor source of information about the rest," said Jasper.

The rain started sheeting down, drenching the Dowlings' suits, running off their bowlers, beading on the barouche, turning the backs of the trotters glistening black. A brilliant burst of blue lightning illuminated the innards of the barouche, followed by a cannon shot of thunder that vibrated through them.

"I shall welcome the hotel. Meanwhile thee might petition God for our safety."

As the muddied barouche wended down the slippery slope the rain turned to hail—pea-sized, rattling grapeshot at first, then balls the size of marbles that smacked the fine running boards of the barouche and dimpled the wood, shattered on the Dowlings' bowlers, and stung the trotters.

"It is no place to live, this Montana. Let the barbarians and rustics keep it," Drago muttered. "This in the summer. Brutal cold in an endless winter."

Then, as swiftly as the rain and hail came, they vanished, and there was only a biting wind teasing its way into the barouche.

They rolled into town, and before they passed the bank, Jasper told the Dowlings to stop a moment. The soaked Dowlings, showing no sign of discomfort, immediately pulled up.

The little bank seemed, in its way, a solid establishment. Artisans had cemented arched brick transoms over the tall windows, adding grace to the building. Inside, they could see Myrtle Phillips in her wicket. She had lit lamps against the gloom of the storm. There was no one else present. The front doors stood open.

"Stop knew what he was doing, hiring that woman. They can be had for less than a man, and are often better at books."

"Better with customers," added Jasper. "We shall keep her. She will lower the overhead."

"I shall send the Dowlings there shortly. We shall want to see Stop's books."

Jasper couldn't resist a faint smile. The Dowlings would be sent for the books. A bank is helpless without its books. It was good mischief, for starters.

"To the hotel, then," said Drago, and the carriage lurched forward. "What are you going to say to that wife, Jezebel, and the wastrels?"

"Depends. 'The wages of sin is death,' I imagine."

"Sin being . . . ?"

"Supporting old Ben. First thing that will bring him to his senses is to put his family against him. That'll be easy. They are all buyable, and cheap at that."

"Eickles says the wife has a temper. An unruly woman without a Christian tongue in her."

"Ungoverned women are simply greedy," said Jasper. "When I contrast old Ben's perilous wealth with ours, she'll see the light. We are the magnet, she the iron filings."

"And the sons, Jasper?"

"Give them more bawds and they will do anything to help us. Say a harsh word against their old man and they will rally to us."

"What if old Ben doesn't care?"

"Why, Drago, that is easy enough. What have I the Dowlings for? A little brass-knuckle work on the sons and old Ben will see the light. A little work on the wife, his little lust machine, and he'll see the light."

"And if he doesn't care?"

"Why, my dear Drago, there are many other options, some of them marvelously persuasive. But the old man is scarcely a problem. Stop is the problem. And I leave it to thee to devise the means. . . ."

Chapter Five

Jezebel was over near the paddocks doing something. From a distance it was hard to tell just what. The newly shined barouche emerged from the shaded lane, and before them lay a sweeping sloped lawn, with the pile of red brick at its crest.

It turned sunny again, and the damp suits of the Dowling twins steamed. Lethbridge steered the sleek gray trotters into the carriage path that would lead to the front veranda. Ben Waldorf's mansion towered impressively, even to the jaded eyes of Mr. Jasper Kennedy and Mr. Drago Widen.

No one met them at the door when they paused, so with a nod to Lethbridge Jasper directed the black barouche toward the paddocks and the distant figure of a woman dressed in bright pastels. The carriage snaked silently along a rutted trail, its brass glinting and blinding and dappling the red brick with shards of sunlight.

Jezebel turned to greet them as they drew nigh, and the sight of her stunned Jasper. Jezebel Waldorf was the most spectacular beauty he had ever seen. Raven hair in loose, silky waves framed a perfect, creamy face, flawless of flesh. Eyes of uninhibited lavender reconnoitered him boldly, and her lips formed a bold and saucy grin and threatened to pout at any second. She wore a summer dress of lavender-and-pink awning stripes with a white ruff at her soft, delectable throat. It was closely fitted at the bodice, revealing a luscious figure narrowing down to a small, girlish waist. For the sake of politeness Jasper hoped not to stare but found himself gaping nonetheless.

"I think you are richer than Ben," she said. "I hope so. I have been practicing with my bullwhip."

Belatedly they stared at the object in her hand, a long, plaited whip with a tassel at its end.

"I begged one from the bullwhackers," she said. "I am very good at it, see?"

With a graceful snap and a crack she flicked the bowler from Lethbridge's head and sent it sailing fifty feet. Lethbridge startled visibly and reddened.

"I see you have brought your matched uglies," she said. "I heard about them. Matched grays and matched hooligans."

Jasper Kennedy found his voice. "Thee are Jezebel Waldorf," he yammered in an unaccustomed voice. "We have come for a little social visit. I am Jasper Kennedy, and beside me is Drago Widen."

"And two matched hooligans," she said. Another flick of her awesome whip sent Paddo's bowler sailing.

Paddo gazed intensely, fascinated by a weapon he had not encountered before. Jasper knew at once that before the day was done, the Dowlings would possess two such whips and begin to master them.

"You may stay in your carriage," she said. "I don't entertain. Especially not pirates. You have come to Pony to steal from us."

Jasper laughed. "Now, now, my pretty, I've really come to steal thee from Ben."

In fact, that became his exact intent, and he had the resources to do it, too. He'd take her East. A little brownstone love nest . . . She'd be expensive, of course, but worth the price. Worth any price. Worth a million. Well, maybe a quarter of a million.

He had the advantage on Drago, whose pocked face repelled the fair sex. Drago either read the Old Testament when he was in need or visited a certain New York parlor, wearing a black cape and a mask.

"Why do you talk like that? Thee and thou?"

"I grew up in the Society of Friends. Quakers."

"I never heard of them. But what the hell. I don't care what you are."

Drago recoiled.

She pouted sweetly. "If you are going to steal me, how are you going to do it?"

"Why, Jezebel, if I may, with money. I have stacks and piles of it, and all just for thee."

"I will think about it," she replied. "I like Ben."

"Thee'll scarcely miss him."

"I said I like him."

A gust of wind lifted her skirt, revealing a saucy white cotton petticoat with a ruffle. The gust sent the bowlers on the lawn rolling like tumbleweeds. Paddo clambered down from the barouche and stalked after them, his suit still steaming in the sun.

Jasper Kennedy was smitten by the most perfect ankle he had ever seen.

"Come back with me to New York," he said huskily. "I will give thee a fine apartment and five thousand dollars."

"I don't hear you," she replied, pouting. "I will begin to listen at a hundred times that. Is that what the Society of Friends does?"

Jezebel stared at the pair of them, her keen lavender eyes studying them, her fine, clean jaw thrust upward. "We have fenced enough," she said. "Why are you here? I hear it is to take away the mine from Ben. What do you want from me? Talk plain or I will invite you to leave."

Mr. Jasper Kennedy was momentarily taken aback by the insolent woman. She'd require some taming once he got her to New York. "Why, yes, we've called Ben's loan, and we will have the mine. And make it pay much better than old Ben did, with his lax ways. We came here to discuss it with thee."

"Discuss it with me? Be plain," she said, blazing. "What's that, Quaker talk?"

"Now, don't be hasty. My colleague here, Mr. Drago Widen, and I are preparing to do better by thee than old Ben does." He leaned over to her confidentially. "Did thee know that he has not made a will giving the property to thee? Or to his sons?"

"You don't know that."

"But we do, Jezebel. We have our sources."

"Probably that turd Murray Eickles."

Jasper smiled benignly. "Let us say, madam, that Ben's life is no secret to us. Which is why we have come. When we have the mine, Pony will prosper, the value of the holding will rise, and production will increase."

"You aren't talking plain. Why are you saying all this to me? If you take the mine from Ben, then we will be poor."

"Madam—Jezebel—have thee no thought for the good folk of Pony, who might prosper?"

"Not in the slightest."

Paddo, two bowlers in hand, resumed his seat and handed one of them to Lethbridge.

"Have thee no thought of Ben, then? We have offered him an endowment. He can live out his life comfortably. Enjoy his old age. But he must turn over the company by tomorrow or we shall withdraw the offer. We thought perhaps thee would persuade him."

"How much? The endowment?"

Jasper paused. "Why, five thousand gold."

Her lavender eyes lit with scorn.

The financier continued suavely, not deigning to notice the flare in Jezebel's eye. "Persuade him. Do thy wifely duty to him, and there will be a reward for thee. I am ten thousand times richer than Ben Waldorf and can buy thee a thousand times what Ben Waldorf buys thee. And that goes for his sons—Willis and . . . whatever the other's name is."

She resumed her pouty smile. "You mean to bribe me," she said.

"Nothing so crass as that, madam. A small reward . . . well, a large one if thee please."

"To help you steal the mine."

"I am pained, madam. We are calling a loan. It is all in the contract, duly signed and notarized."

"You're the crookedest bastards that ever drove up that lane," she said.

"I am shocked, madam."

Drago nodded silently. This was Jasper's party, so he continued to sit mutely.

"Why should you be shocked? My father was a tinhorn and a mountebank who sold shoes from the back of a wagon. I grew up in that wagon. We sold shoes mostly because I flashed a lot of ankle, and some thigh, too, at the rubes. My husband's an old prospector. He can hardly read. We've got this pile of brick on the hill for the fun of it. And don't tell me you didn't know."

Jasper Kennedy gazed at her blandly, but in fact he was becoming irate. The sharp-talking hellcat was showing more feistiness than he'd ever seen in a female. The madder he got, the more determined he was to have her. She needed a good thrashing, and then she'd settle down. He knew what he'd do, then. That's what Paddo and Lethbridge were for. He would snatch her. Once they got back to the private palace car, she'd settle down.

"If thee do not wish to help us in the matter, I have other means," he said coldly.

"Of course you do—matched uglies. I saw plenty of their kind on the road with my father."

"Thee will soon regret thy conduct."

"I suppose you will beat me."

"I have better things in mind, Jezebel. Thee will come with me to New York, and thee will be powerless to do anything about it. And I will show thee what money can do . . . for thee or against thee. Money can turn thy beautiful face into pulp."

Her lavender eyes blazed again, and for an answer she snaked the bullwhip back and snapped it viciously over the rumps of the gray trotters. Stung, they lurched forward at a gallop. Both the Dowling uglies were thrown bodily out of their seats and onto the grass, bowlers flying. The two financiers tumbled back against the barouche hood, and only after a hundred yards of careening travel did Drago Widen scramble forward and draw up the reins.

When he finally turned the barouche around to pick up the Dowlings, he saw them advancing warily upon her, and she was smacking the whip and waiting. Jasper called them off. There would be other times and places to deal with that gorgeous, profane woman.

They drove silently back to Pony, the barouche wheels hissing in the dust. All four of them nursed wounds and were vowing revenge, though nothing was said aloud. It had been a bad day. First Stop and his insolence at the mine office, and now the tigress.

Jasper enjoyed the exchanges. Little did such rustic creatures know what money could do. In his mind he began to envision just exactly what money was going to do, and it balmed his soul to think about it. He had encountered small-timers like Stop before. Brave enough men but without the grand sense of mission that made great financiers. He had crushed them all like bugs. They always thought in terms of contracts and law and courts and justice. Those were the tools of a small mind. Jasper thought in different and grander terms—influence on courts, ownership of politicians and officials, surveillance by paid informers. And of course, the Dowlings and their ilk.

Back at the Goldstrike Hotel, Jasper directed Paddo to hunt down the wastrel sons, Willis and Stanley, who would no doubt be at Louella's establishment. Lethbridge was directed to care for the horses and the barouche. With that the financiers retired to the General Sherman Room for further consultation.

A half hour and two Old Crows later, the financiers summoned the hotel proprietor, Pyle, and invited him to bask in their company and share a toddy.

"I hope you gents are enjoying your stay at the Goldstrike, and enjoying Pony, too," the gaunt, ruddy innkeeper said.

"Why, Mr. Pyle, that is the very thing we have summoned—invited you to talk about," said Drago. "The fact is, we are impressed by Pony. As you may have heard, we have taken over the mine—it could not meet a loan call—and we have great plans. We are going to expand operations up there, double or triple the tonnage. Go for profit. Bring in more miners. And, of course, we want the best of everything in Pony and will be establishing businesses here. Company businesses, of course. Everything at low profit, to benefit our good miners and integrate the local economy. . . ."

Windham Pyle took that all in, nodding and sipping and pulling himself erect in his chair. He tended to slouch, but he tried not to while facing these magnates from the East.

"Now," Drago said delicately, "we will be making offers for local businesses. Splendid offers, I might add. Your hotel, for example. Tell us what it is worth. We shall buy it."

Windham Pyle shook his head. "It's not for sale, Drago"—he was on a first-name basis now—"but I'll consider it. The missus and the two sons and I like Pony. Hotel's doing fine. The mine draws 'em in. Drummers, selling products to the mine and the miners. Nope, I'll just keep her, thanks."

"Well, now, Windham. I can well understand your feelings. But, of course, in the interests of an efficient economy here we do plan a company hotel. Now, if you don't want to sell, why, we'll be forced to build another, and of course charge no-profit, break-even rates, for everyone's benefit. But that takes work. Why don't you just think on it overnight. We'll give you a fine buy-out offer—why, even three thousand for the building and some additional sum for the furnishings and goodwill. . . ."

"That's half what it's worth!" exclaimed Pyle.

Drago Widen sighed. "We don't see it that way. We see it as a favor to you, Windham. A chance to cash out before a new hotel goes up."

The hotel keeper glared bleakly out the window. "You say you're taking over the mine. Old Ben won't be running it?"

"Consider it done," said Jasper.

"I'll think on it," said Pyle curtly. He rose.

"Have another toddy, man," said Jasper. "We want to ask thee about the others. We propose to buy up the mercantiles, too. Spade's place down the street. Bonack's. Barteau's shop. We'd like thee to tell them, let them know we will deal generously with them. Indeed, there'll be a little reward in it for thee."

"What if they refuse?"

"Why, Pyle, much as we regret doing it, we'll build our own stores and compete. We're going to make sure our miners can buy from the company at a benevolent price, generous terms, their bills deducted in a simple manner right from their pay envelopes. In fact, it'll be a credit economy, and we'll just keep track of things in the company offices."

"You have charitable instincts," said Pyle dryly. "Sure, I'll tell them all. But not for a reward."

He left abruptly. Jasper laughed and Drago joined him.

"He got the picture," Jasper said. "Tell me, Drago, does it ever bother thee? The takeovers? Does thee still think thee are doing God's work?"

Mr. Widen swirled the toddy around in his glass, then swallowed. "I do," he said. "On my knees I asked Divine Providence about it, and He assured me I was doing the world a favor. Some are temporarily inconvenienced, like Pyle there. But efficiency is the thing. I can say that with Divine assurance. Efficiency. It makes for profits, which makes for more investment, which makes for more jobs, which makes for prosperity. Jasper, my friend, I am assured whenever I fall upon my knees that you and I, and a few others, are the great engines of the American Dream, bringing opportunity to the masses."

"Thee are right, and someday the world will understand it," said Jasper piously. "During my silences the Spirit led me in the same direction . . . when I was young."

A racket rose in the corridor and a tapping upon the door of the General Sherman Suite. Jasper opened it to find the two younger Waldorfs, and behind them the Dowlings.

"Ah, it must be Ben's fine sons," said Jasper amiably. "Come in, come in. It is high time we met."

Willis and Stanley filed in. The financier turned quietly to the Dowlings at the door. "Thee has business to attend, I believe?" The pair of them quickly dissolved into the gloom.

Mr. Jasper Kennedy turned to examine his guests. He thought they were in their forties but looked older as a result of voluptuous living.

Their hands were white and soft, their grips flaccid.

"Now, then," he said after introductions and the proffering of spirits, "we have matters to discuss. I am told, Willis, that thee and thy fine brother favor fast horses, fast women, fast spirits, and fast money."

Willis smirked. "Also fast food, fast guns, fast talk, and fast times," he added. Jasper stared. Willis was smooth of flesh, devoid of wrinkles. Bulbous-nosed, pig-eyed—the eyes were colorless—and mouse-haired. Also running to fat.

"Well, we just might accommodate thee," Jasper said smoothly, concealing his nauseous distaste for the cretin. He turned to the other, Stanley, who looked even more porcine and billiard-smooth, if possible, than Willis. But Stanley was black-haired, and the gloom of his hair, along with his gray flesh, made him look like a ghost.

"Stanley, my good man. Are thy tastes the same, eh?"

"No, Jasper, old friend, I like 'em slow. Slow women, slow food, slow and easy."

A pair of cretins.

"Now, gents, I regret to inform thee that we have called the loan on thy father's mine and are assuming control."

"What's that supposed to mean?" asked Willis.

"Why, simply that the Waldorf family no longer owns it. Ben will sign it over to us shortly."

Something sagged in the brothers. "Well, we still got a pile to go through," said Stanley nervously.

"Not quite," Drago intervened. "It's all gone, lad. The fun's over."

Now, at last, alarm filtered into the pig faces.

Jasper Kennedy smiled easily. "Now, never fear. We captains of industry take care of our own—always. It is the unwritten rule. We honor old Ben, and thee, too, of course. What Mr. Widen and I have in mind is employing thee. Thy family has a great enterprise, and thee have the knowledge to run it. We'll put thee on a retainer. We'll discuss the amount later. For now we simply want Waldorfs—symbols of power and solidity in Pony—with us for the transition. We are prepared to pay thee a thousand for now—"

"Apiece?" Willis's little eyes danced.

"Nay, for the both, for now. Simply a bridge until later. Safety for thee, you see. A modest stipend for thy skills . . ."

"We'll take it," said Stanley.

"It is thine," said Jasper. "Now, of course, if we employ thee, we will expect thee to do our bidding."

The pair nodded cheerily.

"And thy first task, gents, is to persuade thy father to go along. Ben is troubled, does thee see? Unsure. But thy counsel will persuade him, surely."

"He doesn't listen much—"

"Never mind that, lad. Now let us discuss the things that need doing. . . ."

Chapter Six

Elmer Dudley was feeling testy. Things had been happening all day that he didn't fathom, and that bothered him. That morning the financiers and their two plug-uglies had driven up to the mine in that fancy carriage. In the afternoon they had driven out to the Waldorf place and had returned looking grim. Then the uglies had gone after the Waldorf sons and had brought them to the hotel. That was a rare sight. Not in recent memory had anyone seen the younger Waldorfs by sunlight. And now the uglies were patrolling the street, rapping their canes on the boardwalks. Twice they had passed under the overhang of Spade's Mercantile, taking the measure of the old constable.

Dudley sank into his wicker chair, making it chatter like a squirrel. It was unusually hot for early June, and the shaded boardwalk felt cool. He had spent a goodly portion of his life there, in that wicker chair, in this place. It was where the town constable belonged, with a fine view up and down the street, and a central location just three doors down from the little wooden marshal's office and jail house. With his bum knee it was easier on him than making rounds.

He'd reached fifty, but his hair had long since turned stark white. He wore it long, shoulder length, to the disgust of the town's more progressive element, who thought it made him look like a barbaric frontiersman. Which is why he wore it that way. He peered out upon his small world with keen black eyes that lurked beneath enormous white eyebrows no barber dared trim. The rest of him, muscular and powerful except for his limp, was usually encased in red long johns, a navy-blue wool shirt, tan duck pants held up by thick leather suspenders, and square-toed boots. The silver constable's star always glinted sharply against the dark blue wool.

Occasionally, mostly for show, he wore his black holster and belt, with a Colt .44 hogleg in it. He preferred the .44 because he had the Winchester of the same caliber. He paid little attention to weapons and couldn't tell a finely balanced and smooth-firing one from another. In twenty and more years of lawing, his approach had been to draw it in dangerous situations, before it was needed. He had scarcely heard of fast-draw gunmen, and snorted at the idea.

But there were few of those in Pony. The place didn't draw a lot of people because it was the terminus of a long road and was not on a trail to somewhere else. But more importantly, Old Ben Waldorf did all his own hiring and was pretty good at gauging the character of those who came to his office seeking work in the mines. Pony became a haven for family men; wives and children were here. Only one or two saloons had faro and monte dealers, or poker, or roulette, and only one saloon had dance-hall girls or other painted types. Of course, there was Louella's, but she had a tough houseman, a freed slave, and the place was always orderly. So mostly Elmer Dudley sat and watched, poured water on fighting dogs, hauled a few drunks to his wooden calaboose of a night, and on rare occasions dealt with petty theft—stealing chickens and garden produce and the like.

But if Elmer's life was simple enough, that did not mean he didn't know what he was doing. He had taken one look at those two plug-uglies in derbies and knew they were dangerous and could probably whip him. He had caught a glimpse of their shining shotguns in the barouche. He knew what toughs could do with canes and walking sticks. And he knew the bulges under the left shoulders of those coarse wool suits weren't made by handkerchiefs or eyeglass cases. That matched pair could tear up a town and likely kill or maul him on the spot.

Which angered him. A man gets to sitting in his wicker chair, in his town, for over a decade, and he gets to feeling he owns it. But not today. Today it was owned by those fancy gents and their plugs. He felt glad Millicent was dead. If he had gone home to lunch as he did in the days before she died, he'd have bitten her head off, and for nothing. Just because he was full of steam and lava. It always showed up in his obsidian eyes first, and miners and cowhands in the saloons had come to recognize it. When Elmer Dudley got steamed up, he was likely as not to pound the hell out of somebody and throw him in that calaboose overnight for good measure, bum knee or not.

Now those eyes glittered, but it was not a signal the uglies knew or understood. There were the usual duffers, his cronies, on the bench beside him, gabbling and whittling, but this time he paid them no attention. They brimmed with hot-air speculations today. About the financiers. About the price of that barouche and the gray trotters. About the uglies. They remarked the similarity of the two Dowlings, and missed the hooded menace of them. Which made Elmer Dudley contemptuous, because he saw the other thing and the old goats didn't.

He thought he'd go talk to old Ben later. Ben had always let him in on the important things, and that helped keep the town orderly. Once Ben planned to hire fifty new men, and he told Elmer about it in advance, and Elmer got a temporary deputy for a few weeks just to make a certain kind of show to the newcomers. Things like that. Ben would tell him. But it stuck in Elmer's craw that Ben hadn't already told him what in tarnation was happening. Maybe that was why he felt so irritable now. For once he was in the dark.

It was getting well into the afternoon, and before long the June sun would slip behind the high bulk of the Tobacco Roots, and long after that the low eastern side of the valley would be illumined while Pony would be shadowed in high-country blues. Across the street, the uglies talked softly, laughed, and gazed toward the constable. He could see their expressions even without his eyeglasses on. Dudley had two sets of them, one for reading and one for distance vision. A drummer with two carpetbag valises full of them had come in once and sold specs off the street or in saloons. Elmer had tried out a few and found he needed both. It cost him a week's wages, but it had been worth it. He dug around now for the long-distance specs and put them on. That made the uglies clearer, and he could see what the duffers were talking about. They had to be identical twins, maybe thirty, both built like oxen. Dudley felt a tiny surge of fear, and it nettled him, which made him fume.

He stared again at the Goldstrike, and at the upstairs windows where the financiers roomed. The Waldorf boys still tarried there, up to no possible good. If they hadn't been Ben's sons, he would have run them out of town long since. As it was, he had talked Louella into keeping him informed about them. They had never done anything but satiate their gargantuan appetites, but that didn't keep Dudley from worrying. If their jaded appetites turned to harder things—opium, murder, and things unspeakable—Dudley wanted to know of it, and fast. Galoots like that were capable of anything, he figured.

Then the uglies strolled into the Buffalo Hump. That was not the proper saloon for their ilk, and it immediately worried old Dudley. He hoisted himself from the wicker and tugged his belt around until the holster hung right, then took a tentative step with his bum knee, commanded it to work, and lurched on downslope toward the saloon that, by unwritten Pony code, had been reserved for the professionals and businessmen of the town.

But he needn't have worried. It was a busy time of day and only two merchants sipped drinks. The uglies, who stood at the bar while the barkeep served them, had ordered shots of whiskey neat, and mugs of beer. From the open batwing doors Dudley watched them down the shots, then chase them with the foaming beer. He turned abruptly and headed back to his wicker chair, sulking and refusing to say anything to Clem Witherspoon, the retired mine accountant whose crude false teeth rattled with every word.

Only ten minutes later the uglies emerged, peered up and down, watched an enormous gray ore wagon rumble through, and then began parading uphill, their cane and stick rapping sharply, in mean cadence, on the boardwalk. Their path would take them directly past Spade's, and on parade before the duffers there and Constable Dudley. Through his long-distance specs he watched them, heard the rap of sticks on wood like the volleys of a rifle company, watched them smile blandly at him as they passed, then stalk upslope, west, and turn into the bank.

That did it. He jerked himself out of the wicker once again, got his bad knee functioning with a slap of his hand, and set off behind them. Probably nothing, nothing at all, but he would keep an eye, dammit. He didn't bother to pocket his gold-plated wire-rimmed specs, and maybe that was just as well. Keep an eye on things.

The bank window was open. And inside, Myrtle, looking pleasant as usual. "Gentlemen, may I help you?" she asked amiably. Elmer Dudley paused to watch. They had not noticed him there, in the shadows.

They were eyeing the place, peering toward the rear office, glancing at the safe. Dudley himself looked at the big green safe with the cupids on the door. The heavy door stood open on its cowled hinge. Stop had shown it to him once. Within were a number of lockable compartments. Some of his customers kept their valuables in those locked boxes. But visible in the safe was banded currency, stacks of golden double eagles. Wealth. Dudley's stomach squeezed up against his esophagus.

"Stop. Is he around?" asked one of them, the one with the walking stick.

"Why, no, he rarely is here in the afternoon," Myrtle replied.

"Where does he go?" asked the other.

"Why, I don't rightly know," replied Myrtle. "Did you wish to see him about a loan?"

"Yes, that's a good word for it," said the one with the cane. He smiled broadly. "Might start an account. You got a record book to record it?"

"Why, certainly," said Myrtle. "But I don't know you. Are you new in Pony?"

They ignored her.

She reached for the ledger, dug among her pens for one with a fresh nib, and dipped it in her inkwell. "Now, then," she said, "I'll need your names, of course, and whether you plan to write drafts on this or just save, and addresses and so forth. . . ."

"Think I'll just go back and see if Stop's hiding in there," said one. He ambled to the counter gate and opened it. Dudley ducked below window level for a moment so he wouldn't be in clear view.

"I'm sorry sir, but you can't—" Myrtle's voice had a keen edge to it.

But the ugly passed through, and the other followed, heading for Samuel Stop's office.

"Ain't got much security around here, ma'am," he said mockingly. She stood, frozen, watching from her clerking wicket. They stood in Stop's door. "Not much of a bank," said one. "Country joint."

The pair of them spread into the office, poking and probing. A ledger book lay on the desk.

"Wonder what's in here," said one, tossing it open. "Loans, looks like. Payments, dates, interest charged. Pretty good stuff, eh, Lethbridge?"

"Please leave at once! You are trespassing. I shall summon help," snapped Myrtle, livid, heading for the door.

"Oh, you just do that, ma'am. You just go right ahead, and me and Paddo will have a little talk with them folks you bring."

"Leave here at once!" she cried. "And put that ledger down. It is not yours. If I—if I—the whole town will come here, and you'll be in trouble."

"No trouble at all, ma'am. I like to read. Guess I'll take this with me." The one called Lethbridge tucked the loan ledger under his arm, grinning all the while.

They meandered out toward the safe. "Well, look at that. Greenbacks and gold, right in plain sight." Paddo cupped a pile of the coins and toyed with them, rolling them over the marble counter.

Myrtle said no more and suddenly raced for the door, but

Paddo tripped her easily and she sprawled across the floor. Now she sobbed. Her gray skirts rumpled, revealing petticoat and stout calves. But she was not easily deterred, and ferociously she sat up, then stood, poised to spring. Lethbridge caught her thick arm easily, spun her around.

"Now, now, mustn't leave," he said. "Somebody has to stay in the bank. Back to your post!"

Myrtle was disheveled, her dun hair freed from its bun, her skirt and suit coat stained with dust. She stood tensed, neither returning to her wicket nor heading for the front door.

That was all Elmer Dudley needed to see from the window. He gimped along the redbrick wall to the door, pulling his Colt's revolver as he went. And then he swung in, filling the door frame with a roar, two hundred pounds of pure rage stomping into the bank.

But he had been expected. The hook of a cane caught his bum leg. A savage yank and he felt himself crashing into the hardwood floor, his revolver flying. He rolled over instantly, ignoring the pain in his bad leg and the bruised feeling along his side, where he'd landed. But then a knout glanced off his head, and for the next moment he saw nothing, and after that, pinwheels, dizziness, and wild throbbing in his skull.

When his eyes cleared, he found himself on his back, staring up into the smirking face of one of them. "Thought you'd never come, copper," said Lethbridge. "Now you know, don't you?"

He knew. There was no law in Pony. At least for the moment. These two had toyed with him. They would toy with any others, including the toughs in the saloons, and the strong but unskilled miners, and anyone else who dared to resist. Through his haze of red pain he doubted that even the old frontiersmen in town, the ex-soldiers and scouts, the old mountain man down the hill, could handle these uglies . . . at least not without organizing into an armed troop.

He watched them through blurred eyes. The tears had come involuntarily, rinsing the pain that mauled his skull. Myrtle's square face and indignant gaze shifted from him, on the floor, to the uglies again, and she looked fierce. She had not for a moment surrendered.

Now they were back at the open safe, cheerily scattering gold coins, rolling them smartly across the wooden floor, tearing open packets of bills and tossing them like confetti. They hunted then for more records, found three filled volumes on a shelf, and added them to the current records, five ledger books in all.

"You don't want to spend your life on the floor. That's no place for a man to live," said Paddo, his eyes mocking. He offered a hand to Dudley, who refused it, rolled over onto his knees, and stood up weakly.

"Here's your six-shooter, copper," said Lethbridge, stuffing it into Dudley's holster. "We just wanted to make sure it wasn't accidentally discharged."

For a wild moment Elmer Dudley thought to yank it out and start shooting. He felt mad enough. But he thought better of it. He didn't even know whether it was loaded. He stood there, panting, his head pulsing, his balance out of whack, his bum leg howling.

Still, there were things that needed saying. "You're under arrest, both of you. Drop those ledgers. Get your hands up."

"You wouldn't be thinkin' anything like that, would you? That'd be the dumbest thing a copper could do, old man. Now you just sit tight. We ain't stole a dime. We're going to borrow these here ledgers for a while. The bosses want a little look at them. Ain't no theft in it."

"You're disturbing the peace and under arrest," muttered old Dudley wearily.

The twins stared. "Well, take us in, old man. And if you do, go tell our bosses to post bond."

Dudley saw where it was leading. "Go ahead, then," he said. "Take them books. Me and Mrs. Phillips will just clean up around here now."

He needed time. Time to get hold of Sheriff McDaniel at Virginia City; time to organize a posse and deputize some of the good men in town. No telegraph reached Pony; he'd have to dispatch a man. Get the Madison County sheriff over here with an armed troop. Not even fancy financiers, and their plug-uglies, were going to treat this town, and this bank, like this.

"Thinkin' about getting some help?" said Lethbridge. "It ain't gonna work. The bosses buy and sell help. And me and Paddo here can handle it. Handle anything. You try for help, old man, and you and the one you send ain't got ten minutes of life left in you."

There it is, then, thought Dudley.

"I will go myself," announced Myrtle, and she walked deliberately out of the door and into the sunny street. The twins scooped up the ledgers and strolled after her.

Dudley felt trapped. He couldn't leave the place unattended, with greenbacks and gold scattered to every corner. He checked his Colt; it was loaded. From the window he saw Myrtle flee toward Spade's, then watched the two uglies saunter down the street with the blue cloth ledger books and into the Goldstrike Hotel.

Nothing to do but pick up the money. Every time he bent over, his head spun and the throbbing got to him, but in less time than he had imagined, he had the bills and gold coins picked up and organized on the marble counter.

This was something for Stop, he thought. Why had they done it? Why were they harassing him? What had Stop done? Refused to sell the bank to those two vultures?

It pained him not to know. Dammit, he usually knew everything about Pony, but now he didn't know a damned thing. But he'd find out. First he'd go see Ben. And Stop—if Stop showed up. And he'd get his revenge. Pony's law might be one gimpy old man, he thought, but that old man would find some way to outsmart those uglies, or die trying.

Chapter Seven

Hunkered deep in his swivel chair beside the rolltop desk, Sam Stop seemed calm. Maybe too calm, thought Ben Waldorf. Maybe there was no fight in the young banker, after all. But even as he thought it, he dismissed the thought. There was something about Stop that Ben fathomed instinctively. Behind the quietness, the blandness, and the public civility lay a ruthless warrior, although there was not a shred of evidence for it.

Ben knew his man, or thought he did. Stop would take very little pushing, and when he started to shove back, some kind of hell would bust loose. Ben didn't know what kind of hell, though. Just hell, unvarnished.

The others in the Bank of Pony office seemed less calm. Myrtle's square face and stout body seemed tense, and old Elmer Dudley's white features had settled into a burning scowl. The long June twilight lingered, reaching grayly into the room, but they were all illumined by the warmer light of a pair of kerosene lamps in a brass holder.

"It is bad but not a disaster," Stop said. "I will get the ledgers back. There are ways."

"I'd arrest those uglies in a moment if—"

"You did the best you could, Elmer. There'll be a time for that. Just now you're outnumbered."

"I could git up a posse—"

Stop paused, a distant look in his brown eyes. "You could at that. Strong men, miners. Good-hearted men who would likely die. The Dowlings are professionals, Elmer. Of a sort we've never seen here."

Somehow Ben knew that Stop was familiar with uglies and respected them. And knew the strength and weaknesses of the Cousin Jacks from the pits too. Here was Stop telling old Dudley that a posse might not do; that the Dowlings could handle long odds. It made Ben wonder all the more about his mysterious young friend.

"I will talk to Kennedy and Widen," he said.

"You think that'll get the ledgers back?" Ben asked.

"No, not yet."

Ben waited for Stop to say more, tell what he intended, but the banker was quiet.

"Everything's such a mess," said Myrtle.

Stop's gaze turned to her. "Bad, yes, Myrtle. You did your best, too. But we can reconstruct. I'll have the ledgers back soon, but if we don't get them, we can reconstruct. Most depositors save their deposit slips and receipts. They have copies of loan agreements. We have similar files, duplicate receipts, the loan papers. It'll take time, but not all is lost."

"I must start in. I must have it all done before we open tomorrow. . . ."

Stop smiled. "Not tonight. You've been through more than enough trouble for one day."

"But, Mr. Stop, what will I tell the customers?"

He sighed. "Don't hide it. There'll be rumors, anyway, no doubt started by our New York friends and their uglies, and if we deny that we've lost the books, the panic will be worse than if we tell people what happened. Tell them to bring in their deposit slips. . . . Ben, I imagine you have a record of your entire account up at the company offices, right to the penny."

"Guess we do," he said.

"You see, Myrtle? It'll fill in. It'll feel bad, though. Lots of people will worry. Just tell them I will get the ledgers back."

"I've got to get help down to Virginia City," Dudley growled. "I'll git on down there now, ride all night."

"And be bushwhacked."

"I'll sneak someone out, then."

"They will be watching tonight," Stop said easily. "The moon is almost full, too."

The old constable fumed. "Well, I ain't gonna sit here and let this happen without trying to get help."

"That's a noble attitude," Stop said to the older man. The comment struck Ben as being mysterious. Still, Stop wasn't opposing Elmer Dudley's plans, just gently steering them toward safety. Sam Stop was giving no orders, and old Dudley wasn't riling up. If anything, the look in Dudley eyes suggested that he was seeing the banker in a new light.

Myrtle spoke up. "Mr. Stop, what if there's a run tomorrow? What if all the miners want their money out? What will I do?"

Stop sighed. "I think tomorrow we'll have a bank holiday. Locked door. Put up a sign saying we'll reopen the next day. And we'll spend our time reconstructing. But that's mostly for peace of mind. I expect to get the ledgers back soon enough."

He stood, a quiet figure in the lamplit office. "I think that does it. Elmer, be careful. Whatever you do, give the Dowlings credit."

The old man slammed on his hat and hobbled out wordlessly. Myrtle left as well, half terrified of the evening shadows, but game for what was ahead.

Ben and Sam Stop stared at each other. They had spent the afternoon up at the mine offices making plans and acquainting Stop with the company and its assets and liabilities. Stop would need to know everything, be able to answer any question a lender or investor might ask. When they got right down to it, they had several options. There were substantial banks in Helena and Virginia City, for starters. But closer at hand were the copper kings of Butte, Marcus Daley and William Andrews Clark, powerful, rich, ruthless, canny men who might take an interest in Ben's mine, and whose own restless genius might be a match for Kennedy and Widen.

Butte was a long, hard, one-day horseback ride away, over the Tobacco Roots and toward the Continental Divide. Stop thought he could slip out at night and make it. He kept his horse at his house, rather than at Bonack's Livery, and that would help. Between them they had worked out several proposals to present to the copper kings. To Ben they looked like a good bet, and the Butte financiers were close enough at hand to conclude a deal within the thirty days before the called loan came due. He doubted that the Butte magnates would offer a loan, but he thought they'd jump at the chance of getting a piece of a successful mine.

Now, in Stop's office, they stared amiably at each other.

"You got plans?" Ben asked.

"Sure. Want to come along?"

"A powwow," Ben said, rising. Stop looked pleased.

Stop turned the lamp wicks into their cowlings until the lamps blued out and smoked, and then they locked up and trudged down the dusty, shadowed street. The evening remained warm, and lavender light lingered up beyond the Tobacco Roots.

Of the two upstairs rooms at the Goldstrike Hotel that fronted on Pony's main drag, one was illumined, the other dark. Ben followed along, barely keeping up with Stop, wondering whether Stop saw the Dowlings loitering on the street, each in a shadowed place, their black bowlers giving them away. Not that they bothered to conceal themselves. The opposite, rather, Ben thought. A show of force the town could not mistake. Then he saw Stanley, his own fat son, loitering, too, and suddenly Ben knew that the young pigs had been bought. Ben Waldorf snorted, then guffawed.

"I thought you'd feel that way," said Stop.

Ben glanced into Stop's brown, knowing eyes and was startled. Stop hadn't missed anything. Not a trick on that street. Stop sure as hell was something more than a banker.

One of the Dowlings managed to loiter along behind them as they climbed the steps to the hotel and strode through the lobby. The clerk nodded nervously.

Then, at the foot of the stairwell, Stop paused, hand on the banister.

"Ben," he said, "what do you want?"

"What do you mean, what do I want? That's the confoundedest question I ever heard," Ben fumed.

"It's important, Ben. What do you want?"

"Lissen here, Stop. I'm seventy-five. Does that have any meaning to you? Seventy-five? Don't ask me dumb questions."

Stop stared at one of the Dowlings who was loitering back in the lobby. "Seventy-five going on fifty. Supposing you've got a long time still, Ben. Supposing you go right along to ninety. What do you want?"

Ben muttered and fumed. Life had been simple. He was old and he'd kick off. And here stood this banker, still wet behind the ears, telling him . . . "I haven't thought about it," he replied shortly.

"Well, think now," said Stop patiently. Ben saw that he would not climb stairs until the thing was settled.

"I got everything; hit the bonanza and saw the elephant. I can't think of a blasted thing—"

"What about the hellcat?"

"Her? Aw, hell, Stop. Why, I'd like to keep her in feathers and furs. You know—don't you go spreading this around—but I sort of like her. I mean, never a dull moment for an old goat like me. Yes, I like her. Lots of feather and furs until I croak, and then she can find some other buffler bull."

"What about the boys, Ben?"

He snorted. It was answer enough for Stop.

"What about Pony? The miners? The merchants, Bonack, Spade, and the rest?"

Ben sure as hell didn't know where this was leading, or what had gotten into Sam Stop, but it didn't matter. "Keep 'em going, I'd like to keep 'em going," he muttered.

"What about these aces upstairs?" Stop asked softly.

"Kick their butts back to New York. That's what I want." He glared suspiciously at Stop. "Why do you want to know all this?"

Stop shrugged. "I need to know," he said.

* * *

Jasper Kennedy and Drago Widen entertained prominent guests in the General Sherman Suite. On hand were two of Pony's leading merchants, Martin Spade and Theo Bonack, who sipped Old Crow from ice-filled hotel tumblers.

"We wanted thee to be the first to know that we are assuming control of Pony Consolidated," Jasper said smoothly. "We have great plans for it—and for Pony. There will be higher profits, more miners, a disciplined company. With old Ben out, we will begin some major operations."

"That sounds pretty good. I'll want to hear more about it," said Spade tentatively. He was a seasoned merchant and a wary man, and he peered at his hosts from bagged blue eyes with heavily pouched lids. He had arrived in his shirt sleeves but wore his black broadcloth vest and a blue sleeve garter.

"Thee will have the details in a day or two, when everything is tidied up. Now, my good men, we have invited thee here to talk of other things. Mr. Widen and I are intending to integrate the economy of the town. That is to say, establish a company presence. Which is to say, we'd like to buy thee out."

"Oh, I'm not for sale." Spade's alert face had pinched into wariness.

"Can't say as I am, either," added Theo Bonack. "I like it here; steady trade. Livery business couldn't be better, and it's a pleasant life for my woman and me." He leaned back, his giant hands massaging the arms of his chair.

"We are prepared to make thee good offers, at least now while thee have thriving businesses," Jasper said, a faint suggestion in his voice.

Spade caught the nuance at once. "You're saying they may not thrive soon."

"Why, if we cannot buy from thee, we may start our own. And, of course, pay the miners in scrip, redeemable at our stores."

Spade nodded. He was getting the idea, even if Theo Bonack was still a little slow.

"Wouldn't affect me," said Bonack. "Company people don't use the livery much."

"Thee might find differently," said Jasper. "Thee must buy hay and grain locally. But no matter. We intend to integrate the town. We shall be buying this Goldstrike Hotel as well, and will be dealing with Pyle. And the bank, of course. Especially the bank. If Stop won't sell, we'll have to build our own and require our people to bank there.

"Now, there's much in it for thee. We will buy thee out fairly, then employ thee as managers, company executives, so thee will continue just the way thy life has been, but without the risks, for the risks will then be Drago's and mine, eh?"

Spade was not a man to knuckle under to pressures and threats. "I'll hang on," he said. "Don't intend to give up my own place and not be my own boss. We shall see if I suffer. Unless I miss my guess, my goods will be priced cheaper than yours, anyway."

Mr. Jasper Kennedy reached into the breast pocket of his dark suit and extracted a roll of large bills. He plucked off four of them and laid them on the bed.

"Thee has a fair offer—for now," said Jasper.

Spade and Bonack stared. They were thousand-dollar bills. Neither merchant had ever seen one. Then Spade shook his head.

"That's about half the value of my store and stock. No thank you," he said. There was resolution in his fierce blue eyes, but worry too.

Jasper pulled two more bills off the roll and laid them before Theo Bonack. "A fair offer for the livery, Bonack."

The bald man stared longingly at the bills and said nothing.

"We need, of course, to settle matters before Drago and I head back East tomorrow. We can give thee until then to accept or reject our tender."

The portly financier retrieved the money and restored it to his fat roll.

"And if we reject—?" asked Spade.

Jasper smiled. "Thee will not reject," he said.

Drago said, "It'll be a fine, secure life for you and your ladies, working for us. We expect all the merchants will join us as soon as they are aware of the benefits. And you'll each have a nest egg, too."

"I won't be among them," said Spade. He rose, stared at the financiers icily, and walked out.

"And thee, Bonack?"

"Gotta think about it," he said. "Never made big decisions without some sleeping on it." He rose, too, shook hands, and left.

"They are always like that," said Drago. "Can't accept the gifts of God. Too proud. A sinful pride is the ruin of men."

"I suppose we should talk to Pyle next. What does thee suppose this bedbug palace is worth?"

"What does it matter? Try three thousand."

"Would thee fetch him? He lives in that ground-floor suite. Or send one of the twins?"

"They're keeping an eye on Stop over at his bank."

"That reminds me. What does thee think we should offer Stop for that bank? From a look at those ledgers I'd say he's prospered. About doubled his net worth. He takes a hundred fifty a month out for himself. Not a bad little operation. Good loans, almost invisible default rate. Remarkable, actually."

Drago paused. "Not a thing. He's an insolent sort—we saw that this morning at the mine—and in need of humbling. A little special treatment is the thing."

"Well, of course, Drago, but doesn't thee agree that we should make some small offer first, for obvious reasons?"

Drago sighed. "It would pain me, but I will bend my knee and pray upon it."

At that moment Stop filled the doorway, Ben Waldorf behind him. The door had been ajar.

"What god do you bend a knee to?" asked Stop.

"Why, Stop! Come in. We were just talking about thee," said Jasper.

"I'm sure you were," Stop said dryly as he and Ben entered. His eyes settled at once upon the stack of blue bank ledgers. "I've come to get those," he said without further ado, and scooped them off the far table.

"I think not," said Paddo Dowling from the doorway.

"They are my property," said Stop mildly.

Paddo grinned. "Not any longer," he said cheerfully.

Stop did not put the ledgers down.

"Now, gents, you're just in time for a toddy," said Drago. "We have just had a fine toddy with some of the merchants, Spade and Bonack."

"No toddy tonight," said Stop. "I've got what I came for."

"Interesting ledgers," said Jasper. "Thee knows how to run a bank, Stop. Some genius at it, I say. We will make thee an offer of five thousand for it above thy capitalization."

"No," said Stop.

"Would thee want us to start our own bank? There's a market for only one here. We mean to integrate a bank with our company. It would be most helpful for our workers."

"You don't own the company—and won't," said Stop.

"Thee may accept now, Stop. By the time we leave tomorrow, it'll be too late."

Sam Stop was staring now. "I'll risk it," he said. He turned to leave, only to find himself careening to the floor, his feet ripped out from under him with the hook of a cane. The ledgers went flying.

Stop rolled over and sat up. Above him, Paddo Dowling was smirking. Drago Widen scurried around, collecting the ledgers.

"I think you have made a mistake," said Stop, his brown eyes boring into Paddo's.

Ben Waldorf stared at Stop, plainly disappointed by the mild banker, who sat on the floor, scarcely even angry.

"We don't make mistakes," Paddo said.

Stop stood up and dusted off his suit.

"Until my ledgers are returned, Ben and I will not be available for negotiation," Stop said. "Not tomorrow, not in thirty days, either."

Jasper merely smiled. "It'll all be settled tomorrow. We're leaving for New York tomorrow."

"With nothing in your hands," said Stop.

The financiers and Paddo laughed, but there was a look in Sam Stop's eyes that silenced them. Stop nodded to Ben Waldorf, and the pair of them walked out.

"Small-town fools," said Drago Widen, well within Ben's hearing.

Chapter Eight

Elmer Dudley sulked in his wicker chair under Spade's porch, ignoring the banter of the duffers and whittlers beside him that morning. In fact, he was preoccupied. The episode the day before at Stop's bank—when the derby men had sent him sprawling—gnawed on his mind. He lived and relived it, wondering if he could have done better.

But the bitter truth wouldn't go away: He was no match for that pair of twins, and until he figured some way of mastering them, there would be no law and order in Pony. It galled him, as did the old wound in his knee. The rest of him was as powerful as a bull, and even with the bum knee he had never hesitated to bust up a saloon brawl or haul a rowdy miner off to the little wooden cubicle that passed for a jail in Pony.

Even now one of the Dowlings lounged on the porch of the Goldstrike Hotel, mocking the town. He appeared to be unarmed, save for a walking stick. But old Dudley knew better.

Elmer Dudley had learned humility, and now it served him well. That pair would require special handling. If he tried to arrest one or both, he'd likely end up six feet under ground. Still, twenty years had taught him patience, and some leadership, too. He needed men, a posse, deputies, enough brave miners to deal with this menace. Not that he was sure this menace would be around long. Those financiers might pack up and leave anytime and take their bullyboys with them. Still, Elmer thought, a man could prepare for the worst. It might go the other way. The bullyboys might terrorize Pony, rob it, prevent people from coming and going, or worse. So Dudley thought he'd just do some quiet organizing. One good thing: The town wasn't aware of it yet, didn't know that Dudley was no longer in command, that law had vanished. What had happened in the bank the previous day was private. Those who knew about it, Stop and Myrtle and Ben, wouldn't be announcing it.

"Seems to me that's a mess of Cousin Jacks up there, fillin' the street," said old Witherspoon. "Wonder what that's all about. Guess we'll know soon enough."

The duffer's observation snapped Dudley out of his reverie. Sure enough, a dozen off-shift miners milled up there, in front of the bank. Making loud talk, too, but Dudley couldn't get the drift of it. And that Dowling, too, drifting on up the street, watching, always watching.

Dudley hitched up his legs, yanked himself out of his wicker chair, and hoisted his gun belt around until it hung better. Then he lumbered uphill, pretty much knowing what this would be about but not knowing what to say or do about it. He was a bear of a man, in spite of his limp, and the miners turned to him as he approached.

"Why's this bank shut?" asked one.

"Where's Stop?" asked another. "He's not in there. Off and gone."

"He stole the money, that's what," yelled another. "We've been robbed, and now we can't even get in there to see."

Across the dirt road, Lethbridge Dowling leaned against a porch post and watched the confusion.

The constable lurched through the crowd, seeing scowls and fear in their faces. Myrtle worked inside. The front door was locked tight, the shade drawn. And pinned to the shade was a notice—BANK CLOSED TODAY. OPEN TOMORROW—written in Myrtle's hand.

"Where's Stop? If he ain't there to explain soon, I'm gonna

bust in there and see." It was a thin youth, mine-pit white, with rheumy eyes, who said that.

"You'll do no busting," growled Dudley.

"Where's Stop? He's a crook. I knew it all along," yelled another.

Constable Dudley had a pretty good idea where Stop was. Off chasing down a loan. Ben and Stop had discussed it the previous night while Dudley and Myrtle were there.

"He's out of town today," Dudley yelled. "Probably back tomorrow or the next day. No need to get het up."

"This bank been robbed?"

"It hasn't. Every cent's in there that always was."

"How do you know that, Dudley?"

"I know it."

"This got something to do with them financiers?"

Dudley hesitated. "It does," he said.

"If them and those derby boys are stealing, we should maybe go after them."

Across the street, Lethbridge watched jauntily.

"You ain't told us what this is about, Constable."

"It ain't a robbery."

"How do we know that? I got every penny I own in there!"

Dudley looked at the man who'd spoken, and recognized him. Young Philo Crane, one of the steadiest hands up in the hole. Ben once told him that Philo would be foreman soon. Philo was the kind of man Dudley had in mind to help keep law and order.

"Look," he said easily, "Myrtle's in there doin' some inventory work and accounting stuff. She'll open up for me. Philo, I'm going to take you on in there and show you every penny's there. You'll see it with your own eyes, what's in the safe, and then you can tell the rest here to relax, eh?"

"I'll come on in," Philo said. He turned to his fellows. "I'll tell you exactly what I see with my own eyes."

That didn't soothe the Cousin Jacks much, but it was enough for the moment. Dudley rapped on the glass. In a moment Myrtle peered around the shade, then cautiously unlocked, and admitted Dudley and Philo Crane.

"Mornin' Myrtle," Dudley said. "Philo here's sort of a representative of the fellows out there. They're fearing things that just ain't so."

"Where's Stop?" Philo asked Myrtle.

"Why, he's out of town on business."

"When's he coming back?"

"I don't know. A day or two," she replied cautiously.

"When can we take out our money?"

"Soon," she said. "If there's a run, we can cover it, I'm sure. But there's no need for that."

"What are you doing locked up in here?" Philo demanded.

"Why, inventorying. And working on accounts."

Dudley gimped over to the safe, which stood with its green door ajar. "Lookee here, Philo."

The miner slid behind the counter and stared into the safe.

"Lots there, all right, but how do I know that's all of it?"

"You have my word," said Myrtle.

"That's good enough for me," said Philo.

"Will you tell them that out there?" Dudley asked.

"I will."

"Now I wantcha to come with me into Stop's office. Myrtle, you mind if I talk private to Philo here?"

"Not at all," she said, "I have hardly started putting things together."

Philo stared sharply at her and followed Dudley into the office. As if by some right of possession, the old constable sank into Stop's generous desk chair. Just the way Stop had sunk into Dudley's wicker chair on the porch, three years before.

"You're a good man, Crane, and what I'm saying now is private. I'm not asking you, I'm telling you."

The tall miner settled into a seat, his brogans out before him, and nodded.

"Raise your big paw," demanded Dudley. "I'm deputizing you."

The constable swore in the miner, then told him what had transpired and the purpose of the financiers' visit. The probable result—less safe conditions, lower wages, company stores, wages paid in scrip redeemable in the store . . . a company bank.

Philo Crane scowled. Then the old constable talked about the derby men's bank visit yesterday, the ledger books, the ruthless power of the Dowlings, men who could bury the burliest miners in a hurry. . . .

And then the confession that Dudley could hardly stand to make. "I ain't a match for them. At least not head-on. I'd just get myself planted. I don't fear death so much, but I fear what'd happen to the town. So I'm thinking, get organized, watch and wait for the opening. It'll come, some moment when I can get the drop on both of them uglies with two loads of buckshot. Watch and wait and start preparing. You're in on the preparing, Philo. You're right in, and now I want you to line up a few of the best men you know of in the pits. Don't tell them why yet. Not even what's gonna happen if them money men from the East take over. Nothing like that—I don't want this town torn apart. Just say I may need help and some unquestioned loyalty. I figure it ain't gonna come to that. Stop'll probably raise the money, get old Ben out of his hole.

"But, Philo, they don't want Ben or Stop to raise the money, see. They want to take over fast, now, today, using the Dowlings. And that's what I need you for, you and your men. So get me a dozen, private and quiet, the best men. . . ."

"They're yours. I go on shift at four, and I'll get them all from my shift. By morning, Elmer, I'll have you an army."

"That's the boy," said Dudley, rising. He grinned for the first time that day.

Ben Waldorf was always faintly surprised by Murray Eickles's office. It didn't fit his notion of what a mine office should look like, but as long as Eickles didn't go overboard, Ben didn't care. The carmine-and-azure Oriental rug on the floor matched the flocked wallpaper. Eickles had a walnut rolltop desk, as well as a walnut conference table with plush leather-padded chairs around it. On the walls hung fine hunt scenes—engravings, mostly—long, lean thoroughbreds leaping Virginia fences. And on the desk, a massive brass lamp with four glass-covered wicks.

It fit, Ben thought. Eickles was usually here, never down in the pit, and more often than not, entertaining drummers who rolled in regularly to sell wares to the company. In fact, Eickles was present now, hunched over his desk, dipping his nib pen into a well and scratching and blotting furiously. He'd grown bald on top but had a rim of sandy red hair over the ears, a close-trimmed sandy beard that concealed heavy jowl fat, and a dark suit with heavy white pinstripes that compressed his porcine fat into a cylinder.

Ben stood in the doorway, but Eickles either didn't notice or feigned industry at his desk.

Ben entered and eased himself into one of the stuffed leather chairs, and it felt so soft his bottom quivered as he sat.

"Murray," Ben said softly. At last the general superintendent deigned to look up. "Murray, I been thinkin'. You getting paid enough?"

Eickles straightened up and settled his pen in its stand and stared at a point in space four inches above, and slightly to the left of, Ben's head. "Why, Ben, any man would welcome more money, if that's what's on your mind." He smiled porkily.

"Ain't what I asked," said Ben.

Some faint wariness showed in Eickles's colorless eyes. It was the darnedest thing, Ben thought. Eickles had no eye color. His eyes were a nothing color, not blue or green or hazel or gray or brown or black. Maybe no pupils, maybe that was it. Just a pair of holes into his skull.

"I'm comfortable," said Murray Eickles. "I'm content and have enough."

Enough, thought Ben, to build the second fanciest house in town, a clapboard pile for himself and his equally bulky wife.

"Enough," said Ben. "Enough money. Plenty to keep yourself livin' like a mine super, right?"

"That's right," said Eickles.

"How much are they paying you?" asked Ben.

Eickles looked puzzled. "Paying? I don't follow you, Ben."

"Jasper Kennedy and Drago Widen. How much?"

Now fear laced Murray's face, and the glint of early sweat.

"Don't know what you're talking about," he said curtly. "You feeling all right, Ben?"

"No, matter of fact, I've got a case of the Eickles," Ben said.

There was a long, pregnant silence. Eickles slid deeper into his quilted chair.

"You got anything to say?" Ben asked.

"Is this some kind of joke?" Eickles asked.

"Sure is," said Ben. "Get out. You're out. Pack up and leave right now."

"I haven't the faintest idea why—"

"Neither do I. Just an old man's whim," said Ben. "But I'm the owner and I'm indulging my sporting instincts. So git."

"Right now?"

"You got anything that's keeping you?"

"Why, I have a report to finish—appointment with Walsh of the Mine Owners Betterment League—"

"Out."

"What about my pay?"

"Out."

"You won't even listen to my side of the story."

"Out." Ben stood, a massive hulk of tough old prospector, even at seventy-five. At last Murray Eickles stood, plucked up a humidor and his hat and a silky umbrella, and skittered out the door.

"The key," said Ben.

Reluctantly Eickles dug in his pocket and extracted it.

"The other keys," said Ben.

"Why, that's all—"

"Empty your pockets," said Ben.

"This is outrageous!"

From the central room the two clerks observed all this, astonished. Slowly Eickles emptied his pockets. No more keys. Then, at Ben's nod, he grabbed his wallet and coins and dashed out. Ben locked Eickles's door and pocketed the key. When Stop got back, Ben would have the banker read whatever was in there.

Outside, he heard the footfall of horses and the crunch of a carriage on gravel. From the grimed window Ben saw the black barouche, Kennedy and Widen, and one driver in a black derby. Eickles had vanished.

They'd given him twenty-four hours, and now they were here. No doubt planning to take over. He headed into his office and waited.

"Howdy, gents," he said as they entered. Two rich penguins in starched shirts, and a gray-tusked boar. "Have a seat."

The New York financiers eased themselves down on the bench. The bowler man stood at the door, as if to guard it.

"We'd like to bring this trip to a successful conclusion," said Drago Widen with no preliminaries. Ben nodded. "We have a transfer paper here for you to sign. I'll go over it for you. The first clause transfers ownership of Consolidated Pony to Kennedy and Widen as of today. The second says that the transfer discharges all company debt owing to Kennedy and Widen and cancels the loan . . . . There's a few other details. Giving you a week to vacate your office, agreeing not to bring legal actions against us or the company, that sort of thing. Details."

He shoved the paper across the plank desk.

Ben grinned. "Sorry, gents. Sam Stop does my negotiating, and he's not here."

"That's foolish. Stop can't come up with that kind of money. Just get it over with, Ben. You'll feel better."

"Nope. We won't even talk until those ledgers are returned to Stop. He told you that last night."

There was a long silence while the two bankers assessed him, probed the old man's determination.

"Thee is wasting our time and yours, Ben," said Jasper. "For pride? Thee should know better. This is business, Ben. Thee knows about the hard choices."

Ben Waldorf grinned. He was through talking. Let 'em stew.

"We have been generous with thee, Ben. We could treat thee harder."

Ben said nothing. It was coming, he knew. Something now beyond the rules, the hard things men like this did that startled those who thought in civilized terms: fair play, law, courts, settlements.

"Would thee offer us other terms? We'll listen to thee."

"You can start by returnin' them ledgers."

"No. Young Stop needs to learn some lessons in humility."

Ben said nothing.

Time stretched long, or so it seemed. A minute, maybe. No time at all in an old man's long life. Ben eased back, waiting. He had twenty-nine days left, by God, and he'd take them.

At last Jasper nodded to the bowler man. "We are forced to keep thee here until thy signature is on that paper," said Jasper sadly. "Such a silly thing. All for nothing."

Lethbridge Dowling smirked faintly.

Jasper turned to him. "Thee shall hold him here until he signs. Without fail. No food, no water, no trips to the necessary rooms."

Ben absorbed that and laughed, a great rumble of delight in his throat. "I've been lookin' for a way to kick off," he said, "and now I found it. I'll just lay me down to sleep in the corner. Figger dehydrating to death is as easy as any. Ain't going to sign, though. You'll have a death to answer for, you fellas. And that ain't all of it. This company ain't a corporation; it's all mine, personal property, except for one percent I sold Stop yesterday. All the rest goes into my estate as private ownership. But you know that well enough. Them courts, they may allow you the two hundred thousand against the estate, but that's all you git. In fact, I ain't even got a will, so there'll be a doozy of a fight for it. Those punk sons of mine ain't going to get far."

All of that visibly alarmed the financiers, and Ben watched them, amused. He keenly enjoyed life, and the last thing he wanted was to lose it, but he was old and entitled to a good poker bluff. And so he laughed.

Drago spoke up at last. "Jasper, there are other ways, less risky and more effective. Lethbridge, my good man, you lift old Waldorf here and carry him outside. We'll just take over this property. As they say, possession is nine-tenths of the law. Carry him out, and we'll find Eickles to run it and start diverting the bullion to us. No sense in letting it pile up."

Jasper instantly agreed. It seemed better. If they had the mine, and the Dowlings to hold it, why bother with the papers? The old man would come around eventually.

Lethbridge Dowling sauntered toward the old man. "You walking out or coming hard?" he asked.

Ben said nothing but stood and stalked out, the smirking ugly crowding behind him, the walking stick never far from the old man's kidneys.

In the central office and reception room, Jasper Kennedy turned to the two clerks. "The company ownership has changed hands," he said. "Thee'll take instruction from Murray Eickles. Consider Mr. Drago Widen and myself, Jasper Kennedy, thy employers."

Ben Waldorf blinked in the reflecting mountain light. It was a half mile to his pile of red brick, and he began to walk, keenly enjoying the shining summer sun.

Chapter Nine

When Ben showed up in the middle of the day, Jezebel didn't think it was unusual. Ben followed no set schedule. But Ben didn't pause long at the red brickpile; just long enough for a bite to eat. He seemed preoccupied, too.

Then he headed out to the barns, and with the help of the Waldorf stable and yard men, Alonzo and Gilberto, Latins of undetermined vintage, he harnessed Pegasus to the light buggy. By then Jezebel was curious. Pegasus was her fine harness horse, and the light buggy was usually what she rode.

"Ben, what's happening?"

The old man gazed at her fondly, his white hair and full beard glistening in the sun. "Some trouble up at the mine, Tootsie."

"It's those Eastern money men," she said.

"Yes, it is. And we may have a hard time of it for a while."

"Are we going to be poor?" she asked directly.

He guffawed. "Not very likely. If they take the mine away, what would you do?"

"Leave you," she said, and giggled.

He laughed, a fine bellow on the morning wind. "That's the girl," he said. "You look stunning this morning."

"I felt like dressing," she said. When she awoke that morning, she'd decided she'd wear something that would torment the financiers, just in case they showed up. So she put on her new pink dimity dress with the daring neckline that showed the top of her lush breasts. It had a tight waist and flared down to a white flounce at her ankles. With her raven hair and lavender eyes, she knew she would be irresistible.

"I'm going on down to the reduction plant. Have a little business there."

"What's happening?" she asked, concerned.

He had always told her about business things, and he didn't hesitate now, even though the matter was sensitive. "Kennedy and Widen have taken over up on the hill, or rather their uglies have. I'll drive 'em out eventually. But now I've got to go below and snatch the bullion in the safe down there before they get their pink paws on it. That's why I need the buggy. Must be a hundred pounds of it." He peered around, then said confidentially, "I'll hide it at Stop's. He's not there—running an errand for me—but I have a place there in mind. You gonna tell that to them financiers and uglies?'

"First chance I get," she said. They smiled at each other.

"Make 'em pay you for the information," he said, and winked.

"I'd rather shoot their stones off."

"We'll lick them buggers," he said, and flicked the reins to set Pegasus off.

She watched him go. She liked the old goat. Hated to admit it, but she plain liked him. Even at night.

She had a feeling she would have visitors that day. Jasper Kennedy had that look in eye. She was familiar with it. Half the rubes who bought shoes off her daddy's wagon had the look, and she knew how to deal with it. Still, he had threatened to haul her out of here, and that alarmed her. Not that she'd resist travel, or New York, or fun, but not with him. All those thees and thous.

Well, she thought, she could take care of herself. In addition to Alonzo and Gilberto, there was the skinny, compact Chinese cook. When he had shown up a few years ago, no one could pronounce his name. Finally she had baptized him Hip Hip, and soon enough he had become Hip Hip Hurray. Anyway, Hip Hip Hurray lurked around, a mean little man with a meat cleaver. Maybe he could do other Chinese things, too. She didn't know. He cooked up a storm, threw everyone out of his kitchen, and kept an irate eye on the world.

She walked amiably back to the house and its shade. No one would mess with her. She had the derringers ready. In fact, she had fifty-four of them, which was more than her forty-seven pairs of shoes. She loved the little things. Years before, a traveling salesman had shown up with a black leather case. She always had had a soft spot for traveling salesmen, because that's what her daddy had been. Anyway, that ruddy, chubby man in the checkered suit opened the heavy leather case, and there on the gray felt trays were rows of derringers and a few other gats.

She was enchanted. There were mean little blue-black devils, in both .36- and .44-caliber. There were nickel-plated ones, and two with silver plate. There were one-barrel and two-barrel ones, some with side-by-side barrels, and some with over-and-under barrels. Some had pearly grips and others had filigree designs etched into the metal. One had an engraved naked lady on it. In the end she bought them all, twenty-two of them, plus all the ammunition he had. Then he had sought additional compensation in flesh, but she had kneed him in the groin and he'd left in a hurry.

But that was just the beginning. When she and Ben traveled to Virginia City, or Butte, or Helena, she always bought a few more. Ben had taken to calling her bedroom the Armory. Once, when they were pursuing connubial bliss, she grabbed one on her bedside table and shot a hole in the ceiling, and old Ben had laughed until he coughed. She always had three or four in her reticules, and it made her feel mean and saucy. Indeed, she had one on her person right now. It was a clever one she found in Virginia City. It formed the grip of her parasol. One tug of the shaft of the parasol and she was armed.

She knew how to use them, too. Once in a while she would gather them all up—all she could find, anyway, since they were spread around in half a dozen reticules and elsewhere—and haul them off to a slope back behind the mansion, then massacre an unoffending tin can. They were supposed to be accurate only at a few feet, but she became deadly with them at fifty feet. She liked the naked-lady one best. She supposed it had been made for a gambler, and that's what she was, anyway.

Well, sure enough, a couple of hours later that gleaming black barouche rolled in, those two financiers perched in the rear of it like a pair of sucked eggs, with one of the uglies driving. That didn't bother her. What did was the other company, her two fat stepsons, Willis and Stanley, looking smug on fancy horses. She hardly recognized them by daylight. Obviously they'd been bought; they'd never show up in daylight unless they'd been bought. Ben paid them to stay away. They were really remittance men, staying away, down at Louella's, with Ben's gold. Ben had actually done that for her, so they wouldn't molest her. The pair were many years older than their stepmother, and always suggestive and smirky around her. Once Willis had even said, when old Ben died, that she was going to see what kind of stepson he was. She had told Ben about that, and for once the old man's face had darkened. "Shoot him," he had said. She intended to.

At the foot of the veranda she curtsied slightly, giving the financiers a fine peek at her lush breasts. She enjoyed that. Back on the wagon selling shoes with her daddy, she had managed to flash all sorts of portions of herself, then watched the rubes' eyes change. She noted that Willis and Stanley had gone off to the barns with their horses, and that pleased her.

"Well, well, what a fair, fine day," said Mr. Jasper Kennedy. "Are thee well, madam? Thy fine sons have invited us to stay here while business matters settle, and so we have brought our trunks. So very kind of them."

She hadn't expected that. In fact, it rattled her. The three of them, the financiers and the bowler-tipped ugly, were licking their chops.

"Those jackasses made a mistake," she said. "But you are welcome for a snort."

"Why, we don't imbibe spiritous drinks by day," he said, "but we shall take thee up on it this evening."

He nodded, and the ugly leapt down, attached a carriage weight to the horses, and lifted down the first trunk.

"Which room, lady?" he asked, leering.

She flamed hotly inside, but something told her to stay cool. They seemed to think they owned the place. Maybe they did! Maybe Ben lost this house, too! But, no, he always told her everything, and she was certain Ben owned every brick of it.

"This way," she said tersely. She threaded her way through the first floor, through Hip Hip Hurray's kitchens, to the maid's quarters behind, now vacant. "Here," she said.

He grinned. "I think not. You has got upstairs rooms for the money men." With that he threaded his way back, up the balustraded stairs, and deposited the first trunk in Ben's own room.

Then he hoisted the second trunk from the coach and hauled it in. This time Hip Hip Hurray slouched at the foot of the stairs, narrowly eyeing the parade, his thumb absently sliding along the honed edge of a meat cleaver.

"What's the heathen doin' here?" the ugly asked.

"He is my cook. He is excellent at putting strychnine in guests' food."

The ugly cackled. "We'll have you eat some first, then," he said.

He deposited the second trunk in a spare bedroom, and she felt relieved that her own was unmolested. She vanished into it and hid the derringers lying about, putting eleven under the pillows of her four-poster.

She found Jasper Kennedy and Drago Widen in Ben's den. Drago sat at Ben's rolltop desk, reading whatever was crammed into the pigeonholes. Jasper lounged easily in Ben's big chair.

"Where's the old boy?" he asked amiably.

"Off on a little ride," she said tersely.

"That's fine, fine," he said. "I can talk with thee, my little buttercup."

"You can talk with me if you wish. Getting me to do things is another matter."

Jasper smiled. "I thought perhaps thee would like to win a little profit."

"Money?"

"Gold."

"I like gold."

"Aha!" cried Drago. "Here it is, here it is!" He waved something he had discovered in the rolltop desk. "Just as we thought, Jasper. The old boy has barely a thousand in his bank account. Here's his passbook at Stop's bank."

He handed it to Jasper, who smiled. "Thy husband is not a frugal man. Just a pittance at the bank. Nothing to repay his loans."

"Why should he be? He's got a gold mine," Jezebel retorted. "Besides, I spent it. He hardly spent anything."

"Ah, mistress, thee has no sense of what it means to possess wealth. Stewardship. Even small wealth, such as this." He handed the passbook back to Drago.

"I can spend it faster than anyone can earn it. I can spend it faster than *you* could earn it," she said saucily.

"Hardly," he said softly. "But I will say this: If thee likes to spend like that, forget old Ben. Thy future is brighter than that in the great cities. Now, then, I will give thee a double eagle if thee will persuade Ben to sign the agreement. Then it will be over."

"How shall I do that?"

"Why, how does any wife do it? By withholding the nuptial blessing or whatever thee does best."

She sighed. This was more fun than she had had in years, but she thought not to reveal it. "Why, the old goat hasn't come to me in a century. I think he is . . . ah, retired."

"What a waste!" exclaimed Jasper. "Criminal waste. All the more reason for thee to abandon the old goat."

"I'll take the gold piece," she said. He handed it to her. "I'll go spend it now. You've got the wrong man. Ben said it would be up to Stop. He won't sign anything unless Stop tells him to."

She turned to leave.

"Wait," he said, but she didn't. She was twenty dollars richer and would find something to spend it on. In her bedroom she changed to her split riding skirt and a loose blouse, then ran out to the stables. Ben never liked her to ride to town in that split skirt—it shocked the merchants—but she did so, anyway. And, besides, he had the buggy.

She haltered her black mare, Nightwind, in her stall, led her into the barn aisle, and began to brush her sleek coat.

"Well, look who's playing with the mare," said Willis from behind. She turned. The pair of them, Willis and Stanley, stood near her, pink-and-white and fat and smirking. Both of them wore holstered revolvers, which jutted out oddly from their corpulent hips.

"Why don't you play with me instead? I like to be brushed," said Stanley.

She ignored him and went on brushing.

"Just because you're Ben's, don't go getting smart ideas. He won't last long. And then we'll see. You're his tart; everyone knows that. A bought-and-paid-for tart."

She threw the brush at Stanley, and he dodged it easily with a mincing step.

"Oh, I like women with a temper," he said.

Willis said, "You don't suppose you're going anywhere, do you? You're staying here, you know. Our new employers, who own the mine now, told us not to let anyone leave."

She ignored them. Silence was the sole defense against those two, other than resorting to the bullwhip, which lay close at hand in the mare's stall. The pair of them seemed more loathsome to her than she had ever remembered. She realized she had not seen them in half a year. Well, in a moment she'd be gone. They wouldn't dare shoot.

She dropped an English saddle with silky leather onto the back of the tall thoroughbred mare and cinched it up. Then she bridled the mare and led her toward the barn door.

But Willis intervened, grabbing her arm and spinning her.

"We told you," he said. Then he squeezed her to him, and she pounded on his chest.

"Time for old Ben to share the fun," he said. "There's only the three of us here, just right for a little party."

She struggled, fending off hands at first, and then, when it became difficult, twisted free. Stanley grabbed at her, got a fistful of blouse, and pulled it out of her skirt, but then she escaped. With a bound she was on the mare and slapping the mare's rump even though she couldn't find the stirrups and the reins were trailing. Then she broke away, righting herself in the saddle, and reaching forward for the reins.

It had never been like that. Smirky suggestions, but they had never touched her. They had been emboldened by the financiers and no longer felt dependent on Ben, she thought. The pair of them were screaming behind her, but let them!

A shot cracked, and a tremor convulsed the mare. It stumbled and coughed and wouldn't move. Another shot and the mare coughed and began to sink, slowly, a trembling mountain of black beneath Jezebel. And just before the mare sank to earth, Jezebel leapt free. The mare shuddered on the grass and died, blood pooling in two places beneath her chest and rump.

Wildly Jezebel stared. Willis and Stanley were smirking, blowing smoke from the barrels of their revolvers, chortling.

"We told ya," one said, "but ya didn't listen. Things are different around here. Old Ben's out of it now."

Her wildcat instincts cut loose. She didn't run toward the house, she raced into the barn, straight past the two brothers, who stood there mocking her still. She wanted her bullwhip. She found it, got a firm, mean grip on it, and leapt out to the barn door, where Willis and Stanley still stood and smirked. The first lash set Willis to howling, bloodying his hand. The second caught Stanley across the face, half blinding him. The third snap caught Willis again, just as he was pulling his revolver free, and spun the revolver into the corral muck. The pair of them danced and minced and tried to escape the lash.

Then, from behind, two powerful arms pinioned her brutally.

"You has to stop. They're our employees you is whipping, and we can't allow that."

She struggled, but Lethbridge tightened his grip until she went limp. He continued to hold her in an iron clamp.

Stanley and Willis wiped blood off themselves, recovered their breath, and approached—one with the whip, the other with a stick he had found.

"We're gonna mark you, you whore," raged Stanley. "We're gonna mess your face and scar up the rest of you so bad that . . . you'll never live high off a man again."

Now, at last, Jezebel felt terror steal through her like cold lead in her veins. Behind her the ugly had her arms pinned, and she was totally vulnerable.

Willis giggled. "You're gonna get it, Miss Fancypants. You're just a bought tart for Ben, not a wife. But no more. You're never even gonna recognize that purty face when I get done with you, little fake virgin."

"I think you had better not," said Lethbridge mildly.

"What've you got to say about it?" Stanley asked. He closed on Jezebel now, his stick poised to break her nose and bash her face.

"You didn't hear me. Mr. Kennedy wants her unmarked. He's taking her back East, for a little taming. If she doesn't tame, Paddo and I will do a little marking then. But not now."

Stanley ignored the derby man and started to swing. Jezebel found herself thrown violently to earth, well clear of the arcing stick, and from the dirt she saw the ugly do something strange and alarming. With a few short chops and jerks, and no apparent effort at all, he clobbered Stanley and Willis and sent them reeling across the aisle. The pair of them ended up gasping and weeping and gurgling on the ground.

Jezebel, her heart pounding, stood up. "Kill them," she snapped. "The way they killed my mare. Oh, God, my mare." She wept tears of rage at the sight of the awkward lump of black horse sprawled inert on the grass outside.

"You had better go up to the house and entertain your guests," Lethbridge said. "I got to clean up around here. You ain't going anywhere, lassie. Those two fatsos were right about that. Nobody leaves here until we get this business settled up proper."

"I'll kill you," snapped Jezebel, and she stalked off toward the mansion, furiously dusting dirt off her riding skirt and blouse.

Chapter Ten

When Ben reached the stamp mill and reduction works eight miles below Pony that afternoon, he found no one in the office save for a clerk, and that was to his liking. He sent the clerk on a half-hour errand, then opened the safe where the company's product, in the form of bullion, was stored. Only Ben and the stamp-mill manager, not even Murray Eickles, had the combination.

There was not a lot in the safe. The gold weighed about a hundred pounds or less, with a value of around twenty-five thousand dollars. The company shipped monthly to the Denver mint an amount that averaged close to a hundred thousand dollars—more in summer, less in winter.

The entire contents of the safe would easily fit into two black leather satchels he had brought for the purpose. He dropped five ten-pound bars into each bag and snapped them shut. At his touch the heavy door of the safe swung back and locked. Then he carried both bags to the buggy. The hundred pounds seemed no weight at all for a man who had grubbed rock all his life. He set the bags on the floorboards next to a shotgun.

He debated for a moment whether to confide in his manager

there, Amos Galb, and decided he would. Amos was a man of rocklike rectitude and could be trusted with any confidence Ben cared to impart. Telling Galb would help. Otherwise Galb might find the safe empty and sound an alarm, which would alert Murray Eickles—and Kennedy and Widen—who would swiftly point a finger in his direction, as if they owned the company. Ben told himself that it was, after all, his own gold.

He hopped into the buggy and drove it over to the rumbling stamp mill, where the ore was crushed to bits before the amalgamation process drew the gold from the quartz. Uneasily he left the buggy unattended. It was recognizably the Waldorf buggy, and not in all the years of operating the mine had anyone approached it or stolen anything from it. In any case, it would be in plain sight of numerous windows.

He found Galb at the number-three stamp, supervising a repair, and beckoned to the manager, who followed Ben outside.

"Got some trouble, Amos," he said, then briefly explained the loan, the financiers, the takeover, the thirty days, his refusal to sign over anything, Stop's mission, Eickles's treachery, and the rest. Then he told Galb that the gold was in the buggy.

Galb glanced briefly at the satchels and nodded. "I can keep it quiet for some while," he said. "We just shipped last week. I always put the gold in the safe myself and do a count each night. No one is ever in the office, because I don't want anyone figuring out the combination from watching me. So I'll just continue. Glad you let me know, though. I'd have raised hell if I'd found the safe empty."

"You may be accused and abused by those buzzards," Ben warned.

The manager straightened and stared at Ben through rimless glasses. "Right is might, and not the other way around," he said. "Now, I got a question: Have you sent to Virginia City for the sheriff? Seems to me those uglies are outside the law. Seems to me I could send someone from here, and even if Pony's being watched, they'd never know it, Ben. In fact, I'm thinking of my son, Bob."

Ben wasn't happy with the prospect of an outsider coming in

and listening to Kennedy and Widen lie. But maybe it'd work. "Okay, Amos, do it. But before you do, I want to go over it all again so you got the story exactly right and can tell the sheriff the whole thing proper. You ain't seen those uglies in action, either, and I don't think that numskull McDaniel over there has any idea what he's stepping into."

Ben went over it again. "You have your boy bring the sheriff to you, not to Pony. And you tell him. Just have Bob summon him, without sayin' why. Might take a day or two."

They shook hands. Ben clambered wearily into the buggy and began the hard trip upslope, knowing it would wear down Pegasus, especially with the gold aboard. No one followed, and he drove for miles through empty foothill country under the low, slanting sun. By the time he reached Pony, it was dusk, and he welcomed it to conceal the next step, which would take place over at Sam Stop's, well in view of the red mansion up above if there was someone watching up there. Like one or two disgusting and disowned sons whose blood may have been his but nothing else.

On the main street, still unnamed, he paused and watched the saloon men light lanterns, and watched Pyle, over at the hotel, walk from room to room plucking up glass chimneys and scratching sulfur matches and lighting wicks. He sat in his buggy, looking in particular for either of the uglies but not finding them. Neither was there a light in the upper front windows of the hotel where the financiers stayed, which struck him as odd. Could they have gone back East? Satisfied at last, he eased Pegasus out into the road, and at the bank corner turned left, southbound toward Stop's house, a half mile out. It wasn't full dark by any means, but it was murky enough so that no one would identify him at any distance. Pegasus was weary and walked listlessly, and that suited Ben, too, because the Waldorfs were usually seen with spirited, high-stepping horses.

Stop's was dark, a gray hulk of high-peaked house looming in the gloom. He eased slowly past the house, regretting the tracks the buggy was leaving in the dust. Stop had a small barn, the sort that private households employed to keep a horse and buggy, and some hay in an overhead loft. Ben thought about burying the bags in the hay, but that seemed pretty ordinary. Hiding something in hay is what the run-of-the-mill crook would think of, and Ben figured he was smarter than that. There was a small cistern in the back that caught rainwater off the roof. It was used to water the horses and was boarded over to keep the dust and dirt out. He would drop the bags in there, right smack into that cold water in the dark gloom under the boards. Might damage the bags, but so what? What was a gold mine for, anyway? But not the gold. That gold under that water would stay exactly the way it was, glinting yellow bars in the soaked bags.

Night settled as he eased the buggy close to the barn, where shadow would blot out the last of the western twilight.

"You hiding something, Ben, or stealing something?" asked Stop. Ben jumped a country mile. "Hiding something, I'd guess," Sam Stop added.

"Old men ain't much good at sneakin' around," Ben said. "I thought your cistern here might be the right place for a hundred pounds of gold."

Stop pondered it. "Let me help," he said, lifting a satchel from the buggy. Together they pulled away the planks and slid the satchels into the tank, watching the bubbles glimmer in the dusk. Then they replaced the boards and retreated to the porch of Stop's house. He did not light a lamp. Instead he dragged a chair from inside and set it beside his own, and the two men settled into them quietly. But Stop was not satisfied. He rose, did a quick tour around the house and its environs, then settled back into the chair. Ben watched him, thinking that Stop's panther prowl didn't at all resemble what one would expect from a banker. It sure as hell was a mystery: who Stop was, how he got his money, and how he'd come to be a banker.

"I guess you got news for me—and I got news for you," he said. "I'll go first."

"Suits me," said Ben.

"I thought I got out of here unobserved. I left late enough, after midnight sometime. I made camp north of here, maybe around three, and got some shut-eye, and got into Butte the next evening. But, Ben, I was followed. Not closely, and not by anyone very expert at it. I doubled back at one point, middle of the day, and watched from a ridge, and sure enough, it was one of the Dowlings. Don't know which. Chunk of beef under a black derby on one of Bonack's horses."

"How'd you know to do that? Double back? You been followed before?" Ben blurted.

There was a long pause, and in the dark Ben could not see the look on Stop's face, and didn't know whether the young man was angry or what.

"You've been probing around for years, Ben. It doesn't matter, really, what you think. But I'll tell you a little. I was a banker once in a place I'll not name. It was my own bank, too, built with hard work and some good loans. My beautiful sable-haired wife and I lived a little outside town in a home I'd built. I love the outdoors, and I wanted a place for horses, for hunting pheasants, for my children to spread their wings. Three miles, a quick trot, from my bank . . .

"They came one day from across the river, men whose names you'd know as train robbers and bank robbers, men who struck and run. They came in the rain, struck my bank, and left in a deluge of hail and wind as terrible as I've known . . . and, Ben, they didn't go far. Only as far as my house . . ."

Sam's voice changed, and his eyes peered into distance.

"They stayed two long days. Abused my beloved wife before my eyes, all of them. Threatened me, then left. After that, my wife was demented, my son melancholic. He got a fever and died. I knew who they were; I'd seen them enough. I was a sportsman who knew weapons. I put her . . . into a hospice run by nuns where she remains, not knowing me or anyone else. I hunted them down and shot four, four human beings, loathing it. I'd been a Catholic until then. I put the revolvers away and have not touched them since, nor will I."

"I shouldn'ta picked and probed, consarn it," Ben muttered.

"Protect my privacy."

Stop picked up the thread of his report then. "I tried William Andrews Clark first. Checked into a hotel, got cleaned up, and headed for Clark's offices. I couldn't get in. Told the secretary, man named Stinson, who I am and why I'd come and all the rest. Stinson was in there maybe fifteen minutes, then came out and said Clark wouldn't see me—sorry, he had bigger fish to fry in Butte, and he didn't deal with anyone but principals in a venture, anyway, because agents always were powerless and had half the facts.

"Out on the street I spotted Dowling. He had kept tabs on me the whole time, it seems—on my hotel, my visit to Clark. He didn't even bother to conceal himself. That black derby sitting on all that meat was there for me to see."

He paused, staring into the sky, glittering with stars now. "I went to Marcus Daley next—Clark's rival, you know, and maybe smarter than Clark. A lot more flexible, and a happier man, too. A little more like you, Ben. I laid the thing out to Daley's secretary and got ushered in fast. We took the measure of each other for a while. Daley was cool, reserved, and ready to like me, I think. Also . . . well, ready to listen. So I talked and he listened. I rattled off the whole thing. Tonnages, profits, grades of ore, and the call loan with Kennedy and Widen—he knows the pair of them, Ben—and he scowled a moment.

"Daley lit up a fat stogie and said he was pretty tied up, especially when it came to that kind of cash. Then he stared at the ceiling awhile, keeping me guessing, I guess, and allowed that he could raise the money fast enough. He'd only deal for a majority interest in the company, but he said you'd still have a respectable chunk left. . . . I just sat there. I figure that's between you and him. Then he said he never trusted a single report from someone like me, and he'd send a trusted man down to look things over. That's where it stands. He's sending someone. Refused to describe him. But someone is coming, and he'll have credentials and will get in touch soon."

Ben nodded. That made sense. Look it over and the deal might work. Give up fifty-one percent and get the bail-out money. A bargain for Daley, if the mine was worth the two million Ben figured it was worth.

"I talked to a couple of bankers, too. Ralph McElroy at Butte Federal and Kermit Willems at the other one, uh, Daley's bank.

They were a pair of head shakers, like most bankers"—Ben could see Stop's teeth in the dark—"and I didn't get anywhere. Slipped in here an hour ago, after shaking off the Dowling. I didn't want him knowing where I was going, so I headed north out of Butte, as if I were aiming for Helena. I don't know where he is. Maybe back here. He probably just hightailed it here to report to our friends Jasper and Drago."

"There's a chance for some financing, then—if we can hold out almost four weeks," Ben said.

"A chance. No promises, Ben. Just a look from a copper king. . . . I got more to say—something's going on up at your brick pile. But let me hear what you've been up to."

Ben told him about the morning's takeover, threatened violence and the prospect of being detained in his office until he signed. Sam Stop's face went dark with that news but relaxed when Ben told how he had bluffed his way out of that jam. Ben narrated the rest of it easily enough: the trip down to the stamp mill, cleaning out the bullion, confiding in Galb.

"Galb's son is on his way to Virginia City to get the sheriff," Ben said. "I figgered this had got far enough."

"McDaniel is no match for those two Dowlings," Stop said quietly.

"How do you know that, Sam?"

Stop paused but said nothing. Then, "You've got visitors up at your place. Did you know that?"

Ben looked at him sharply. "No, I didn't."

"Coming in, I swung around above the town, not wanting to be seen. Past your house. It looks to me like you've got a couple of financiers for guests, and a couple of sons with side arms on. As an offhand guess, I'd say that Jezebel and the rest are prisoners, and you might well be if you go back up there."

Ben pondered that, his gall rising. "I spawned two pigs," he said roughly. "I suppose the hellcat can handle herself—but maybe not. Those are rough customers. I imagine they've got an eye for her, too. What they want, they take."

Ben slipped into silence, not knowing what to do, feeling like an old silver-tipped grizzly.

"You're welcome to stay here, Ben."

"No, dammit, that's my wife up there, and that's my home, and I won't run. I'm going in there and order them out. That's a few steps too far. McDaniel will get here to enforce it eventually. I ain't runnin', Sam. I ain't signin' anything, either."

Sam sighed. "What if they threaten Jezebel—you understand what I mean—to force you to sign?"

Ben laughed, a deep rumble in the dark. "Hell, Sam, she'd enjoy it! And if she didn't—some or all of them wouldn't come out alive."

"The derringers?"

"That and getting a catamount by the tail." Ben laughed uproariously.

"Wouldn't that bother you?"

Ben hawked up phlegm. "Guess so. I don't know. I never figgered she was some church lady, showing leg like that from her pappy's wagon. I tell you what, Stop. Them money men and their uglies and those two turds I sired ain't a match for an old prospector that fought Injuns and rattlesnakes of all species—and a hellcat. I'm goin' on up there."

Stop was silent for a while. Then, "Your bedroom faces this way, out over the town. If you have trouble, hang a sheet in the window. Or any window."

"And what's a banker going to do to bail me out?" Ben said, faintly mocking.

Stop didn't answer. But in the dark Ben could see amusement on his tanned features.

Ben stood up then and said his good nights, and left. Pegasus, refreshed, pulled the buggy briskly up the hill and into Ben's own acres.

There appeared to be no one present. Ben lit a lamp at the barn and forked hay into Pegasus's manger, then wandered toward the big house. Sure enough, the black barouche was parked off to one side, and a pair of trotters stood in the corrals. He thought for a moment of disabling the barouche but decided against it. He also thought of slipping to the rear door, cornering Hip Hip Hurray and getting some information, but he dismissed the notion. This was his own brick pile, and he would enter by the front door.

At first he thought no one was present or awake. But in his den—the builder had called it a study, and the old semiliterate man had laughed—sat Mr. Jasper Kennedy and Mr. Drago Widen, apparently reading. It was a scene so pacific and serene that for an instant it fooled the old man.

"Why, Ben, good to see thee," said Jasper Kennedy kindly. "Thy good sons have invited us to share thy fine home, and we hastened at once, since the hotel is less than accommodating."

Over in the other chair, Drago Widen grinned like a weasel at meat.

"Where are they?" Ben asked blandly. He had kicked them out years ago, and he would kick them out again. "And where's Jezebel?"

"Your lively young wife has retired to her room," said Drago. "As for Willis and Stanley, we have employed them. I don't know where they are at the moment."

Probably off to Louella's for the night, Ben thought. "You gents here to do business? Staying up late?"

"Nay, not really. We just finished our evening repast," said Jasper. "Thee must discipline thy heathen cook, Ben. The insolent Chinese refused to cook for us. Most inhospitable."

"What happened?" Ben asked warily.

"Why, one of our assistants persuaded him," Drago said.

"Well, gents, I'm going to disinvite you. The boys made a mistake. This here's my own brick pile, and I do the invites. Now, we'll just get your things together and harness up them trotters, and I imagine old Windham Pyle over at the hotel will be mighty glad to take care of you."

They made no response, and it was quiet save for the clacking of the grandfather clock.

"Thee doesn't understand, Ben," said Jasper gently.

"What don't I understand?"

"We are forced to take measures." Jasper Kennedy smiled crookedly. "We wish to hasten thee along toward the fulfillment of our purposes here. Now, if thee would sign the transfer papers,

94

why, Drago and I will pull out right smartly in the morning. . . .
I'm sure you understand."

Ben contained himself, though he felt like bashing in their
heads. If he tried it, he knew, one or another Dowling would
materialize from nowhere. Still . . .

"Stop does my negotiating. And you'll pack up now and git,
before I summon the law."

Jasper sighed. "Thee won't be summoning anybody, I'm
afraid, Ben. Thee must stay, thee and thy lady and servants."

"Thin ice, Jasper," Ben said. "Someone might get hurt."

Ben refused to remind them of his rights of ownership. They
would know all about those, and they had chosen to violate them
at will. A man's rights meant nothing.

"Thee are comfortable here; no one is abused," said Jasper.
"Drago prays most devoutly for thy salvation."

He was a prisoner, then, and would be until he signed . . . or
until the call loan was due. Well, he could weather that. It didn't
look like Dudley would be of much help. Maybe McDaniel from
Virginia City, if he wasn't overly dumb about it.

"Guess I'll retire, gents," Ben said. He would work on some
things in the night.

"Thy sons gave me thy room. Perhaps thee could spend the
night with Jezebel," Jasper said blandly.

Ben glared. "I'm movin' you into a spare room," he said. It
went unchallenged. "You'll find your stuff."

In a huff he dumped Kennedy's black valise, carpetbag and
trunk into the hall. He tried Jezebel's door. It was locked. Then
he locked his own door and lit a lamp and sat down to think.

Chapter Eleven

Two things caught Dudley's attention. Across the street, Louella was on her way to the bank. She made that walk occasionally, on no set schedule but always late in the morning. This morning she had dressed as she usually did, like a preacher's wife, except that everything was much more costly. Even in the summer she wore suits rather than dresses, and the one she had on this morning was a deep green without a wrinkle in it. In her hand she clutched her reticule, no doubt with several days' earnings in it. As usual, her path led up the far side of the street so as not to pass the constable and the duffers lounging under the porched roof of Spade's Mercantile. Whether it was to avoid ribald or impolite comments, or whether it was occasioned by some natural delicacy, Dudley didn't know. But for years now, no one had ever seen Louella walk to the bank on Spade's side of the street.

Louella was still a young-looking woman but going heavy, and it was said she could be bought just like her girls, but for more money. There was always talk and baloney about Louella and her girls and her place. She had glossy brown hair and must have been a beauty ten years ago; indeed, Dudley remembered a prettier Louella when she'd first arrived in Pony and had had the log place, the first hotel in town, rebuilt to her specifications. No doubt it was profitable. On the two occasions he had been called there by Louella's freedman to stop a quarrel among drunk miners, he had found a passel of them in the front-room saloon. Mostly single men, he knew, but not all. Others he pretended not to recognize. But that's the way it is with a town constable. You don't see things.

He remembered those two forays amiably, in part because he had gotten eyefuls of some awfully pretty girls, young, so young they seemed adolescent, and he had wondered about that. He had gone home and teased his wife about what he had seen, and at first she blushed and ignored him, then turned merry and laughed and gave him a hug as a reminder. He had always been faithful, and after she died . . . the need had died. Mostly.

The other thing that caught his attention was more unusual. Coming downslope—in the direction opposite to Louella's travel—rolled the Waldorf buggy with Pegasus in harness. A perfectly familiar sight to the old constable, except that the two uglies were driving it, side-by-side twin slabs of red-faced beef. Dudley frowned. Not in a hundred years would Ben Waldorf have loaned the buggy to those uglies, or their employers. Not in a thousand years would the hellcat, whose buggy it really was, have agreed to it. And that spelled grief of some sort, and Dudley instantly had that pang of not knowing, which irked him so much these last few days. Even though Ben had been candid enough, and Elmer Dudley had a pretty good idea of the building pressures, he now knew that the town was out of his control.

Louella had reached the place where she always crossed the street to enter the bank, which was on Spade's side, the southern side. And just at that moment the Dowlings reached the spot where she would cross. One of them reined in Pegasus, and the buggy stopped. Dudley scrambled to pull his long-distance specs out to see all of this, because it was a block and a half away, and he did manage to see one of the Dowlings doff his derby and say something. But what was said, he had no idea. Louella shook her head—he could see that, at least—and crossed in front of them and on into the bank. Even that far away Dudley could see their mocking eyes as they watched her. He decided to keep his specs on, even though they made his nose sore.

"I suppose they want her business, too," said Spade. Dudley startled. He had plum forgotten that the merchant had come out and settled beside him. The morning trade had been slow. "I'll wager she grosses two or three times what I do, and that's temptation of another sort for those pirates from New York."

"Reckon so," said Dudley absently. The buggy was rolling again, coming their way.

"They wanted this place, too," Spade was saying. "Tried to buy it for half price. Threatened me. Said I had to decide by yesterday or there'd be trouble. Just vague like that. Trouble of some kind. Something more than competition—building their own mercantile and whipping me with it."

That caught Dudley's attention.

"I told them they'd reach Hades before I'd sell, or something along those lines. But they were going after the rest—Bonack and Pyle—and I imagine they've been bought."

Dudley wasn't listening. He was wondering how the uglies had gotten possession of the buggy, and why they were pulling up right there in front of Spade's.

The closest one—Dudley thought it was Lethbridge but wasn't sure—addressed Spade. "You has had time to think it over and the gents want an answer," he said amiably.

"Same as before," said Martin Spade. "Same as my answer will be tomorrow, too."

"I guess we'll have a little lookee at the merchandise," said the other Dowling, who was driving. He jumped down and attached a carriage weight to the horse's bridle. And the pair of them sauntered into the store. Spade leapt up and followed. Dudley sat a moment, unsure of how to handle what was bound to happen. Maybe the way he always did, he thought, with his revolver out before he began asking questions or giving commands.

Spade's emporium displayed foodstuff along the right side, dry goods and clothing along the left, and hardware at the rear. When Dudley swung into the front door, his Colt in hand, things seemed peaceful enough. The uglies were wandering through, peering into pickle vats and cracker barrels, observing neat rows of airtights on shelves, eyeing heavy cotton bags of flour and sugar, noticing boxes of salt, a counter jar full of licorice sticks, and rows of boxed spices.

Then they wandered amiably over toward the dry goods, peering at bolts of cotton and wool and linen, racks of ready-made shirts and pants and shoes and jeans, flannel and wool and denim. There were straw and felt hats, ladies underthings discreetly to the rear, stockings, sheets, blankets, pillows.

Dudley holstered the old Colt. The uglies were casing the place, maybe to give their employers some idea of what was here.

"Anything I can help you with?" asked Spade nervously. The proprietor stood behind a counter in his usual black vest, white shirt, and sleeve garters. Dudley knew that beneath that counter Spade kept a loaded shotgun. He hoped Spade had the sense not to touch it.

"Just lookin' around," said Paddo. "Want to see the hardware, too."

At the back of the store were bins of nuts and bolts and screws and nails, a rack of rifles and shotguns, shelves of ammunition, plowshares, buggy and wagon hardware, lanterns, jackknives, silverware, frying pans, milking stools, latches, Majestic cooking ranges, tin tubs, stock tanks, rolls of barbed wire, flue pipe, stoves, hinges, doorknobs, and more.

"You've had your look. If you ain't buying, you can vamoose now," said Spade.

"What did you say your stock here is worth?" Paddo asked.

"I didn't say."

Dudley slipped his Colt out again. "The man wants you to leave," he said, the heavy revolver in his hand pointing steadily at the Dowlings.

"That ain't very friendly," said Lethbridge.

Dudley grew wary. The Colt was a damn-fool thing, and he should have left it holstered. He knew that.

"Don't much care to have old geezers pointing gats at me," said Paddo.

The pair of them smiled amiably as they approached the door. Dudley stood off to one side, behind a pickle crock. They exited peacefully, and Elmer Dudley could scarcely believe it. He had faced them down. The uglies clambered into the buggy easily, and then all hell broke loose. They each lifted a ten-gauge Stevens and fired through the plate-glass windows, shattering glass, sending shards flying. Dudley was slashed on the neck by one piece, on one hand by another. Some of the buckshot caught the flesh of his arm, and pain bit him. He tumbled off-balance to the floor. Spade ran toward the counter, and his shotgun, after a moment of paralysis.

On the floor, Dudley struggled to unholster his Colt again when a foot pressed against his hand, pinching it hard to the wooden floor.

"You should know better than to point gats at us," said one of them above him. Dudley raged; it was a replay of the bank debacle, he on the floor staring up at those two smirking chunks of beef. Dudley twisted his head and saw Martin Spade, hands in the air and fear etching his face, under the gun of the other Dowling.

Paddo—he thought it was Paddo—plucked the Colt from Elmer's holster. "You and the storekeep can stand over here," he said, pointing to a corner in the grocery. "Too bad you didn't sell when you had a chance," he said to Spade. "Tossed away real opportunity. Great future."

People gawked outside now, women mostly, all of them afraid to come in. The Dowlings ignored them. The fresh summer air whirled in through the shattered windows.

Lethbridge found a pair of sickles in the hardware area and handed one to Paddo.

"Seems there'll be a little earthquake," he said. "You mighta sold before the quake hit."

With the sickle he swept a whole shelf of airtights to the floor. They clattered and rolled and bounced and dented, spewing up dust that caught and hung golden in the sunlight.

"You'll pay," cried Spade, choking on his own words.

Elmer's arm was bleeding hard. He reached for his handkerchief to stanch the flow and saw the bore of a Stevens shotgun following his hand.

"I'm bleeding, consarn it," he roared.

The sickle swept another shelf, and cracker boxes sailed across the aisle. More swipes and sacks of flour were gutted, the soft white powder mushing out and swirling into the air. A bushel of onions flipped and rolled like great marbles down the aisle. A fifty-pound bag of potatoes flew across the store and mashed into a shelf of women's hats and veils. A crock of molasses sailed toward the shelf with bolts of wool on it and shattered there, sending a wild brown spray across the wools and into the bolts of cotton, too, the stain almost invisible on one brown cotton print.

"You'll pay," cried Martin Spade hoarsely. "It may kill me, but you'll pay."

Spade reached the point of blind rage and started toward the counter with the shotgun beneath it.

"Don't!" snapped Elmer.

But Spade was there now, ducking beneath the counter. A blast of buckshot blew just over his head, insanely loud inside the store, balls embedding themselves into the counter and beyond it, in bolts of flannel and linen, tearing jagged holes in them.

"If you sticks yer head up, Spade, the next load catches you in the mug."

Dudley feared Spade would leap up, anyway, but sensibly Spade stayed low. Outside, the crowd thickened, and Dudley spotted Sam Stop in it, in his shirt sleeves, drawn from the bank up the street. Dudley wished he could read Stop's mind or interpret that dark, enigmatic gaze in Stop's face. But the young banker did nothing, stared at the increasing devastation within as the Dowlings continued their demolition. For some unfathomable reason Constable Dudley raged at Stop, as if Stop were the answer to this holocaust.

Ten minutes later, when the store was a shambles, the Dowlings emerged, swaggering victoriously toward the silent crowd. There were miners there now, powerful men ready to rush the Dowlings but afraid of their lethal shotguns.

Standing at the doorway, Lethbridge said, "You can all go

home now. You can come to an understanding now with Mr. Kennedy and Mr. Widen.''

Sam Stop said, quietly, "I think you've made a mistake."

"You said that once. If you say it again, you can kiss your bank good-bye."

"I think you have made a mistake," Sam Stop repeated.

The Dowlings stared at Stop. Everyone in that terrified crowd knew that the Dowlings would make good their threat.

Sam Stop continued to face them down, his black eyes impenetrable, hard, and unafraid.

"You're a damn fool, Stop," said Elmer Dudley roughly. "Here, now, get the doc. I'm bleeding bad."

The Dowlings boarded the buggy, pointing the great black bores of their shotguns at the cowed mass of people.

"Did the Waldorfs lend you their buggy, or did you take it?" asked Stop.

Dudley watched the bore of the Stevens swing toward Stop, and was afraid.

"We dint ask, if that's what you mean, Stop."

Stop smiled thinly. Then Paddo slapped rein over Pegasus, and the buggy clattered out, wheeled around, and started up the hill, its beefy occupants flaunting their backs to the crowd.

"They'll pay," snapped Martin Spade. He stood in the doorway, his shirt peppered red where shards of glass and some buckshot had hit him. "We'll get the sheriff. And a posse. We'll have law again . . ." He held his hand to his bloodstained shirt and sat down abruptly.

The doc, Havelock Frede, arrived with his black bag. He wasn't really a doctor. The town was too small for one, and too remote. Actually he was a mortician, pharmacist, and veterinarian, but he had read medicine, subscribed to eastern journals, and some citizens thought he was more up-to-date about modern practice than any real sawbones. But others refused to go to him, saying that no mortician would ever be allowed to treat them. Frede, a short, lean man with a black spade beard and a frock coat with a fresh handkerchief poking from it, started on Dudley first, because the ball wound in the flesh of his forearm was the most serious.

A miner's young wife—Dudley realized it was Mrs. Crane—peered into the store with horror. "I think," she said to Martin Spade, "you need some help here. We will all help." She pushed inside, and others followed her, spreading out in the store, beginning the dolorous task of restoring order and salvaging the merchandise. Spade slumped weakly on the bench in front of his store, tears overflowing in his eyes and wetting his pale face.

Elmer Dudley sat on the boardwalk, his shirt off and his massive, gray-haired chest exposed, while Havelock Frede nimbly bandaged him after dabbing carbolic on his wounds. Stop watched quietly, then walked back to his bank, as if he were miles removed from the cataclysm that had stricken Pony. The constable watched him go, and raged, sore as a bad tooth and not knowing why. The man was a banker, after all.

The crowd around him grew as off-shift miners appeared, looking faintly accusatory. Dudley knew what they were thinking, and it pained him worse than anything else in twenty years of lawing. His failure was reflected in their eyes, in their stares, in their fear, in their frightened glances uphill, toward the mine, toward the Waldorf mansion. It graveled him. There was no explaining or apologizing in him. Any one of them with brains could see what he had gone up against. Some had seen him try to drive the Dowlings out of the mercantile at gunpoint. But he knew there was more to those glances than his own failure.

Now every miner would think about his job, and the future, and the company stores he might be forced to buy from. Some darkness had descended on Pony, even in the bright midday sun. One or two smart ones headed for Stop's bank, intending to withdraw their meager savings before they were stolen, or the bank collapsed, or Stop was killed. Dudley watched them as Frede bandaged him, knowing where they were going and feeling his own failure paining him more than his wounds.

At last Frede was done. "Your arm'll be stiff. Drink a lot of liquids; you lost a lot of blood. But you'll do," he said tersely. "Now I got to patch up Martin."

Dudley disdained to put his bloodstained, shredded shirt back on. Tenderly he unpinned the shining badge, praying in some small way that he might still be worthy of the trust reposing in it, and then he walked angrily to his cottage to get a fresh flannel shirt. He had failed. Twenty years of lawing and he couldn't handle two uglies.

He was aware, at last, of cadenced steps beside him. He had been so absorbed in his shame and defeat that he had failed to notice the big square-toed miner's boots. And then he glanced to his side and found himself walking with Philo Crane.

"I have the men," Philo said quietly. "Not twelve. I couldn't find twelve I thought were right. But I have seven. Fine strong lads, Cornishmen who braved the high seas to come here, men I'd trust with my life, Constable."

Elmer Dudley sighed. "Any of 'em ever faced a gun, been fired at?"

"Nary a one. But every day they brave the pits, go down into the cold earth, and if they'll go into that danger, they'll stand with ye in other danger."

Dudley nodded. "You've done well. Are they armed?"

"Three have shotguns. Two have hunting rifles. Two have only their big fists, but don't you make light of their hands."

They reached Dudley's cottage. The constable motioned the miner in, and they talked while he donned a fresh shirt.

"Good men," Dudley said. "But you'll teach them something about the Dowlings' cane and walking stick, eh? And the things they do with their feet—Oriental kicks and chops of some sort? They'll flatten your men, Philo. Strength isn't enough. Your good Cornishmen'll walk into these uglies and find themselves flat on their faces with their heads ringing. And that's not all, Philo. Gats in shoulder holsters, dirks, eye gouging. Tell all that to your boys. And they ain't the only two, either. Waldorf's sons have been bought. Worthless, but they're armed and vicious and can pull a trigger as well as the next man. And them two financiers, too, Philo. I imagine they're no easy marks, either. You can bet on them being well armed. Six men, two of them the most dangerous that ever come to Pony. You got seven and yourself and a lame old constable with a hole through his arm who ain't feeling good."

104

"I'll talk to my boys. They got jobs and safety to think about. And their women and lads and lasses to feed. And they ain't going to take this here trouble lying down."

"If I need you, how do I get you?"

"All of us go on shift at four, and off at two in the morning. By day, come to me and I'll roust out the lads. By night, send a man into the pit and we'll put down the jacks and come on out, foreman or not, and meet you where you will."

Old Dudley stepped out on his sunlit porch. "Every man of you is brave beyond your knowing," he said gravely. "Have them clean their weapons and put in fresh charges or cartridges. Tell them the whole truth, lad. And we'll choose a time. It may be soon, Philo. As soon as the uglies move against Stop's bank."

Chapter Twelve

Jezebel stayed in her room until mid-morning because she didn't want to breakfast with Drago Widen, or worse, with Jasper Kennedy. She loathed Jasper Kennedy. But in a way he seemed a fascinating man who radiated power and civil manners and a will that would not be brooked. Whenever his gaze settled on her, she felt his desire and his barely controlled possessiveness.

And that part of it she enjoyed. Men's desire and possessiveness attracted her, even though in Kennedy's case she knew that she was the moth and he the flame, and that the closer she fluttered, the greater was her danger. From her wardrobe she selected a snowy cotton frock that had arrived from Paris only the week before, one she'd never worn. It was a saucy dress with rows of ruffles climbing the skirt and waist and bodice, making her look like a snowflake. The white turned her lavender eyes and jet-black hair all the more vivid. She admired herself in the looking glass, admitting nervously that she wanted Jasper Kennedy to see her in it and lust his heart out, then tripped downstairs.

It was quiet. Sun streamed through the towering windows, whitening the ivories of the piano and making the gold thread in the settee gleam. Outside, the purple flanks of the Tobacco Roots loomed brightly.

Ben sat in the dining room sipping coffee. The sun caught his white hair so that his head glowed and his beard shone. There was no one with him; no sign of the financiers or the Dowlings or—God help her—Willis and Stanley.

He looked up and beamed. "I married the sweetest thing on the American continent. And halfway pretty, too. Good morning, Tootsie."

She kissed him.

"Now, is that one of them Paris doodads you got? So much foolery on it, I can't see where the cloth ends and you begin."

"You always know where I begin," she said. "Where's everybody?"

Ben's face sombered suddenly. "Off and gone. Plumb disappeared, I reckon."

Hip Hip Hurray appeared. He had a mysterious way of placing an entire cooked breakfast before her only seconds after she appeared in the morning.

"Good morning, Missy Waldorf."

That was his ritual greeting. Anything more strained his English. "Chop heads off," he added.

"Not today," said Ben. Hip Hip vanished into the kitchen.

"Where'd they go?" asked Jezebel.

Ben smiled faintly. "Kennedy and one Dowling went up to the mine in their barouche. Eickles came over here first thing, saying the boys in the pits were restless. Rumors are flying that the whole shift might walk off. So our friend Jasper hastened away to pour his oil on those waters. Widen had already taken off with the other Dowling to inspect the reduction works, and I suppose he'll be gone all day. So, Tootsie, we're alone for a moment—unless Satan and Beelzebub show up—in which case I will pitch them out."

"Good!" she cried. "I'm going to go riding!" Then she remembered the sight of her black mare's comatose body sprawled outside the barn, and the idea of riding faded. There were other horses, fine mounts, but the idea died in her.

"Seems to me," said Ben amiably, "we might just walk down the hill and take the ledgers back to Stop. They're heavy, but if I carry three and you take two . . ."

"Where's the buggy? And Pegasus?"

"I'm afraid the great Mr. Drago Widen borrowed them. Or his ugly did." He sighed. "I fear what they'll do to Galb. He's too honest to lie. If they ask whether he can open the safe, he'll set that jaw of his and say yes. And then he'll be in for it, Tootsie. We're all in for it, I fear. . . ."

Jezebel was indignant. "You know what he told me?"

Ben cocked a white eyebrow. "Who?"

"Jasper. He told me he would take me East whether I wanted to go or not. And he's going to 'tame' me, whatever that means. And make me his mistress."

"You'd have fun, Tootsie."

"No I wouldn't, Ben. No one's ever told me what to do and where I'm going to live. And that Jasper Kennedy isn't going to be the first."

Ben's face grew grave, and she saw some strange somberness in his twilight-blue eyes. "Tootsie, that kind of man breaks people, destroys the hopes and dreams of others . . . their wills."

It was a tone of voice she had not heard Ben use, and she wondered about it. Old Ben was saying something to her.

Then he laughed. "You're a hellcat, Tootsie."

"I can handle him. I can handle anyone. When I was with Daddy selling shoes from the wagon, I handled worse."

Ben beamed. "I believe you did," he said. "You handled me, and I ain't been the same since."

This conversation troubled her. She knew that Ben was a lot more worried about her than he let on. Never had he opposed her in all the years of their marriage. She had run free, bought what she chose, lived as she chose. That is why she liked him. Could she ever like someone like Jasper Kennedy? Maybe she could, if he gave her lots of money and left her alone.

"Are they going to get the mine?"

"Looks that way," said Ben. "Unless Sam Stop can bail me out."

She grew alarmed at last. "What'll we do, Ben? I mean, with no money?"

"Tootsie, I'm seventy-five, and it ain't no problem for me. I could sit and whittle with them duffers at Spade's and enjoy myself just as much. But you, Tootsie . . . maybe you should scram outa here, right now while you can. Catch a hoss up and git on over to Butte and get set up with Daley and Clark or one of them that can fend off these bloodsuckers here. No, not Clark. He's cold as a pickax in December, and so stuffy a man can't breathe around him. Daley, now . . . you go bat your eyes at old Marcus, and maybe it'll all turn out fine."

"But, Ben," she wailed, "I like you."

"Tootsie, I ain't gonna be here long, and you got to think of your future. You're young and wild as a March hare. Now you just think to your own needs and none of this lovey stuff."

"Who's being lovey? I'm not," she insisted indignantly. "I wouldn't love you for a million dollars."

Ben beamed. "That's good, Tootsie. You promise you ain't gonna get dolled up in widow's weeds. You promise me you'll kiss this old goat good-bye and get hooked up with someone else."

"Why are you talking like this?" she asked, still indignant.

Ben shrugged. "A man gets to be old and he's thinking about kicking off all the time. I do. Sometimes I want it. I got rheumatiz or arthritis or lumbago or whatever it be—in every joint, almost. Comes from living outside, digging in cold, hard-rock pits. I get so cold in the winters that I can't warm up even sittin' in front of a hot stove in a hot room. I get to creaking like an old windmill, and then I figger I've had my fun and I ain't of a mind to sit around and decompose like an old compost pile."

"Why are you talking like this?" she demanded.

"Death, Tootsie. It gits in the mind of the old. Not like you. You shouldn't be thinkin' about it. You just keep figgering how to live high on the hawg. But me, I'm lookin' at this thing, losing the mine, and the fun I had—I figgered to kick off after my three score and ten, and here I got five more already—and I, well, I got a different view of all this than you got. I ain't afraid. I might do

109

a thing or two to them money men that I'd never dream of before."

She tried to make sense of all that but couldn't.

He flopped his snowy napkin on the table. "Come on, Tootsie. Let's carry those ledgers back to Stop."

She glared at him sourly. "Why should we do him any favors? He's a big milksop. Of all the people in Pony I don't like, he's the worst."

Ben chuckled. "What you got against Stop?"

"He never even looks at me, that's what. I prance in there all gussied up, and he pays me never no mind, like I'm a preacher's wife. He just stands there grinning and treating me like a little girl. Next thing he'll do is pat my head and offer me a nickel for a lollipop. And, besides, he's weak. Never raises his voice, never gets mad at people—like he's scared of everybody. He's scared of me, that's what he is. I scare the pants off him."

"Guess you're right, Tootsie. I keep expecting there's more to him, but there ain't."

She giggled. "Not that anyone can see, anyway."

Ben guffawed.

They hiked down the lane under the dappled shade of the newly greened cottonwoods, then down the creek road into Pony, taking the air and the sun and enjoying the early zephyrs. She didn't mind carrying two ledgers, but she was going to give them to Myrtle and not Stop. Damned if she'd give Stop the time of day.

The bank was open today, and a small queue of miners gathered at Myrtle's wicket. Word of the bank's dilemma had spread through town, and its customers had receipts or savings passbooks with them, and Myrtle was making entries in a temporary ledger.

They stared as Ben and Jezebel entered, and not a few were so entranced with the white-gowned goddess that they failed to notice the blue-cloth ledgers. Jezebel enjoyed the attention. Her flouncy dress was a radical departure from frontier style, and she wiggled a little in it, just for fun.

Ben steered her straight through the counter gate and into Stop's office. The banker was creating a new loan ledger from the pile of loan agreements on his desk. He looked out of place there, as if his hard, lean body and sun-browned flesh demanded the freedom of the sun and wind and high meadows of the mountains.

He looked pleased, first upon seeing the ledgers and then at seeing Jezebel. Then his black eyes searched Ben.

"It ain't the way it looks," said Ben. "We ain't come to any agreement with them hornswogglers. They just got into a little difficulty—boys up at the mine is getting restless about all this—and we just galloped on down here with these here ledgers."

Ben placed them on the desk.

"You've bailed me out, Ben. You and Mrs. Waldorf."

She glared at him. "Mrs. Waldorf, my ass," she said. "Don't you 'Mrs. Waldorf' me. Call me the hellcat, since you're too scared to call me anything else."

Stop's pleasant manner irritated her. He never had the hunger in his eye that she kindled in other men. Maybe he wasn't really male. The thought was suddenly delicious to her.

"You havin' any trouble with your customers, Sam?" Ben asked.

"Some," said Stop. "Some are cashing out. A lot are upset, and that is understandable enough."

Myrtle appeared in the doorway. "Are those the books?" she asked.

Stop nodded. Myrtle found the one she wanted and hastened back to her wicket with it.

"Guess we'd better make a duplicate of the current ones and hide them," Stop said absently.

Jezebel was bored. "I'm going shopping," she said. "There's nothing in a bank that interests me except money." She aimed the barb at Stop.

"I'm glad of that, Mrs. Waldorf," he said blandly.

"Why don't you do something about those men? Those . . . those bullyboys! Those big crooks in their suits and cravats?"

He shrugged. "I'm a banker, Mrs. Waldorf. That's for the sheriff or Elmer Dudley to do."

"Then why's Ben expecting you to help?"

"We got to find money somewhere, Tootsie. That's what banks is for."

Stop said, "If you're troubled about something, or you think I'm not doing what you expect of me, please tell me what is troubling you, Mrs. Waldorf."

He waited quietly while she fumed. But in truth she hadn't the faintest idea what to expect of him. He just seemed . . . capable of somehow driving all those financiers and bullyboys away.

"I don't know what I'm expecting. A man, I guess," she said hotly, not understanding her own temper. She suddenly loathed him. "I'm going shopping," she added.

"That's fine, Tootsie. Me and Sam here are gonna talk about some things, get some idears together."

She stormed out, despising Stop, scorning the big helpless hulks of miners in the queue—not a man among them to resist two greedy financiers and two toughs.

She had Kennedy's double eagle with her, and she intended to spend it at Spade's, and as she stormed down the boardwalk she didn't notice the incredulous stares that her flouncy white frock drew from both women and men. She had never been more gorgeous, and with her temper reddening her cheeks, she was any man's dream of paradise.

Elmer Dudley slumped in his battered wicker chair, his arm in a white sling that Havelock Frede had rigged up for him, his face gray with pain. She spotted him there, lazing the way he always did, and halted before him.

"Fine constable you are," she began. "There you sit, a weak old fool, while a pair of bullyboys frighten the whole town. What's the matter with you? Aren't you man enough to keep order? You should quit—no, we should fire you."

Dudley did not reply for a moment. He stared into her enraged eyes and thought some, then blinked patiently. "Could be you're right," he said gently. "Can't say I'm very proud of myself so far. I've been outsmarted, outfought so far. . . ."

She felt her indignation leak from her. Dudley was in pain. Still, he was just an old duffer, and the town needed a *man*.

"Got shot yestiddy. Right through the underarm flesh, here.

112

One of them Dowlings did it. It's swollen up pretty bad."

"How did that happen?" she asked curtly.

He told her about what had happened in Spade's Mercantile while she was trapped in her brick pile on the hill.

"What are you going to do about it? Nothing!" she raged. "There isn't a man in this town that'll stand up to them. They should be shot. If you and the rest of the boys around here won't do it, I will. I'll shoot them both."

"Likely get you into some trouble," said Elmer.

"Not if I'm being beaten or imprisoned or ravished or—" she sputtered.

"Like as not that'd reduce the charges some," Elmer agreed.

"Well, one thing's for certain—you'll just sit in that chair and do nothing."

He looked stung. "When the right moment comes, I'll do what I can," he said softly. "If I can't meet them head-on, maybe I can get around behind. Those two roughs ain't here for Sunday school picnics. I got some things going that'll help."

"I'm sure you do," she said tartly. He was helpless and she knew it.

She stormed toward Spade's door and found it locked.

"They're cleaning up that mess," Elmer said. "It was god-awful. Martin says he's going to lose seven, eight hundred dollars, even after salvaging what they can."

"I want to buy something," she stormed. She peered in. Spade was shaking his head at her. He looked old and ashen and was bandaged on his neck and arms. There were two women helping him. His wife was one, and Jezebel thought the other was the wife of that miner, Crane.

"Why'd they do that to him?" she asked suddenly.

"He ain't selling out. Them Easterners want a company town, everything here owned by Pony Consolidated—"

"But they don't even own the mine!" she exclaimed.

"Looks like they will soon enough, or maybe now since Ben ain't showin' much resistance," Dudley said.

"Then I'll go buy at Barteau's," she snapped.

"He sold—word is, at half the value of his store—and they've lowered prices over there to run Spade out. Don't expect it to last long, though. Barteau ain't in there. The word is, he and the missus and kids is packing up."

"There isn't a man in Pony," she said, and stormed across the street. But gliding down the slope from the mine was the black barouche with Jasper Kennedy in it; one of the Dowlings was driving. They saw her. They saw that she was not up in the mansion. She feared they would make her return there and that her brief liberty was extinguished. She stood in the street staring, wanted to flee. Toward the old constable? No, he offered no protection. Toward the bank, then, toward Ben. And Stop. Not that Stop, the milksop banker, would do any good. But Ben was a man. She whirled back to the south boardwalk and began the uphill trek to the bank. It grew quiet. There were people—housewives, ranch women, off-shift miners—watching the progress of the shining barouche with paralyzed awe, for all of them knew now about the mine, and Spade's and the rest.

Jasper Kennedy leaned forward and said a word, and the barouche wheeled gracefully in the wide road and drew up beside her, hissing in her direction.

"Would thee like a ride?" asked the financier.

"I will walk."

"I will take thee home. It is a fine day for a ride," he said blandly.

The barouche slid along beside her, keeping to her pace.

"I am not your prisoner," she snapped.

"Of course not, madam. We are thy guests. But there are matters to attend to until the transfer is done. Where is thy husband?"

She ignored him.

"No doubt consulting with Stop," he said in response to his own question. "Do join me, madam, I have great things to discuss with thee. Things concerning thy future."

She stared straight ahead.

At a nod from the financier, Lethbridge Dowling halted the barouche, leapt down, and took hold of Jezebel's arm to steer her.

She exploded. With one hand she raked his face with her nails.

With the reticule in her other hand she bashed his head and knocked off his derby. And with her mouth she addressed him in unladylike terms she had acquired from her father. A miner's wife gasped.

In spite of the blood welling on his cheek, Lethbridge smirked. Then he lifted her up as easily as if she were a sack of flour. She kicked and bit, and he carried her toward the barouche, where Jasper Kennedy stared blandly.

Then she bit his ear, clamping her teeth down viciously, feeling the lobe part under them and tasting his blood in her mouth. She spat out the bitten-off lobe, even as he howled hoarsely and threw her savagely into the street and into its filth and manure.

A thick, massive hand stunned her, throwing her head back as she fell, and then another chopped into her throat, choking her until she couldn't breathe.

"That will be enough, Lethbridge. I don't want her marked— yet," said Jasper. It was the last thing she heard as she gasped for air, then went black because her lungs wouldn't work.

Chapter Thirteen

For the first time in his recollection Elmer Dudley hated sitting in the wicker chair under Spade's porch roof. It had always been the perfect place for a constable, the central spot in town where he could keep a watchful eye on anything that mattered. But now people averted their eyes from him or glared at him coldly, with blame written darkly upon their faces.

He had failed them, failed Pony. They knew him for a weakling and a doddering old fool, and the hurt of it was more than the old constable could bear. He never had seen that look in people's eyes—that look of disappointment, ended friendship, disgust, revulsion. Mostly that afternoon, town people simply avoided him. Spade's store was closed, anyway, and Dudley sat alone. Even the old duffers and whittlers who passed the days with him had vanished.

The events of the last two or three days rankled, but nothing rankled more than the mauling and abduction of Jezebel Waldorf earlier, while he had stood watching, helpless and—dammit—plenty afraid. He had done nothing but watch through burning eyes. He didn't know what people expected of him; he was shot up, his arm in a sling, his shooting arm, too. The ugly had simply picked the girl up out of the street manure and dumped her in the barouche beside Kennedy, who shrank away from her filth and dusted off his suit. And then the ugly had driven the barouche off to the mansion, and in the silence that followed, there must have been fifty people staring at old Dudley.

Steeped in his self-disgust, he scarcely noticed a careening buckboard labor upslope into Pony, its dappled gray dray sweated and weary and foaming around the harness and between its legs. It was Mrs. Galb, the stamp-mill superintendent's wife. She was a strange one, Dudley had always thought. She wore her usual brown dress now, her hair carefully braided as usual, with the braids coiled around her head and pinned down. She was Pony's literary light and poet, and she had a weekly gathering at the Galb place, downslope a ways, where they read books and talked about them and wrote verse and carried on the way blue-stockings do.

But now she seemed desperate, and Dudley could see misery in her eyes, even behind her gold-rimmed glasses. She wheeled the buckboard to Havelock Frede's mortician's parlor and halted, stumbling out. It was only then that Dudley noticed an inert lump of male human sprawled in the buckboard's small bed. The dappled horse heaved, trembled, and struggled to stand. It had been used hard on that long uphill run. Mrs. Galb stumbled, righted herself, and plunged into Frede's place.

Trouble, Dudley thought, rising. Trouble again, fast and heavy these last few days. He banged on the gimpy knee to get it straightened up, then began thumping down toward Frede's. Not that he could do anything about trouble anymore, he thought. He reached the buckboard about the time that Mrs. Galb—Cora, he thought her name was—plunged out, with Frede after her. What brought him up short was the sight of the man in that buckboard bed—or what was left of him. It was Amos Galb, on his side, moaning, his hands holding his crotch, his face purple-and-red pulp, his lips and nose mashed and bleeding, his shirt torn and bloody. But what raised the hair on the back of Dudley's neck was that groaning, which rose to a sobbing shriek and subsided, like a man demented and suffering the final agonies of brutal torture. Never in all his years of lawing had Dudley heard such an eerie howl, like the scream of starving wolves in a January night.

"Help me," cried Cora Galb. "He's been beaten. He's 'most dead. They hurt him beyond . . . beyond . . ." Words failed her then.

Frede studied the pulped, gasping, howling person in the bed and hastened inside, returning a moment later with a small purple bottle and a spoon.

"Laudanum," he said. He poured a spoonful while Dudley lifted the huddled hulk up enough to let Galb swallow it. Galb gurgled and lost half of it, and Havelock Frede meticulously poured another and made sure it drained down Galb's throat. It took three more spoonfuls of the tincture of opium before a certain release eased the convulsed features of the stamp-mill supervisor. Then at last old Dudley and the dapper Frede were able to carry Galb in and set him on the mortician's slab table inside. Those few people who had witnessed these events in the street fled, fear becoming more urgent than their curiosity.

"He's alive, anyway," muttered Dudley.

But Havelock Frede had swung into action, jerking off his black frock coat and drawing water. Mrs. Galb cowered in the door.

"I'm not so sure he will last," muttered Frede. "Help me get this shirt off. And the pants."

"Mrs. Galb, what happened?" demanded Dudley. It wasn't a question.

"He was beaten. That's all I know. By an awful man in a bowler hat."

Then she wept.

Dudley ignored her. He already knew the answer and had a pretty good idea why, too.

Cora Galb slumped into a chair and buried her head in her lap, not wanting to see her husband's torso, which was a mass of purpling bruises and red welts. In a few days it would discolor and look even worse. Even in his half-comatose condition, Galb clutched his groin, groaning and nauseous.

Frede caught Dudley's eye. "I'd say a boot or a knee, but probably a boot. Enough to cost a man his manhood."

Mrs. Galb sobbed anew.

"He's been injured internally. Not much I can do about that except kill the pain some. But we can clean up the rest," Frede muttered. He began washing Galb's face, each gentle rub of the warm, water-soaked cloth bringing a sob from Galb.

Outside, there came the clop of a harness horse and the crunch of carriage wheels, then silence. Dudley gimped over to the window of the parlor. In front stood the Waldorf buggy with Pegasus in harness, and sitting in it were Drago Widen and one of the Dowlings—Lethbridge, Elmer thought. Pegasus was not lathered and scarcely showed sweat after the long climb from the valley floor. Neither was the driver, Lethbridge Dowling, lathered. He sat in the carriage, as tidy and immaculate as his employer beside him, with not even road dust visible upon either man.

"Git outa here before I kill you," roared old Dudley from the door.

Lethbridge tipped his hat, smirked, and indolently flicked the long reins, and the carriage rolled languorously upslope once again. It was all Dudley could manage not to draw his heavy Colt and blast them both in the back. He cursed himself for not doing it, but backshooting was not in his book.

Inside, Doc Frede worked diligently and expertly, with swift, adroit flicks of hand, cleaning wounds, binding lacerations, salving bruises with concoctions from his pharmacopoeia. Galb's grating breath had quieted as the laudanum took effect, and little by little his choked sobbing slowed and stopped. Then, for the first time, he grew aware of something beyond his mad, red pain, and his eyes focused first on old Dudley, then on Frede, and then sought out his wife but didn't find her, for she had fled from the gargle and agony of his breath. Galb closed his eyes again.

"It will take a lot of laudanum," he said. "If I live."

The words came indistinctly, through mashed lips, loose teeth, and a pulverized nose that nearly cut off his air and made his breathing whistle.

"You'll make it, man," said Frede.

"Don't know that I want to . . . manhood gone," Galb muttered.

"Not gone. Swollen up pretty bad, though."

Galb closed his eyes for a while, then tried to explain.

"They came in . . . said they were the new owners. . . . I said no they weren't. . . . They said open the safe. I said no. Shipment just went out last week, anyway. . . ."

Galb sighed and sunk into silence. Any sort of talking wearied him.

Then, "They demanded I open it. I said I wasn't authorized to . . . only Ben . . . only Ben could give that permission. . . . We went back and forth like that for a while, and I told them to get out; this was Waldorf's company . . ."

"Then?" Elmer asked gently.

"They said they'd give me an hour to think it over—or else."

"Nice of them," said Frede.

"I told them I'd already thought it over."

Galb lapsed into silence again and asked for more laudanum. Frede frowned. He'd obviously gone far beyond the prudent dosage.

"Just a little," he muttered. "Elmer, maybe this should be put off. This man's had enough. He needs total rest now."

Galb peered up at Dudley. "You know the rest, anyway. They have the combination, and they know Ben's got the gold and how much . . ."

Galb closed his eyes and crawled back inside himself. But it was all that Elmer needed to know. They'd hammered it out of Galb, and the good man had resisted to the last, until his body collapsed. And even then he had taken the punishment hour after hour, until the pain had broken him in two. And Elmer guessed that Galb, being the kind of man he was, hurt more from giving up secrets and surrendering than he did from his physical wounds. Probably was punishing himself and had no idea of his own courage.

"You're a good man, Galb. A better man than you know," Dudley barked, but Galb had slipped into a rasping sleep as the added laudanum stole though him.

"Galb's a good man. Take care of him, Doc," Elmer said.

Frede looked pained. "Good care. Everyone asks for good care. Someday I'll give someone bad care. Help me move him over to the bed."

Gently they lifted Galb, settled him on a bunk at the side of the room, and pulled a blanket over him. "That's my hospital bed. Only one in Pony," Frede said. "The sick can watch me prepare the dead."

Frede stared sourly. Dudley nodded and stepped into the sunny street. The Galbs' buckboard stood there, and the worn-out gray dray still heaved and hung its head. Cora Galb had disappeared. Probably at the hotel, Dudley thought. He took hold of the gray's bridle and led it gently toward Bonack's.

The Waldorf buggy was up at the bank, which alarmed him. That meant that Widen and his ugly were in there with Ben and Stop, and God only knew what was happening. Maybe old Ben and Stop were taking the same sort of mauling that had been given to Amos Galb.

Fear crawled in Dudley's gut again. Fear and helplessness. At the livery he found a new man, a tough-looking customer as burly as a blacksmith, with mean white eyes.

"Where's Bonack?" Dudley asked.

"Sold out. This is Kennedy and Widen property now."

Dudley stared at the man. "Rub down this gray and walk it out. Horse may be ruined. When it's cooled down, water it. Maybe some feed later."

"Six bits—in advance," the hostler said.

Dudley growled and dug in his britches. He would have made a fight of it, but there was trouble up at the bank.

He gimped his way up there, dreading every moment, and thinking that perhaps his own life would come to a sudden end here on this fine June morning. It seemed a long walk. The block stretched out to a mile and a league. Dudley felt ready to die, ready to take—which one, Widen or the ugly?—with him if he could. Then at last he was at the bank and swinging into the corner door and walking past Myrtle and into Stop's office, filling the doorway with his wrath.

Standing just to his right side was Lethbridge Dowling. The other three were seated, Stop behind his desk.

"This doesn't concern you, Constable," said Drago Widen.

"I'm staying," Elmer retorted.

Widen shrugged. Dowling glanced expectantly toward him, but Widen faintly shook his head.

"Maybe it does concern you, Constable," Widen added smoothly. "Ben, here, has made off with company gold—gold that now belongs to us. A felony theft."

Stop said, "You don't own the company."

Widen said, "You're not in this, Stop."

"I don't figure a crime's been committed. Show me some ownership papers," said Dudley truculently.

"A technicality," said Widen silkily. His lips were compressed, and he seemed to be a man out of patience and ready to explode. "We will have the signed papers today."

"Not with my signature on them, you won't," Ben Waldorf roared.

"Constable, tell Mr. Waldorf and Mr. Stop what happened to the mill superintendent."

"You don't have to," rumbled Ben.

"It can happen again," said Widen. "It took no time at all. The safe was opened. We found out how much was gone and that Ben took it."

Stop said, "If you touch Ben, you will make a mistake."

There was a long silence. Widen gazed at the banker with lidded eyes. Lethbridge Dowling smirked and pulled at his leash like a pitbull terrier.

"You've said that before," said Dowling. "Twice too often."

Stop gazed quietly. "I know where the gold is," he said. Ben stared at him, stunned. "Pick on me," Stop added.

The banker eased back into his chair, his black eyes resting first on Dowling, then on Widen, showing only mildness and no fear.

"You are a party to the theft, then. There is a Commandment against it."

Stop said nothing. Seconds passed, ticks of an executioner's clock. Dudley gaped in the doorway.

Widen steepled and unsteepled his hands.

"I think the Bible also says that those who live by the sword shall die by the sword," Stop said amiably.

Dudley wondered, Was it a threat? Was Stop finally showing some steel? After all these enigmatic years, was the banker going to reveal something? There rose some faint, instinctive feeling in Dudley that if Stop ever cut loose, there'd be a fire storm.

Then it all seemed to recede. Stop sat up. "Gentlemen, we have more than three weeks to meet your call loan. We are expecting a representative of a capitalist, a man more than able to raise the funds in exchange for an interest in the company."

The menace in the room seemed to evaporate, at least a little.

For some unfathomable reason Dudley felt disappointed. In truth he had wanted Stop to do something, wanted to see whether Stop had violence in him, wanted Stop to spring over his desk and maul that ugly, pound on Widen . . . but it was gone. He should be grateful that the peace was preserved, but he wasn't.

"We know about your visit to Daley," Widen said. "You won't get anywhere. No one's coming."

"Oh?" Stop's eyes rested alertly on Widen. "How is that?"

Drago Widen smiled thinly. "No one is coming."

Elmer thought he detected the faintest smirk on Lethbridge Dowling's face again.

Stop said, "You know more than I know." He rose. "Ben and I have matters to discuss now, and if you will excuse us—"

Ben said, "Where's Jezebel? Elmer, did you see her walk home?"

Dudley realized then that Waldorf and Stop had no idea of what had happened two hours earlier.

"She was hauled off by Kennedy and the other one." He nodded toward Dowling. "Knocked out and kidnapped are the words for it," Dudley blurted.

They stared at him.

"By God! Is she—is she all right?" Ben roared, bolting up from his chair.

"She wasn't when I last saw her."

Lethbridge Dowling leered, but Widen looked concerned.

"I'm going up there, and if you've touched a hair on her head—"

"I'm sure things are fine. I was just going to invite you to join us, Ben. We have matters to settle alone—apart from Stop, here, who seems to not wish to come to terms—"

"Don't go, Ben," Dudley snapped.

But the old miner straightened himself up with some dignity and said, "I will go. It is my home. It is my wife." His wide blue eyes showed no fear, only concern for Jezebel.

Stop addressed Lethbridge. "If Mrs. Waldorf has been harmed, then your brother has made a mistake he'll regret." He said it so blandly that Elmer Dudley at first dismissed it—only something lurked in that quiet tone the banker used that seemed different, odd. Deadly.

"I will walk," said Ben. He pushed out of the office, looking at no one.

Drago Widen smiled. "For the sake of your health, Mr. Stop, it would be good to confess where the stolen gold is. I'm sure the company will find it soon, and press charges if you don't return it at once."

Stop said, "We bankers respect the privacy of our clients."

Dudley sighed. He had hoped for something better from Stop. Wouldn't the young man ever stop backing down and fight? Was the man a coward? A fool?

"You can think it over for an hour or two."

"Don't hurt Ben," said Stop. It was a command.

Dowling didn't respond, and he and Mr. Drago Widen walked out.

Elmer Dudley stared at the banker, disappointed and angry.

"Something troubling you?" asked Stop.

"Yes, dammit. You're troubling me. And I'm troubling myself. I'm a fool, I guess," the constable retorted. "A damned fool."

Chapter Fourteen

Louella Peregrine barely tolerated those two pigs, Willis and Stanley Waldorf. They were loathsome, and some of the girls refused to do business with them. Louella didn't force the issue. They were a major source of her income. She had remodeled the summer kitchen, a lean-to at the back of the log hotel, into an apartment for them and charged them plenty for it, and she had instructed the girls to charge them double. They brought other income, too, from the meals and drinks they consumed gluttonously. Since Willis and Stanley usually engaged a girl, sometimes two girls, all night, they were star boarders. But that was only midweek, when the trade ran slow. On weekends Willis and Stanley were not permitted to monopolize the girls.

On several occasions girls had left Louella's house because of Willis and Stanley, and on those occasions Louella had had acute misgivings. But in the end the outpouring of gold from the mine owner's sons decided her in their favor. But now she felt doubly anxious about them. They had announced themselves the top lieutenants of the two Eastern money men who were devouring the town piece by piece, and their new position and the bouncing revolvers at their fat hips had made them insufferably arrogant.

The rules that Louella had laid down were being violated—especially that they should make themselves as invisible here as possible, and do their saloon drinking elsewhere. They lounged out in Louella's saloon each night now, insolent and arrogant, and it had affected trade.

Then, last night, they had brought Louella tidings. On behalf of the money men they offered to buy the place for ten thousand dollars. Louella had laughed. In her better months Louella had grossed that amount and often netted a clear profit of two thousand. When she had flatly told them no, they had gotten smirky and said the next offer would be lower, and if she didn't sell out, she'd be ruined.

Now, as she sat in her private office, a businesslike room compared to the luxurious and florid decor of the front parlors, and the Victorian elegance of her private rooms, she worried about it all and had no solutions. Like most people in her trade, she knew exactly what was happening in the community, albeit vicariously. She may not have been present at the demolition of Spade's Mercantile, or at the beating of Amos Galb, or at the abduction of Jezebel Waldorf, but she learned of them soon enough, and in minute detail, from her talkative clients. Now it would be her turn, and she was as loath to sell out for a fraction of her worth as any of the businessmen in town.

She might just shut down and leave, she thought. If Pony became a company town, and the company mercantiles charged exorbitant prices and kept miners in debt, there'd be no future for her here, anyway. She could take her girls and her possessions elsewhere—one of the Nevada camps, maybe—and do better.

But she hated that. In fact, she liked Pony. She felt secure here, or at least she had until the last few days. As secure as anyone in her profession could. There were always ambiguities, occasional cries for reform, people whose palms she greased when necessary. Those did not include the old constable, Elmer Dudley, who simply ignored her. Pony was not a riotous town full of bad and wild men. Not like that Arizona camp she'd heard so much of, Tombstone. Not even like Butte. It was quiet here. The miners had cash to spend, they were by and large burly and healthy in their manhood, and her girls seemed happy. Once in a while she let herself be bought—her price was triple—and more often than not she enjoyed it, even with rough men.

Louella Peregrine had been born in gentle circumstances in Syracuse, New York, the daughter of an administrator of the Erie Canal. The great canal had been a lucrative venture in her childhood, and its administrators were paid handsomely. But with the advent of railroad competition, canal revenue fell, and so did her father's income, until the family was reduced to genteel poverty. Charges of corruption in the canal's administration—which her father vigorously denied—nonetheless prevented him from finding employment elsewhere, and so the family eked out a living while still dining with the finest china and silver. And, Louella discovered, as her parents slipped into poverty, their social status declined so that the doors that once opened were now closed.

She had a practical bent. She saw at once that money was the key to everything. With money itself came respectability and position. She resolved in her teens to have money and to keep it. But there was only one way for a woman to have it, and that was to marry it. There was no prospect of earning it—not for her sex. There was one unthinkable exception to that, but she dismissed it from her mind because she was high-minded and not given to folly. Then, within the course of three weeks, she lost both parents to cholera. Miraculously she escaped, perhaps only because she was young and in robust health. Then she was alone, with almost no inheritance but with a houseful of elegant things and fine furniture—damask linens, Tiffany silver, Royal Doulton china, and more. All that and no money. And no suitors because her independence scared them off. The house itself had been mortgaged, and she had scarcely buried her parents when Joshua Grubbe, the town banker, had called at teatime and told her he was forced to foreclose.

She sat quietly that night, weighing her options, while a single candle burned low. She could sell the household treasures piecemeal and survive for a while. She could find a husband—she was handsome enough and knew she could bag one, perhaps a clerk or accountant or a teacher at the academy. All of which could be perfectly respectable, and the thing most women in her circumstance would do unhesitatingly. But Louella was a freethinker, as well as a young lady of practical bent, and as the hours wheeled past on the grandfather clock she turned to bolder ideas. And why not? What was left and who would say no?

She was a virgin. She had not the slightest inclination to become a soiled dove. The very thought was ghastly. But she thought she might become a madam and supply a house richly furnished with the things that were now her sole wealth. She, herself, would remain a virgin, untouched and untouchable, and that was all the respectability she cared about, and it would be for her own sake, and not the sake of others.

She scarcely considered that she knew nothing of the trade, or its pitfalls or diseases, or delicate positioning in any town, or the ways to deal with unruly or drunken males, or equally unruly or violent women, or just what it was that made a house attractive and profitable. But she surmised, correctly, that her genteel upbringing would serve her well in these areas. She would deal with the world as a gentlewoman might, with good English, cultivation, social ease, and assurance.

Her own plan had shocked her, and for weeks following she wavered about it. Once across a certain great divide, she would never be the same again, nor have the same claim upon the world. For the sake of wealth she would give up virtually everything she was. But in the end, as the last of her funds dissolved, she resolved to do it. She hadn't the faintest idea where to begin or how to recruit the girls, but she knew that Denver City was a raw and lusty place. She would go there, learn something of the trade, then pick a site to set up her own business. And so it happened that Louella Peregrine vanished one day from Syracuse, taking a large load of furniture and china and linens with her. And nobody back there ever heard of her again, and she never again used her last name.

Now she sat in her office, thinking of that fateful decision and wondering how to cope with what would come. The office was a shadowed place, the shade drawn. She disliked the sun, which somehow reminded her of her girlhood and her other life, and she welcomed the night, when her warm flesh gleamed in the amber lamps, and she welcomed every species of male familiarly, from Pony's leading lights to shabby drifters with strange, bruised faces. She would not sell. She had decided on that. She would pack up and leave. Pack the fine furnishings in barrels and crates, and take her girls, Esther, Maria, Candy, Lulu Lee, Lacy, and the big Bavarian blonde, Matilde, with her. There'd be an empty log hull, and she'd even burn that, just to spite those avaricious money men. Partridge, her powerful freedman, would see to their protection en route to . . . wherever.

There would be money enough—over a hundred thousand dollars, all in gold bullion and coin, in her own locked compartment of the bank's safe. Only Stop and Myrtle and herself knew of it, and they were reliably silent about the hoard. She distrusted banks and paper and had put none of it out at interest, even though she might have earned a great deal over the years. No. Gold was gold, and it survived depressions and folly and bad times better than anything else. It would be enough to retire on if she chose. Enough to establish herself elsewhere if she chose. Enough. It was there in the safe—most of it—because that was the safest place in Pony.

There came a firm knock on her office door, and she opened it to . . . Stop. His presence startled her. He had never been at her place. In fact, his refusal to come had always piqued her. He was a bachelor, with a bachelor's hungers. Had he no needs, no desires, no lust? How often she had wondered about him. Bland banker, correct, mild. Rarely did he take a drink, and then only one at the hotel saloon, with the town's better element. No known vices. A wooden Indian, passionless. Or maybe just timid, clamped down by some terrible Puritanism imposed upon his youth? She didn't know.

"Miss Louella, I desire a word in private," he said. "I trust you are well?"

She nodded, and he entered, his gaze quietly taking in the Spartan office. This was a countinghouse and an administrative room, and what it lacked in elegance it made up for in command.

"It reminds me of Ben's office at the mine," he said approvingly. "A no-nonsense place."

"I am a businesswoman—first, last, and always," she said. "May I serve you a beverage? Coffee? Spirits?"

He shook his head amiably. She wondered at him. It was a mystery how a banker could look so lean, tanned, muscular, and virile. She caught herself wondering how he would be in her arms, in her great four-poster in the next room, and then let it pass. He seemed sexless. Still, now that he was here, she intended to probe, just out of curiosity.

"You have never been here," she said. "I have always expected you . . . in your circumstances."

"Your young ladies are attractive," he replied.

"I'm glad you find them so," she said. "But you never indulge yourself."

"I am committed," he said.

The answer surprised her. Never in his years here had he had a woman on his arm. Surely there would have been something. Letters, perhaps. The postmaster, Lacy Philhorn, was a gossip. He would have talked. Or Stop might have taken long trips somewhere, but there were only short ones. A woman in Butte? Virginia City? Those were possibilities. And yet . . . he baffled her.

"You keep your lady a dark secret. I trust she is well?"

"And very comely, too," he said.

"Is she nearby? And will Pony see her soon?" Louella felt annoyed by her own curiosity and disliked her own probing.

His face went blank. He sat across from her, tanned and handsome and blank, as much a stranger with her as with the rest of Pony.

"To what may I ascribe the honor of your company?" she asked, turning to business at last. "I trust my gold is safe."

"It is safe," he said. "At least for now. If the Dowlings and their masters choose to ruin the bank and pillage the safe, your gold might not be secure at all."

"I have been worrying about that. Have you no security?"

"There is Dudley," he said.

"And yourself?"

"I'm a banker, Miss Louella. Security is something to be hired."

"I keep having the feeling that you could take care of yourself, and the bank, too, if you would choose to."

"You are flattering," he replied. "Other people seem to entertain that notion, too. I don't know where it began."

She eyed him shrewdly. She had gained a bit from this fencing but not much. Still, she guessed she understood him better than the respectable citizens of Pony ever would. "You are more than a banker," she said, her dark eyes firm upon him. "But you are a young man with lines, borders. Lines you once crossed. I know all about lines myself."

She waited. He listened politely.

"I will tell you things I never talk of. Lines. I grew up in gentle circumstances in the East, never dreaming of this profession. I had a taste for good living, comfort, security, freedom. Then it vanished. I decided to pursue this profession, but there were lines—do you follow me? Lines. Once I crossed a line, I could never turn back. For days I deluded myself. I would be an owner, a manager, but not one—not one of the girls. I thought I might make money that way and not cross the line. But in the end I crossed the line, and a gulf separates me from the rest of Pony. All I know of you is that there is a line in your life, Mr. Stop. You either crossed it in the past or you are living a false life now, by staying within lines. I don't know what you have been or will be, but you are channeled by lines that only you know of. I understand lines, and in a way I understand you, Mr. Stop."

She paused. Stop's eyes had become contemplative and gentle. At last he smiled. "Perhaps you are right," he said. "I think you understand me better than the rest. But what does it achieve, this understanding?"

He had her there. There was nothing to it, except some salve for her curiosity. She hardened, sorry she had revealed as much of herself as she had. "You are here on some business, I am sure," she said.

"I represent Ben Waldorf in certain confidential matters," he said. "We are offering a negotiable share in the company."

"And so you have come to me."

"Yes. You have large and very liquid assets in the safe. Enough, I think, to purchase a generous portion of the mine, and probably improve your position."

"Seams of ore can pinch out tomorrow. There's no way of knowing," she said.

"I have reports from mining engineers and geologists. There appears to be several years of reserves left, and maybe lots more."

She understood well enough what he wanted. Word of what Kennedy and Widen were after had reached her ears, earlier, if anything, than the ears of most in Pony. "My assets are not available for investment," she said tersely. "And in any case they run half of what you need immediately."

"We think they might be enough," Stop said.

"They'll want it all," she said. "With that type they'll settle for nothing less, and be disappointed if they get it because they wanted the whole thing."

"Perhaps you're right," he said. "But your bullion, plus the mine itself as collateral, might make the company eligible for a loan among Helena or Virginia City financiers."

It was tempting. If the mine remained in Waldorf hands, she could stay on. She wouldn't be squeezed out, either by violence or competition or, at the worst, the deepening debt and poverty of the miners in a company town. But her hoard in the safe was her entire security, the thing she had patiently built to the point where she was almost ready for her next step. She might indeed cross the line again if she could, into respectable, rich widowhood in a place where people had scarcely heard of Pony, Montana Territory.

"It is tempting, but I think not. I do not trust investments, or companies run by others. And it's half what you really need."

"It would buy you a quarter of a mine valued at two million dollars," Stop said. "And you would not actually commit until the second hundred thousand dollars is raised among capitalists to meet the call loan. So Jasper Kennedy and Drago Widen would be out of it, their bullyboys and themselves gone. At least that's what Ben and I are hoping. And in turn you would have a valuable and profitable property. Whoever offered the other hundred thousand would also have a quarter. Ben would retain half, except for the one percent I bought."

"You have an interest?"

"As of a few days ago when this came upon us. It put me in a better negotiating position with them."

"You tempt me," she said. "A hundred thousand in bullion for a half-million share, at least by your estimates."

"By the estimate of these reports," Stop said, reaching for papers in his portfolio.

"Reports can lie," she said. "And when it comes to mining, they often do."

"I am prepared to supply the names of independent geologists and engineers in Butte or Virginia City," he said. "But you would need to act fast."

"It is tempting," she said. "More than you know. I've been approached to sell. And with the usual threat about it, too. If this becomes a company town, I see no way of hanging on. I am still shy of my personal goals, though. I want two hundred thousand, which I hope to have in a few years."

"You would have gotten it faster lending it at interest."

"I don't like risk."

He smiled gently. "Nothing could be more risky than a hoard like that in a safe in a small-town bank," he said. "You have depended on my silence—and Myrtle's. But now the Eastern gents have seen the books. They will know that you have no account. No account in the bank."

It alarmed her. "I had not thought of that," she said. "Perhaps I could hide the bullion."

"Amos Galb refused—as long as he could—to give them the combination of the stamp-mill safe," he said.

He had made his point. The Dowlings could torture it from her—she dreaded pain above all else—easily enough.

She sat, undecided and distressed. Then at last she addressed him. "I'm sorry, Mr. Stop. Investing in the mine is too risky. Especially now. With those uglies terrorizing the town, not even a full two hundred thousand payment of the called loan is any guarantee that Mr. Kennedy and Mr. Widen will leave. I happen to know Mr. Widen. He was a neighboring boy. How I give myself away to you! I'm sure you could trace me now, if you wished . . . but I knew him. And even then I could see what he was, and what he could be, and Mr. Stop, I shudder to think of him here. I am very afraid he will walk in here and recognize me. . . . No. Mr. Stop. The answer is no."

Chapter Fifteen

Jasper Kennedy never got angry. His Quaker upbringing had bred such feelings out of him, and now it always amazed him when others lost control or turned choleric. That Quaker serenity was why he knew he was superior to Drago Widen, who sometimes lost his temper.

Whenever Jasper felt frustrated, he practiced the spiritual centering and calming and godliness of his former people, and soon enough he would feel better. He thought, rightly, that it gave him enormous advantages in life. Instead of making bad mistakes in the heat of frustration or rage, he quite coolly thought things through and found ways and means to reach his ends.

The Dowlings, of course, were an important factor in all of this. They were almost magical. Whenever events threatened to upset his Quaker serenity, the Dowlings found solutions and the trouble passed. He always got what he wanted in the end. He couldn't remember a time—at least an adult time—when he didn't get what he wanted sooner or later. Time was the only variable. Some things had to be waited out. Ben Waldorf, for instance. The stubborn old reprobate had forced Jasper to wait, and that was displeasing. The financier supposed he might be a little more vulnerable to temper if he did not employ the Dowlings—he saw it as a weakness, a potential testing of him. Jezebel, too, had forced him to wait, but that would be a problem easily solved. Too bad she was not a Quaker. No, he corrected himself, he felt glad she wasn't one. Jezebel was deliciously unlike Quaker gentlewomen. He would have to break her like a bronc horse, but carefully, so as not to destroy that vital spirit.

The pair of them stayed upstairs in their rooms. Jezebel had recovered soon enough from that chop to her throat and had slipped wearily into her room and locked the door. Soon that heathen Chinese had carried buckets of hot water up there, and brought her meals as well. Jasper had thought about stopping that traffic but decided to let her wash and feed herself. She would be more tractable and perhaps grateful.

Drago, who perched tensely in the other wing chair in Waldorf's study that evening, interrupted Jasper's musings. "It's time to deal with Stop," he said. "I don't know why we keep putting it off. The instant Stop caves in, the old man will, too."

"I think thee are optimistic," said Jasper amiably. "For an old wastrel and reprobate, Ben Waldorf shows a lot of steel."

"Stop's the key," Drago insisted. "Arrogant, godless young man without an ounce of humility in him. There are men walking the earth who need a whipping. Invite a whipping. He's deceived us with mild words. Never saw a blander man, and that has put us off. But I see through him. I know his ilk. He'll fold fast enough when we turn the screws. He's a country banker, after all. A banker! A little persuasion from the Dowlings . . ."

Jasper could follow Drago's turn of mind easily enough. Perhaps it would be the thing to do. But there was some indefinable quality about Stop, some hidden power in him that made Jasper hesitant.

"I think we may underestimate the banker. Perhaps thee should entertain other options. . . ."

"Tomorrow the bank," said Drago. "There are only three people of any consequence left: Spade, Stop, and the madam, Louella. We'll have the bordello soon. And in the name of those idiot Waldorf boys, too, so we can remain silent partners in that enterprise. The woman will cave in as soon as she thinks it over. We must wind this up and leave. This little burg is wearisome."

"This Waldorf manse is amiable enough," said Jasper. His thoughts were more on Jezebel than on other amenities.

The amber lamplight seemed to deepen the pocks in Widen's ferret face, and Jasper, always the aesthete, found him singularly unbecoming in the shadowed room.

"Let's try Ben again," Jasper said. "Thee and I can try some new tacks."

"Such as?"

"Jezebel."

"What else?" Drago asked testily. He behaved like a man ready to explode.

"The Dowlings."

Drago waited tensely, alarm crawling across his face and then receding.

"Yes, Drago, the Dowlings. The old man has bluffed us, you know. Ready to die and all that. We've been snookered like a pair of rube poker players. . . ." Jasper Kennedy scowled faintly. "We can always call the bluff, see how willing he is to sign under a little pressure, a little wrench of those old bones . . ."

Drago shook his head. "It won't work. The old goat is a brave man, if ever I saw one. Devils never lacked courage, God knows. I pray on my knees that the old reprobate will come to see God's design and purpose."

"But we won't know until we try," said Jasper amiably.

Drago sighed. "He's old. What if . . ."

"That's up to God, wouldn't thee say? We are only the instruments of progress. Are we not freeing valuable property from an old lecher and reprobate, the scum of the earth?"

Drago was agitated. "But we lose, we lose . . . there's no will. The courts, the heirs, the tangle, the legal expense, the, ah, embarrassment—a whole town suspecting things, twisting facts." He leapt up and paced Waldorf's den like a caged jaguar.

"What heirs?" asked Jasper mildly.

Those two words arrested Drago in midstep. He stared.

Jasper Kennedy smiled deferentially. He always knew he was

the brains of Kennedy and Widen, but he took pains not to let it show. The younger man lived on the razor's edge, and a valuable partnership could be fatally damaged with an unkind word.

"No will. Only common-law heirs. The girl, Jezebel, with dower rights—easy enough to handle, since I'm taking her East. And who else? The sons. Tubs of blubber. Not the slightest problem after the Dowlings are through with them. Mere whiners. Drago, you need only say the word."

"But the courts. The territorial courts. Rough justice here. Circuit-riding judges, delays . . ."

Jasper smiled. "Come now. Does thee forget that judges can be bought and sold, a dime a dozen? It is a simple matter."

"Stop has a small interest. Enough to make trouble. He'd have standing in court."

Jasper simply smiled. Stop was really not worth discussing. What resources did the man have?

Drago, reading his mind, objected. "Stop, himself, said he knows where the mine bullion is. He and Ben know."

Jasper shrugged delicately. "What's twenty thousand compared to two million, or ten or twenty million? Ben will reveal it, I'm sure, as soon as the Dowlings ask him to."

Drago paced now. "Let's invite him down. Try him one more time tonight. Where are the Dowlings?"

"Lethbridge is here. Paddo is out prowling again. His scouting has certainly been successful. I suppose he's keeping an eye on Stop. It is of interest to know where the man goes, who he sees. Thanks to our good man Paddo, we've kept Marcus Daley out and headed off that Virginia City sheriff—what was his name? Rafe McDaniel? Not that I worry about sheriffs. The other, Daley's man—"

"It was a woman."

"The more the pity, but that's life. I suppose he's wondering now what happened to her, and his lackeys will soon discover the buckboard wreck . . . yes. At any rate, the Daley interest was the only serious menace, and Paddo dealt with it."

"How'd Paddo know who Daley would send?" Drago asked.

138

"Who knows? Thee can only guess. Money buys almost everything," Jasper said, delight on his tongue.

They directed Lethbridge to bring Ben from his room and, if Ben resisted, to smash the bedroom door and bring the old man, anyway. But Ben came without resistance, looking virile and alert when he walked into his own den to confront the uninvited guests.

Jasper eyed him and wondered if it was an old man's bluff. Surely the pressures of recent days would drain an old man's vitality. And that was for the good. Perhaps the old reprobate would be softened and ready now.

"Why, you're looking chipper, Ben. I hope thee are enjoying thy company as much as we enjoy being here."

Ben Waldorf grunted. He didn't look particularly hospitable.

"We thought to have another talk with thee. A last chance, if thee can understand that."

"Sam Stop's doing my dealin'," the old man replied. "And nothin's changed. We're not signing anything until the contract time expires. Likely have you paid off good and proper by then."

This was all familiar, and Jasper pushed aside a faint annoyance that rose in him.

"Let's bring Stop up here then, and settle it."

"Suits me. Go ahead and hunt him down," said Ben.

"Are thee suggesting he's not available?"

Ben shrugged.

"You and Stop spent the afternoon in his office. Did thee achieve much?"

Ben eyed the financier, then snorted. "A will. Drafted and executed a will good and proper—and a few spare copies, besides."

Jasper Kennedy was delighted. "Why, Jezebel would be an heiress if you had any property to bequeath. Of course you do still have this splendid brick pile and all the trimmings."

That would make it all the easier, he thought. When he took Jezebel East, he would have the whole thing, and not a dower right . . . if it came to that. He hoped it wouldn't come to that. Beatings, bruises, death—all could be embarrassing and might require all sorts of cash. On the other hand, at times that sort of persuasion was the only way to do proper business.

Ben laughed. "Maybe I cut the hellcat out and willed it all to my sons."

"But time's run out, Ben. Run out for thee." Jasper nodded faintly toward Lethbridge, who lounged at the door.

The old man settled himself in a wing chair. He looked barely clean, barely kempt, and Jasper thought Ben smelled of fear, despite his seeming ease. The old miner's rough hands were resting softly on his knees as he waited.

The grandfather clock began to gong sonorously, ten times. Ben said nothing.

"A handsome piece," said Jasper. "I admire good things. Thee hast collected beauty around thee."

"Hired it done," said Ben. "My turnip watch is just as good."

"Beautiful things," continued Jasper easily. "Such as Jezebel. Truly a woman worthy of thy wealth."

Ben wheezed, but Jasper saw his eyes turn wary.

"In fact," said Jasper, pacing easily in the amber light, "she is causing us much distress. She's been most . . . inhospitable. Indeed, biting off the earlobe of poor Lethbridge, there, scratching, bullwhipping. A terror of a woman. My two gents are steaming about it and want justice. I've had my hands full keeping them from punishing her for her . . . indiscretions."

"Say what you're sayin' plain," Ben said.

"Why, Ben, only that I can't guarantee her safety anymore. No telling what terrible things are in store for her. These gents have their dander up, and I fear the poor woman might be, well, ah, bruised a little. But, of course, if we could just come to a quick agreement right now, why, ah . . . we'd hustle these gents out of here and be on our way back East in the morning."

Ben cackled. "Jezebel now, eh? That hellcat can take care of herself well enough. Give as good as she gits, I'd say. Turn 'em loose and see the fun. It'd be better than a cockfight."

It startled Jasper. "Surely thee art married?" He knew the answer. Murray P. Eickles had written him all about that. The marriage was valid.

"Ain't a woman like her in the world," Ben said. "Likely skin them Dowlings and hang the carcasses up to dry."

Jasper sighed. "Why, Ben, I fear her virtue might be compromised. There's no telling when the beast in men gets the upper hand."

Ben laughed again. "Likely as not, she'd enjoy it. She weren't any angel selling shoes and showin' leg off her daddy's wagon."

Ben eased back into the chair, his blue eyes sparkling. It irked Jasper. He wasn't sure if Ben really didn't care about Jezebel, or if it was another bluff. But, in any case, it wasn't levering Ben toward giving up the mine.

Mr. Drago Widen jumped in. "Look here, Waldorf," he said testily. "Unless you turn over the collateral right now, three things will happen in the morning. We will not be responsible for the health and safety of yourself, Mrs. Waldorf, and Sam Stop."

Ben snorted. "We still got three weeks, according to the contract. You fellers ain't doin' business; you're doin' claim jumpin', and I've seen your kind before, not duded up so fancy . . ."

Hoofbeats and voices sounded in the yard, and a moment later, a resounding rap on the door. Lethbridge disappeared into some shadowed place, while Hip Hip trotted to the door and admitted two men, both armed.

Jasper knew one of them—the old lame town marshal, Elmer Dudley. And he quickly surmised who the other one was, from the steel star pinned to his chest.

And in the shadows just beyond them he spotted Paddo, following like a wraith. So both the uglies were on hand, if necessary.

Ben sat quietly.

"Ben, welcome them," commanded Jasper, but Ben shook his head amiably.

Jasper took the measure of Rafe McDaniel, and he liked what he saw. The man was plainly as dense as a block of pine, burly, long-eared, with narrow-set eyes that peered stupidly at one man after another. A florid bull of a man but clumsy, and a pushover for the Dowlings. He had obviously been primed by the town marshal about events in Pony, and there was a certain truculence in his gaze.

He wasted no time, either. "There's been a heap of trouble up here, and I got the story of it. I'm taking you buzzards in, and your two bullyboys. Got a list of charges long as my arm. Destroying property, assault and battery—you name it and I got it. Mr. Waldorf, you want I should get these buzzards out of here?"

Ben guffawed. "Rafe, go ahead and try," he said.

"I think thee makes a mistake," said Jasper hastily. "We are Ben Waldorf's guests here, working out the final details of the transfer. We have the mine, sheriff. Yes, indeed, Mr. Widen here and I are assuming control of Pony Consolidated. My friend, I imagine we'll have a bit to say about the administration of the county."

Rafe McDaniel eyed him darkly.

"We do admire your work, Sheriff. Why, Drago and I were thinking, as we drove here, that we'd make a modest campaign contribution to keep you in office. Why, would ten thousand help a bit at election time?"

Ben Waldorf laughed. "They ain't got the mine," he said. "Ask 'em if they got a bill of sale. Hell, ask me if these turkeys are invited here, or if they just moved in."

"I already got the whole story from Dudley," McDaniel said. "I don't need no more talk. And I don't accept no bribes, either."

McDaniel pulled several sets of handcuffs from his belt and tossed them to Elmer Dudley. Then he pulled out both of his Colt revolvers.

Jasper was pained. He much preferred to talk his way through difficulties. It was never hard. But this blockhead hadn't come for talk; his mind was as closed as a jail door. The man could be bought, too. That was easy enough to spot. But Kennedy and Widen would have to own the mine, good and proper, before there'd be any buying of Rafe McDaniel.

Rafe turned one Colt toward Lethbridge, who lounged in the shadows of the dining room. "In here," he snapped. "Elmer, you throw a cuff on him."

Dudley approached warily, watching for fancy kicks and canes that tripped.

Then it all came unglued. There was a thump, and Rafe McDaniel dropped as if poleaxed, his Colts flying across the blue Oriental carpet. And old Dudley found himself sprawling once again. Just behind where McDaniel had stood was Paddo, a Stevens 10-gauge in one hand and a knout in the other. Lethbridge stood leering. Whatever he had done, it happened so fast that Jasper hadn't seen it. He knew only that old Dudley was sprawled on the floor and groaning.

Ben Waldorf stood still.

Old Dudley they didn't bother with, but the sheriff was another matter. The Dowlings hauled him outside. Blood caked the back of his head, and he was obviously in a daze. Then, from out on the dark lawn came thumps and grunts and anguished howls, then bloodcurdling screaming that ricocheted out of the dark. The sound was most distasteful to Jasper, and he bore it impatiently. It was necessary. Some things were necessary in business that were distasteful. The clock chimed the quarter hour, and the thumping continued, along with gargled screaming. Old Dudley stared from the floor, dazed and appalled and afraid he'd be next.

Then, at last, silence outside, and the crickets began to creak again.

"Thee must leave," Jasper said to Elmer Dudley. "And let it be a lesson to thee. If thee wishes to be the law in Pony, thee must learn."

The constable stood up shakily, stared violently at the financiers, and limped into the night. Jasper thought the man would bear watching. He followed the constable to the door. The Dowlings were loading what was left of Sheriff Rafe McDaniel onto his horse and tying him down. Dudley mounted his horse and rode down the hill, tugging the burdened sheriff's horse behind him.

Jasper turned to Ben. "Let it be a lesson to thee," he said.

"I'm ready," said Ben quietly. His eyes blazed disgust. "I been ready to kick off for years."

He walked quietly up the long stairs, his hand on the banister, up into the unlit second story, and then Jasper heard the old man's door click shut.

"Whom God loves, he chastens," Drago said. "It is always an ordeal to have to see such things. Upsets me. I must go bend a knee. Business is a heavy cross. . . . Good night, Jasper."

Then Jasper Kennedy was alone. He would sit in the quiet den for a while, preparing for sleep, enjoying the peace, and enjoying the triumph that would come on the morrow. But his thoughts would not hold on business, or focus on what must be commanded in the morning. His thoughts were on Jezebel, beautiful young Jezebel, of the wild jet hair and lavender eyes and glowing young flesh . . . all alone in her room. The thought of her made him tremble. He sat rigidly for several minutes, having an uncharacteristic inner struggle. The Dowlings had vanished, and he sat alone. The house was silent and darkened, save for his lamp.

At last he turned down the wick until the flame blued out, then found his way upstairs by moonlight. He did not turn toward his room but stalked softly in the other direction, toward her room, across from Waldorf's. Lamplight illumined the run at the base of the door.

"Tootsie," he whispered. Eickles had once reported that Waldorf called her that. "Tootsie, let me in."

The door opened silently an inch or two. Swiftly he pushed in. She reeled back under the force of it while he clicked the door shut behind him. He stared.

In the light of her bedside lamp she was stunning. She wore a revealing wrapper, and perhaps nothing else. Her jet hair fell in disarray, enchanting. Her eyes were bagged—she was tired—but the lavender caught the light, and her gaze followed him as he approached. There was a purple bruise at the base of her throat, marring her golden flesh, but other than that she looked unharmed. A scent—lilac, perhaps—rose subtly from her. Her lush lips compressed into a thin line, but she did not scream. And then she looked amused, and he felt encouraged and stepped forward.

"I dream of you," he said hoarsely, his pulse beginning to pound in his temples. "I'm taking you with me. You're the most beautiful woman on earth. I've seen them all, New York, Boston, Saratoga Springs, Philadelphia . . . and there's none, none, your match. I'll give you everything, I'll make you happy. Your wish is my command. Within reason, of course. You're my Tootsie, too, my Tootsie . . ."

She was smiling now. She stood, arms akimbo, letting her robe part, letting the golden rise of her breasts show a little. She smiled and her lips parted, and she licked them provocatively. She said nothing, but her eyes danced and her lush hair glinted.

"Tootsie!" he cried, and gathered her into his arms. But just as he felt the soft warmth of her breast, her knee connected. He felt his insides fold and his legs buckle. He felt white pain burst out of his groin across his stomach, down his legs, out his arms, and explode a second time in his skull. He felt himself folding like an accordion and scarcely heard his own shriek. She caught his arms as he collapsed, and that fine-shaped knee caught him a second time, a second comet burst of insane pain, and he fell into oblivion, gargling vomit as he slid into blackness.

"Tootsie, my ass," she said.

Chapter Sixteen

Elmer Dudley was afraid. He had been afraid many times before in his decades of lawing, but never like this. Every time he had confronted a stranger in a saloon, he had been afraid. Every time he had prodded a wild cowboy or miner off to the little wooden hoosegow, he'd been afraid. He had often dealt with his fear by drawing his Colt beforehand. There was a school of law enforcement that admonished lawmen never to draw unless they intended to shoot. Dudley snorted at that; he would long since have been planted in the town graveyard over on the north hill if he'd listened to fancy advice. He felt proud that it was no boot hill up there, with rows of nameless outlaws buried in it. Pony had always been an orderly town . . . until now.

No, this was another kind of fear, and it crawled over him like a hundred spiders this morning. This was a doomsday dread, and in the back of his mind he wondered if he'd see the sun rise again. He had no inclination to die, he told himself. At the very least he hoped to join the whittlers and gossipers in front of Spade's emporium when the time came to retire. They were good company. And he was still young, in his fifties.

Rafe McDaniel groaned out in the front room. Dudley's wife had called it a parlor, but that was a pretty fancy name for a room in this cottage. Dudley had brought him here, eased him onto the brown horsehair sofa, and then had fetched Doc Frede.

"I'm not equipped for epidemics," Doc had grumbled. "Contagious beatings." But he had hurried along behind Dudley, barely keeping up even though Elmer limped.

"Keep this under your hat, Doc," Dudley had said. If it became known that the Virginia City sheriff had been pounded half to death, there was no telling what sort of panic might ensue.

Dudley had lit every lamp in the house, and Doc had cleaned up the sheriff, extracting two dangling incisors and one molar from a mashed gum, and spooning another heavy dose of laudanum into the groaning, delirious man.

"Can't do much about the internal injuries," Doc muttered. "He's been beaten by experts. Keep him down. Give him lots of liquids. I'll leave some laudanum—use it sparingly, and only if he's half crazed with pain—as he will be when he comes to."

There was no expense budget for the constable, so he dropped a couple cartwheels of his own into Frede's hand. "Shouldn't take it," Frede muttered, but then he slid the coins into his pocket and left, muttering.

Now McDaniel mumbled and groaned in the front room. Dudley stropped his razor, brushed lather into his beard, shaved, then braved the front of his house and the patient. The sheriff's face was blotched red and purple, and grotesquely swollen on one side.

The man's speech was so slurred, Dudley couldn't make it out.

"You got to stay put for a few days. Ain't going to do any traveling. Sure ain't going back to VC soon. Here. Doc says give you a spoon of this."

He poured a spoonful from the purple bottle and slid it into the raw, swollen mouth, and watched ease and drowsiness return to the mauled man.

Then the sheriff was mumbling again—posses, shooting, hanging, law, judges, kill, Greeners, Winchesters, Colts—but Dudley scarcely could make it out. Rafe wanted war—that much seemed clear—and through his haze of pain was planning one.

"I'll check in on ya soon, Rafe. Gotta do my morning rounds now," Elmer said.

He slipped out into a cold, hard sun. Pony had changed. He stood for a moment, staring at the familiar town. He wasn't quite sure how, but Pony felt different now, unfriendly, hard-bitten, dour. It was time to find Philo Crane, put together a posse of brave and foolish young miners, and try to play his only hand. He didn't doubt that the boys would bleed and die, but it was the only card he had, and he would play it today. With his own shooting arm still paining him, it wasn't much of a card. He'd play jokers, not aces.

When his woman was alive, he usually tanked up on a hot breakfast before starting his day, but now his bachelor life had changed all that. He usually did his round, then settled into a familiar chair at Thornton's café, where the widow woman silently laid a heaping plate before him.

It was the sun, he decided. Usually the morning sun shone warm and amiable on this eastern slope of the mountains. But today it drove down in lances, splintering light painfully from tin roofs, stirrups, nail heads and glass windows. Pony cowered under the hard sun. The little mining town was quiet, and there were few people abroad.

The Bank of Pony was open and looked peaceful enough. Myrtle hunched over her books. She'd be there alone today, Dudley knew. Sam Stop had left for Butte the previous day and wouldn't return until the next. Stop would try Daley again and find out whether Daley had sent an agent to Pony to look over the mine. Ben and Stop had told him that. And told him they suspected foul play, too, because Daley's man had never shown up. Elmer figured Marcus Daley was their last ace. If Ben Waldorf couldn't trade a piece of the mine for some of Daley's cash, it was all over.

Dudley's gut churned. He didn't like the idea of Myrtle in there alone, with the door of that big safe gaping open. But Pony looked quiet enough, and the constable eased into his seat at the café and slurped up the coffee he had spilled into the saucer.

One thing about Thornton's: its big plate-glass window afforded him a fine view up and down Pony's commercial district. And now, through that acre of glass, he could see the glistening black barouche, gleaming in the hard sun, ease down the slope and draw to a halt at the bank. Elmer Dudley sighed. He gazed longingly at the eggs, oatmeal, and sidepork and gave up. He paid the Widow Thornton her three bits, jiggled his gun belt around, and walked out into that mean sun, his gut roiling. He hadn't even had time to put his posse together. Those lads went off-shift in the wee hours and were all asleep. There were times, he thought, that a man feels alone in the universe, and just now he felt more alone than he ever had.

The Dowling were in the bank. Their pin-striped suits looked newly brushed and pressed, and the pants had sharp creases. The bowlers were brushed, too, and not a speck of dust lay on them. Elmer took all that in, as well as the sawed-off Stevens tucked in Lethbridge's beefy arm.

The safe was closed, he noted. Myrtle must have seen them coming and shut the heavy green door. She stood not altogether calmly as the uglies wandered through the polished oak gate and into the rear of the bank.

"Where's Stop?" asked one.

Myrtle did not deign to answer.

"You'd better say," one warned. Lethbridge spotted the old constable in the door and lazily swung his Stevens until its double bore was casually aimed at Elmer.

Paddo took a single step toward Myrtle.

"He's out of town," she said. "He won't be here today."

Paddo grinned. "Off to Butte. Off to see Uncle Marcus."

He stepped into Myrtle's teller's wicket and began ransacking the cash drawer, dumping coins and bills into a cotton feed sack.

"Stop that! You're stealing," Myrtle snapped. "You're common crooks!"

"You have it wrong," Lethbridge said. "Stop stole twenty thousand in bullion from the company, and we're just taking it back. Open the safe."

"I will not," she said. "Mr. Stop can open it."

"Leave that safe alone," Dudley growled from the door.

"Come on in, Constable, come on in," Lethbridge commanded.

Dudley felt himself sucked into the vortex of hell as he stepped in. Almost insolently the Dowlings turned their backs on him, daring him to interfere.

"Lady, I think you'll open the safe now," Paddo said.

In answer Myrtle turned to leave. She would leave the bank to the uglies if she had to. But Paddo's walking stick snaked out, and once again Myrtle crashed to the floor while the Dowlings grinned.

"I think not," Paddo said.

She sat, refusing to stand, and glared at them.

Elmer Dudley was incensed. "You'd do that to a woman," he yelled.

"We're not particular," Lethbridge replied. "Lady, open that safe. Or give us the combination. If not, you'll regret it."

She glared silently. Paddo approached her.

"You touch her and I'll shoot," growled the old constable. "You'll kill me, but one of you will be dead."

He tugged at his big Colt, but before it slid half free of the holster, a cane slammed into his sore arm, then a walking stick jerked his arm high and the Colt clattered away. It was the nightmare he had lived through before. These uglies darted with uncanny speed and rendered him helpless.

"You never learn, Dudley. You could die that way," Paddo said, leering. "Now, lady, the fun's over. You open that safe."

She stared, disheveled but defiant.

He grabbed her glossy dark hair, demolishing the careful bun, and lifted her bodily until her head hung by it. And then, just as swiftly, he dropped her and spun her, so that she hit the hardwood floor with a brutal crash. She wept.

"Open the safe."

On the floor she drew herself into a small ball of gray, watershot silk and covered her head with her arms.

Lethbridge flicked a button in his walking stick, and the spring-driven dagger at its base snapped out. Then he jabbed it into her ribs, severing her dress. Something white showed.

"You'll open the safe or I'll push harder," he said.

Brave Myrtle refused to move. Lethbridge jabbed the dagger harder, until red blood welled through the cloth. She sobbed.

"Myrtle, for God's sake, obey the man," Dudley cried.

She sobbed and wouldn't move. Some stubborn thing in her resisted the pain.

"You'll have to kill me first," she said through her tears.

"You kill her," Dudley cried, "and I'll never stop hunting you two down, even if I have to go to New York to do it."

Paddo grinned. "If you are alive to do the hunting."

"Lady-killers don't last long out here," Dudley roared.

He glimpsed a frightened face in the window, then it disappeared. That was good. Someone in Pony had witnessed these things.

"I've got better ways than this sticker," Lethbridge said. He lifted his walking stick and retracted its blade. Then he squatted beside her and twisted an arm behind her back, hard, higher and higher. A seam unraveled.

She screamed.

He twisted more, cruelly, and her screams rose and broke and rose higher, and echoed through the bank. Then there was a snap, the arm went akimbo, and she fainted.

Lethbridge was irked. "What'd she do that for?" he demanded. He found a carafe of drinking water and dashed it in her face. She came to, moaning and sobbing.

He flipped her onto her back. When her sobbing slowed down a little, he took her jaw in hand and forced her to look up at him.

"You are getting the picture, lady. Now tell us the combination."

She shook her head.

"For God's sake, Myrtle," Dudley cried.

Lethbridge simply squeezed her jaw, his pink, meaty hands clamping harder and harder.

"If you break her jaw, she won't be able to talk," Dudley snapped.

But Myrtle had had all she could bear. A dullness slid into her eyes. "Left two turns," she whispered. "Right to twenty-seven. Left to forty. Right to twenty-seven again." Then her eyes closed and she wept.

Moments later Paddo swung the heavy green door open, grinning.

"Lookee here. Ain't that pretty," he said. Currency and gold coins were stacked neatly on shelves. He scooped up the green bills first, then began tossing shimmering yellow coins into the bag. They thudded heavily.

"Where's the keys to those two lockboxes on top?" he asked her.

She didn't reply.

"I asked you a question. Do you want more?"

She blinked back tears. Dudley thought she looked terrible, pain radiating from her eyes and tormenting her face. She was streaked and grimy with dust.

"One box is empty, unused. The other is rented. We don't have a key. She . . . she has it."

"No key? Is that the truth?" asked Lethbridge. He snapped out the dagger blade again.

She nodded.

"Who?" said Lethbridge.

She stared up at him, all the fight out of her. "Louella," she mumbled.

"Fancy that. Louella. Earnin's of sin, wouldn't you say, Paddo?"

"Can't have some godless woman getting rich like that. Mr. Widen and Mr. Kennedy would call it tainted money. I guess we'd better take it."

Lethbridge hurried out to the barouche and returned with a small brown satchel full of specialized tools.

Dudley protested. "That's not bank money. That don't repay what Ben Waldorf and Stop got hid."

Paddo smiled. "You ain't bright, copper. We're just borrowing it. It's a lever. Maybe we'll give it back when she sells out. We're just cleaning up Pony. Sinful town, copper. You should be glad we're doing a public service."

He inserted a jimmy bar and jammed it. But the strongbox didn't give. The steel was heavy-gauge, and the lock was a stout one. Lethbridge tried his hand, but between them they could only dent the box a little and the lock held.

"Blow it," said Paddo.

Once, when both uglies had their backs turned, Elmer sidled

toward his big Colt, which had been kicked into a corner. But then Paddo caught him.

"Stand where you be," he said, covering the constable. He plucked up the Colt and took it back to the safe with him.

Lethbridge drew a snub-nosed nickel-plated revolver from his shoulder holster, aimed carefully at the lock, and fired. The report rattled glass.

The bullet went true, but still the lock didn't give. It was a good safe. Then they jabbed the honed-down prongs of a thin steel lever into the keyhole and began to twist, and at last the lock snapped and they slid the safe box open.

Inside was solid gold, mostly ten-pound ingots, and the rest double eagles neatly stacked in glistening rows.

Dudley was astonished. A fortune in there.

The Dowlings were astonished, too. "Looks like sin is rightly profitable," said Lethbridge, smirking. "I should go into the sin business instead of living upright."

"Ain't the misters going to be entertained?" Lethbridge said. "It'll take a mess of praying before they keep it."

The cotton bag proved much too weak for a load like that, so they filled the satchel and wrestled it to the barouche and dumped the gold in a covered luggage bin. Then they filled the satchel again.

The gleaming gold mesmerized them. It mesmerized Dudley, too. He had never seen so much. But for once the Dowlings' attention was entirely focused, and the old constable saw his chance. While they were at the safe the second time, he wheeled out the door as fast as his bum knee would allow, and lumbered down the road, half expecting a shot in the back. There was no one on the street. Mid-morning and not a soul. Behind him, he heard the Dowlings' nasal laughter. They stood in the bank door, watching his flight. But he didn't care. He needed to get Doc Frede again, this time for Myrtle, who probably had a dislocated shoulder. And then get his young miners together. The thing had gone beyond endurance, and he cursed himself for not acting sooner, much sooner.

Behind him, he heard the crash and crunch of a bank being vandalized, and he knew that when he returned with Doc Frede, he'd find papers scattered, files dumped, furniture savaged, maybe on fire, and Myrtle in the middle of it.

He heard the hiss of the barouche, and from the corner of his eye he saw the trotters wheeling around and the barouche sliding upslope, back to the Waldorf mansion. By the time he reached Doc Frede's, he was trembling.

Doc was waiting. Like many others in Pony, he had witnessed it all from afar.

"Myrtle's hurt," Dudley said.

Doc fell in stride, carrying his black bag. "It's an epidemic," he snapped.

"Jabbed in the side with a spring-loaded dagger. Arm busted or dislocated or something," the constable muttered.

Frede nodded. "Experts," he said. "First-rate bullyboys. How's McDaniel?"

"Full of pain this morning, half out of his head. How's Galb?"

"Coming along," said Doc. "Changed man, though. Something weak and defeated about him now. Hope that part of him recovers along with that white carcass of his."

They found Myrtle on the floor, lost in a haze of pain, and the bank a shambles. She barely recognized Frede. Swiftly he probed her twisted arm and probed the small wound at her ribs, slitting the dress apart to get at it.

He sighed. "Experts, experts. Myrtle, I'm going to snap your arm back. Going to be a bad moment. Worse than ever, and then the pain'll die down."

She nodded.

He positioned himself, gave a sharp, deft tug, and something thumped inside her shoulder, and her arm seemed to hang normally again. She gasped and sucked in her breath.

"Take care of her, Doc. I got things to do," said Dudley roughly. He stared sharply at her, and the mess across the bank, and stepped into the empty street. Two things. Give Louella the bad news, and get Philo Crane and his boys. Some posse, he thought.

Chapter Seventeen

Constable Dudley stared at his posse, such as it was. They had assembled at the bank. He wanted them to see the destruction and chaos, the safe hanging open, drops of Myrtle's blood dried brown on the waxed wooden floor. He wanted them to see and feel the raw evil that was unloosed in Pony, the ruthless ambition and greed masking itself as corporate business, the stain of terror spread by two thugs and their pious masters.

There were only five. The rest suddenly pleaded family responsibilities. One forthrightly said he was afraid and backed out. No one condemned him for it. They were all afraid. They had heard stories that grew worse in the retelling, seen Spade's torn and bleeding emporium, whispered of the wounded. And now the bank.

Five pale young men whose livelihoods hid them from the sun and the golden meadows and the blue peaks. But brave and burly men nonetheless, who fearlessly descended into the bowels of the earth and tore quartz rock from dark, cold walls. They had their own kind of courage, Dudley thought, hoping it would be enough, a match for the brutal skills of the Dowling twins.

The Dowlings had taken his Colt when they abandoned the

bank, but he had other weapons, his own, not the town's. Two Winchester repeaters and a shotgun. He had chosen the shotgun, loading it carefully from a fresh box of shells containing double-ought buckshot. In all his years of lawing he had not resorted to scatterguns; he had never confronted a mob. Now the heavy shotgun rested painfully in the crook of his wounded arm. His rifle and his saddle carbine he gave to young men who scarcely knew how to use them. He instructed them briefly. "Hold steady and squeeze the trigger," he said patiently. "Take your time."

One of them wore a red flannel shirt. "You're the color of a bull's-eye, son," Dudley said. "Hold on a minute." He lumbered back to his cubicle of an office and jail, just below Spade's, and found a denim jacket. It probably wouldn't fit the burly youth, but it'd have to do.

They were afraid. Worry leaked from their faces and eyes and mouths. Some of them he knew, especially Philo Crane, with the bright, alert eyes and upwelling courage. There was Kraemer, hard-muscled and fair and tense; Hyde, a broth of a man, bulging from his dungarees and ragged shirt; Gil Collins, fear on him and thoughts of his red-haired bride and newborn son; and the black-haired Norwegian Pedersen, a bachelor and frequenter of the saloons. He was the toughest and roughest and knew weapons. Crane, Kraemer, Hyde, Collins, and Pedersen—his army.

Now, he thought, the tougher part. He had to devise a strategy. He had one small piece of information he knew would be helpful. The Waldorfs' buggy was up at the mine. He had walked up the hill to reconnoiter while his posse breakfasted and assembled. It was likely that one, or both, of the financiers were up there rather than at the Waldorf place. He intended to grab at least one, and then he'd have a lever. The thing he dreaded worst was a confrontation at the Waldorf house itself, where Ben and Jezebel could be used as hostages and placed in great danger. He could almost hear one of the Dowlings rasping out at them, "You had better drop your weapons, gents, or this lady here gets a bullet in the head. I'll count to three, gents . . ."

Yes, the mine first. They would try for Kennedy or Widen, and throw in Eickles for good measure; if they got one of the uglies, too, all the better. Some cold emotion swept through him: if it took killing a Kennedy or a Widen, he'd do it. If that would be the way to save Ben—or the hellcat—he'd do it. The thought shook him. It would end his lawing, no matter how justified. Maybe his life. The rich heirs would persecute and prosecute.

"Are we ready, then?" They stood silently before him, three with rifles, one with a revolver, and one with a twenty-gauge shotgun loaded with birdshot. They nodded. "We're going to the mine office," he said. "I think one or both of the money men are there. Eickles may be armed; consider him dangerous. I'll want a man outside each window, but out of sight. Sneak up to it on the blind sides of the building, the two ends. Crane and me'll go through the front door. When you hear that, cover through each window and don't worry about broken glass."

They nodded, and he led them up the road. Some army, he thought. Some army.

It was a bright June day, with puffball clouds hanging on the western peaks. His miners blinked in the sun, unused to its glare. A southerly zephyr brought the scent of smoke with it, and he thought that odd.

"Something's burning," said Crane tautly.

Where the road twisted up a slope, they had a sudden view and saw the column of gray rising from Stop's home.

The recognition hit them all. The constable knew what his men didn't—that Stop wasn't there; that Stop, by now, probably was returning from Butte. Or was he? Was Stop back so soon? Was the fire an accident . . . or was it the handiwork of the Dowlings? Whatever the case, it changed his plans.

"We've got to put it out," he shouted. "You boys with legs run over there; I'll be along. Find buckets. Look to see who did it, and stay alert."

All the miners broke into a hard trot, and Elmer limped along behind, as fast as he could. When he got closer, he saw that it was the summer kitchen, the lean-to at the rear of the house that was ablaze, as well as the east facade of the house itself. But maybe with luck the rest might be saved. And in the yard behind the house stood the black barouche, the gray trotters pawing restlessly because of the fire.

"Go slow, watch out," he cried, but the miners were too far ahead, racing recklessly now, heedless of everything except dousing the fire. One Dowling, maybe two, and a house blazing. Fear roiled his stomach. He paused, panting. From a knoll he watched the miners find buckets, organize a chain from the cistern at the barn to the house. He watched the first pail splash effectively on a fiery rear wall, and saw steam billow. Then another pail. The disciplines of the pits helped them, and each man seemed to know exactly what to do. Their weapons lay in the grass, forgotten for the moment. And somewhere nearby were the Dowlings. . . .

The constable approached warily, his shotgun at the ready, checking windows, studying brush and trees and especially the barn, where two ruthless men could easily observe everything through wide cracks in the reddened planks. Where were the Dowlings? In the house, the barn or shed, the brush and trees to the north and west? And where was Stop? Beaten unconscious inside that blazing house? He studied the windows and saw nothing. No glint of a barrel probed through the rough planks of the barn. In the brush, then . . . or perhaps fleeing to the Waldorf place, having seen the posse. But he doubted that. They were somewhere near, and his lads were in peril. His skin prickled at the thought of it, the sudden scattergun blasts mowing them down. Still, he saw no sign of trouble, and the miners were slowly bringing the blaze on the east wall under control, even though the summer kitchen flamed violently. Part of Stop's house might be saved, unless those brave men died under a withering blast of shotguns.

In the yard he cornered Crane, who was sweating as he ran a pair of slopping buckets to Kraemer. "This may be is a trap," Dudley shouted. "Philo, let the others handle it. You and me . . . you and me. Get that rifle. Maybe Sam Stop's in there. Maybe others, but I doubt it."

Philo Crane stared, spoke quickly to Kraemer and Hyde, then picked up his rifle. Stop's front door was flapping open. They saw it had been forced. "Stand back, Philo. I'll go in first. Know how to do this," he said. Crane nodded.

Elmer leapt in and dived to the right, arcing his shotgun, ready for anything that moved. Nothing. The front room had been ransacked. Furniture was overturned, a heavy horsehair chair was cut open, its guts spilling out.

"They're looking for something," Crane whispered.

Dudley nodded. Through the door was a smoke-filled dining room, virtually untouched. But off to the right would be Stop's study, with its desk and shelves and closets.

"We'll swing right. Shoot on sight," the constable hissed. Crane nodded. Smoke drifted through, searing Elmer's throat, making him cough. The dining room wall flared into flame, radiating fierce heat.

Heart pounding, the old constable swung into the study, his finger one hairtrigger from blasting whoever was there. No one. The dark room was chaos. Stop's big rolltop desk tipped crazily. Every drawer had been pulled and dumped, every pigeonhole emptied. Papers were strewn on the floor. The desk had been tipped over by someone looking for hidden compartments underneath or behind. Bookshelves had been stripped. A smashed tintype lay on the floor, and Dudley paused briefly to stare. It was of a lovely dark-haired young woman, smiling enigmatically, set in a gilded oval frame. She did not look like Stop.

The study had been brutally ransacked. Outside, Dudley could hear the hoarse voices of the miners and knew they were losing ground. The east side was flaming clear to the eaves, and up onto the roof. But the lads didn't give up. Pail after pail splashed against the wall, hissing and steaming as the water hit burning wood. And now a wall of heat pushed through the house from the left, the east. They had only moments left to search, or they'd be trapped.

He doubted that the Dowlings—or whoever it had been—were upstairs. They wouldn't trap themselves in a burning building. They would have shot their way out long since. Perhaps they had fled, abandoning the barouche, which still stood in the yard, its drays restless and stomping.

He nodded to Crane, limped to the stairwell, and ascended slowly, glaring at shadows, his ear aching for the faintest whisper up there. A haze of blue smoke hung through the upper floor, caught in the sunlight. They probed the three rooms. Each had been thoroughly ransacked, dressers emptied, closets disemboweled, beds brutally slashed open. Clothing heaped and torn. Dudley wondered whether the bullion had been hidden here, and whether the uglies had found it. Maybe they had. Maybe they simply had hauled it off as the posse arrived, dragged it on up the slope to the Waldorf mansion. The more he thought about it, the more it made sense. Outside, the voices had grown quiet. The miners had lost, and the fire was scaling rafters and eaves high above them. He heard them swing around to the veranda, bringing water up to rescue those inside. It was time to get out. The roof was ablaze. He nudged Philo, and they raced down the stairs, hitting shocking blasts of heat and lung-scorching smoke, and then they burst out on the veranda, gasping. It had only been minutes, but the frame house had turned into a torch.

"No one in there," he gasped to the others. "Place ransacked. Looking hard for something." He thought to tell them about Ben's gold but decided not to. Philo Crane knew; the others didn't.

They backed away, mesmerized by heat and flame. The inferno worried the trotters, and they began to sidle in their traces, then began to drag the barouche and even the heavy carriage weight attached to a bridle. Elmer, still wheezing, saw them, and the rolling barouche reminded him that they could all be in mortal danger, and that the Dowlings could easily mow them down from somewhere close.

He stared at the sweat-soaked, gaping miners. "Get your guns. Fast," he snapped. "We're sitting here like ducks."

The exhausted miners scrambled for their weapons.

"We've got to search. We've got to cover every square foot of this place," Elmer rasped. "By twos. Pair up. Philo, you join me. You two"—he pointed at Kraemer and Hyde—"search the barn and sheds. Be ready to shoot and be careful. You two"—he pointed at Collins and Pedersen—"that brush; the woods. Philo and I'll head up the slope, see if they fled toward Waldorf's place."

Wearily he watched them spread out, his mind crying against it, against sending these raw recruits into the maw of death. Behind him the house thundered and cracked, and great chunks of roof caved in, sending smoke and embers billowing high above them. Everything Sam Stop possessed would be gone. Crazily Elmer wished he had scooped up that tintype of the young woman, the nameless woman in the study of the man no one knew. But it was far too late, and the image would be a cinder. This malicious destruction sickened him. He would shoot either Dowling on sight. His lungs hurt and his nasal passages were raw. It made no difference. He was old: let the young enjoy their health. He ran a grimy hand through his scorched hair, and a lot of it fell into his palm.

He wished he knew where the Dowlings were hiding.

"Philo," he snapped. "First, before we go up the hill, that black carriage. No one looked in. We all been too busy with the fire. They could be in there. We've got to take it somehow. They'll have the advantage on us for certain. Plenty of room for the pair of them below the seats."

Philo nodded, his eyes taut.

Elmer Dudley was at a loss for a good plan. No cover. The horses had dragged it out upon a meadow a hundred yards from the inferno, then had stopped, feeling safe. There was only grass. Not a tree or a ditch or a shrub.

"Could just put some holes in it. You got a rifle."

Philo nodded reluctantly. "Hate to damage an empty carriage like that," he whispered.

From the corner of his eye Elmer saw his men emerge from the barn. Nothing in there. The other two were back in the brush and out of sight.

There was no help for it. He and Philo would have to rush the barouche. He gave thought to borrowing Crane's rifle and shooting the horses. But it didn't make sense. The horses weren't going to take it anywhere, not dragging a carriage weight.

He stared at the young miner, who had a sweet young wife at home.

"I'm doing this myself," he said. "You stay here, cover me with the rifle. Shoot at anyone bobbing up from in there. My shotgun's for close work."

"I'm going with you."

"No you ain't. Your rifle's no good at close hand. Might shoot me. You just set down there in the grass and aim."

"I'll do better closer," Crane said.

There was no arguing with that. He could come another fifty yards.

The constable stalked across the meadow, arguing with himself, angry, muttering. "Ought to just blow it full of holes," he said. "Ought to just blast that black wood fulla holes. Ought to blow it up with giant powder. Ought . . ."

It was a long, long walk. He halted. "Let's get around behind. They got that top down, all folded up in back. The thing rotates up for bad weather, and they can even string up isinglass windows."

Crane nodded, and they circled to the rear of the carriage, which loomed larger and larger until it seemed a black giant in the middle of a verdant meadow. It was an evil thing, a haughty symbol of wealth and power. Its brass glinted brightly in the high sun. Zephyrs rocked it, or was it just the wind? It was Satan's own carriage, he thought. A devil's own carriage, mocking his every lame step, exuding power and wealth, shaking in the wind and laughing at a frontier constable.

He stopped. His mind ran riot. Probably it was empty and abandoned. The grays trembled. One's head twisted back, pulled by the carriage weight attached to its bridle.

"All right, Philo, this is far enough for you. You jist set yourself in the grass here and rest that rifle of yours on your knee, and try almighty hard not to shoot me."

"I'd prefer to come with you. We could rush from two sides."

"Lot of good your rifle'd do in a rush," Elmer retorted sarcastically. "You jist better do as I say."

Still, he didn't want to go. He turned, scanned the country

behind him. The house had collapsed into an orange heap, and the smoke had turned white. The others were coming now, too. "Stay back," he cried. But they stalked on, anyway. Damn, he thought, they'll be like ducks, walking in like that, not even spread out, not even setting up a crossfire, a flanking move. Miners! he thought.

He had to walk now. Fifty yards. He limped up a step, then another, and another. He studied it. He was coming in dead from the rear. He could see wheels and springs and the axle. Above all that, the black bowl of the carriage. Above that, neatly folded down in accordion pleats, the polished black leather hood.

He checked his shotgun. Loaded, ready. Sweaty finger on the trigger. Then he trotted, a lame lunge, one leg working and the other not. Closing to ten yards.

Then, too late, he saw the blued double barrels, four black bores, thrust between the coachwork and the hood, perfectly camouflaged.

The first blast caught him square in the chest, and he felt the large-caliber balls, buckshot, thump into his ribs, pierce flesh. No hot pain at first, just some wild pulsing of his heart, and lungs that wouldn't draw. He looked down, feeling his legs buckle, feeling his shotgun slip from his hands. And then he looked up. There were shots now, and behind him he heard Philo cry.

And then he lay in the grass, seeing the sky turn black and the world revolve. His lungs quit, but his heart thumped spastically, irregularly, its wounded muscle not quitting now, so young . . .

There were shots, he knew that. Rifle shots close. Dowlings had rifles. Laughing. Picking off ducks. Hoarse cries in the distance.

And then Elmer Dudley began to choke on a hot fluid in his throat, and he coughed, and then he didn't hear anything, and then he heard the Dowlings laugh and the clop of horses and the creak of wheels before the blackness settled.

Chapter Eighteen

Later Doc Frede would remember it as the busiest day in his life. At almost the crack of dawn one of the East Coast uglies banged on his door, summoning him to the Waldorf mansion. He was taken there in the black barouche, which rolled silkily up the grade behind the two gray trotters.

"Epidemics," he muttered. "We have epidemics." He grabbed his black pigskin satchel from the padded seat and was escorted into the quiet house.

"It's Mr. Kennedy," said the ugly. "He's hoping you can help."

Jasper Kennedy was about the last person Havelock Frede wished to treat, but duty was duty. As he climbed the wide stairs he wondered where Ben and Jezebel were. Neither was in sight, and the house seemed to be occupied by the financiers and their men. Prisoners, perhaps, he thought.

Jasper Kennedy lay abed, his portly self covered by a snowy sheet and a thin woolen blanket. He looked gray of face. A nod from the financier dismissed Lethbridge Dowling, who had brought the doc.

"Thee are a doctor, my good man?"

Frede allowed himself a certain pleasure. "Actually, a mortician."

Jasper Kennedy paused.

"I've read medicine. If I can't cure 'em, I bury 'em," Frede said. "Usually the latter. I can do the new thing, formaldehyde, keep the deceased intact until the funeral. I conduct funerals as well. Read from the Good Book and then shovel in the dirt."

"Thy bedside manner could stand improving," Jasper said reprovingly. "I have suffered a painful accident, but I don't know whether thee art the one to deal with it. A mortician?"

"We all croak sooner or later, rich and poor."

The man did look gray, Frede thought. He was overweight and obviously a voluptuary. Probably dyspepsia. A good dose of soda . . .

Jasper Kennedy sighed, making up his mind. "I have suffered a most painful and worrisome accident," he began distrustfully. "I have been, ah, kicked by a horse. The hoof caught me, ah, in my private parts. Twice. I, ah, fear I am unmanned. Great pain."

Doc Frede nodded somberly. "That'll do it," he said. Being kicked twice in the private parts by a horse was beyond the realm of probability. Being kicked by a hellcat seemed more likely.

"A mare, no doubt. Mares tend to be kicky."

"Why, yes, I believe so. A mare. Doctor, I cannot bear an examination. I can only tell thee that everything is all swollen up and black and blue, and I suffer every minute and every hour. There is the pain, and my greatest fear . . . that I am . . . well, thee would understand."

"Well, being kicked by a mare will do it. There was the famous case of Jones, written up in several medical texts. Caught a shod hoof right there. Nothing medicine could do about it. A year later his wife divorced him, and two years later he put a gun to his head and committed suicide. That can do it, all right. Put you right out of the husband business. I always figured the wild horses had it figured out about right. The powerful stallions all have a harem, lots of mares. They fought a lot of other stallions to get those mares. The defeated stallions, well, they just band together into their own little herd and get along nicely. . . . Then there's the case of Anneck. He was a rancher down in Texas, got to dallying with another man's lady, and the local boys didn't like it. They lassoed Anneck and performed a small operation on him. Last I knew, Anneck was getting along . . . turned rather porky and his voice changed, but he was thriving."

Kennedy stared. "Thee offers no comfort to a man in distress."

"I'm sorry," said Doc. "I usually talk to the stiffs I'm preparing. One-sided conversation always tempts me. None of them on that slab ever argue with me. Now, let us see here. Stick out your tongue."

Kennedy did.

Doc Frede probed and examined. "Coated tongue, hmm. Yes. Ear wax. Hmm. You eat too much."

"I know my vices. I plunge into my foods, yes. And I indulge in spiritous drinks on occasion. But for the rest, I live as careful a life as mortal can . . . all the more grievous that I should suffer this thing."

"So I have heard. How are Ben and Jezebel this fine morning? I didn't see them."

Kennedy winced. "Late risers, I suppose. Fine hosts. The transition is going splendidly, and we hope to wind it up today. We, ah, will be employing a company doctor. Much as this fine town has enjoyed thy services, we have other plans. . . ."

"Why, yes, I imagine you do, sir. Now then, I shall leave some laudanum for you—quite a demand for it lately here, and I'm running low. But here's a quarter of a bottle. One spoonful now. As for the rest, a mare's kick can be fatal, but that's uncommon. You'll know about your manhood after one to three years. Sometimes there's a long delayed effect, you know. Like the case of Wilburforce, a famous cleric—"

"That long?"

"Well, sometimes six months will tell the tale."

"I will need to travel tomorrow."

"No difficulty. Take a cushion or two. I'll leave something to keep the vomiting under control."

Kennedy stared. "Thee probably are a good mortician," he said.

166

"That'll be ten dollars," Frede said.

"Ten dollars! Thy usual fee is two, I happen to know."

"I charge what the traffic will bear," said Frede, repacking his kit. "Like the ladies of the night."

"I will have it sent," Kennedy said shortly.

One of the uglies met him at the foot of the stair. "I'll drive you down," he said.

"Nice day for a stroll," Doc said. "In fact, I have a patient to visit."

One round for the hellcat, he thought as he strolled down the slope. But there was something radically wrong there, with neither of the Waldorfs in sight. He decided to mention it to his next patient.

Dudley had left for the morning, but Rafe McDaniel was sitting up in the front room of the cottage, looking pale. His face had started to color up now, yellows and purples and other interesting shades. It was still grossly swollen, and the man could scarcely talk.

"You're looking chipper," he said.

The sheriff muttered something almost unintelligible.

"But you won't be traveling yet. Dudley's gone, eh? How are you feeling?"

McDaniel growled angrily.

"Looks like the Waldorfs are out and these Eastern gents are in. Looks like they'll have a bunch of power in Madison County," Frede said. "I suppose you'll be making peace with them soon enough."

Rafe stared. "I don't know what I'll do," he muttered. "This here is my county and I'm the law."

"I'm sure you are," said Doc, sympathetically. "You might just run on up there and pinch them all. More cases of assault and battery last few days than I can remember. Open your mouth, what's left of it, and say ahh."

He peered around. "What a mess!" he said. "You'd better get on back to Virginia City tomorrow, before they bust the right side, too."

"I'll think on it," said Rafe. "Maybe I'll just shoot to kill."

"Your face'll never be the same. It's a wreck. Hope it won't mess up your elections, Rafe."

"Lemme alone," Rafe muttered.

"Two dollars and four bits for the laudanum," Doc said.

"I'll send it," the sheriff muttered.

That was how the morning went. Back at his office, he looked in on Amos Galb, who was up and about now but found it painful to move. His bruises were coloring up handsomely, turning yellow and gray, and he looked like the color plates in medical texts. One chest bruise reminded him in particular of the tints in a diagram of the upper intestinal tract.

Things were pretty quiet after that. He supplied Mrs. Coulter with some powders for her female complaints, ordered more laudanum, posted his letter, and settled into a quiet day. When he saw a column of smoke and heard the shooting south of town, at Stop's place, he knew he'd be busy again, and he hastily discharged Galb, put fresh linen on the bunk, and wiped down the mortuary slab. His instincts were right.

The pale young giants from the pits burst in. Two of them carried terrible burdens; another was bloodied but staggered in under his own power. The dark-haired one who was carrying Elmer Dudley lowered the constable onto Frede's mortuary slab. Frede saw at once that the old man was dead. The other bad one, young Philo Crane, was lowered onto the bunk so recently occupied by Galb. Crane was ashen and barely breathing. Doc Frede undid his trousers, took one look, and knew it was hopeless, only a matter of time. Gutshot and bleeding internally. Even now Crane was unconscious. Nothing to do. He turned to the one with a shoulder wound, a clean hole through the forearm.

"Look after Philo first," said Kraemer.

Doc shook his head. "Nothing to do. He's unconscious and not in pain."

Swiftly he probed Kraemer's wound, cleansed it, and wrapped it tight.

"Who did it? Tell me the whole thing," he said.

Haltingly they told him the story: Elmer's posse; Stop's house

ransacked and burned; the barouche; Elmer's leap into the booming barrels of the shotguns.

"Epidemics," said Frede, staring at his old friend Elmer Dudley. "I can't deal with epidemics."

Mrs. Crane burst in, followed by two other distraught women.
Her eyes focused on Elmer Dudley first, and then found Philo
over in the bunk, rasping his last breaths. She raced to him and
grasped his limp, cold hand. Mrs. Kraemer, bonneted and
dressed in brown gingham, found her husband and rushed into his
arms, exclaiming at his wound. And fat, puffing Mrs. Hyde
rejoiced to see her husband untouched, scarcely noticing the
death and injury around her.

"Help him!" implored Annabelle Crane.

Doc Frede shook his head. "Nothing I can do."

Philo opened his eyes briefly, stared into his wife's tear-
streaked face, and then closed them and died. His mouth fell open
and his rasping breath simply stopped.

She sat stunned. She was a pretty woman, Doc thought, a
bloom on her cheeks and hair the color of a carrot, and a way of
turning simple, cheap cloth, such as the green cotton she wore,
into something that drew the rays of the sun to her. Now she
stared, scarcely absorbing death. Everything transformed in
moments; a live young husband, good provider for herself and
two children, thoughtful and steady and not a drinker, gone. It
was too much for her, and she groaned.

"He done it," shrilled Mrs. Hyde, jabbing a finger at Elmer
Dudley. "He done it. He took them poor boys out to be slaughtered. Him and his posse! Him and his law, puttin' a demand on
simple folks like Philo. Him and them highfalutin ones like Stop
and Waldorf, refusing to pay up a debt they owe to these people
that come here . . . . Him and Stop and Waldorf, we know their
kind, using up common folks like cannon fodder . . . . We know
their kind, putting up banks and companies just to bleed us
all. . . ."

Havelock Frede frowned. "I don't recollect Ben or Sam Stop
pulling any triggers or breaking up any business around here,"
he said gently. "Don't recollect Elmer, God rest his soul, laying

a heavy hand on this town, hurting the innocent, or letting the crooks and bullies run wild."

That was the way of distraught people, he thought, getting their blaming all cockeyed. You'd think that Elmer and Ben and Stop had caused all the grief.

It angered Hyde. "You stop that, Mabel. Elmer Dudley tried to stop trouble and paid a price worse than any other. He was a brave man, going against them toughs, and I'll not hear you say otherwise."

Mrs. Hyde subsided into weeping then, her sobs and sniffles loud in the room. At the bunk Mrs. Crane stared woodenly at her man, her cheeks wet. He lay quietly, his face composed in death. "I've loved ye, Philo," she whispered, oblivious to the others. "There was never a man swept me off my feet so grand."

Doc addressed the others. "We'll go into the front room now and leave Mrs. Crane to herself," he said. He ushered them all through the door and into the street-side room, which was an apothecary shop with benches to sit on while he ground up his powders.

The town was a shambles, he thought. Not a dime in the ransacked bank. Unless these people had a few dollars squirreled away in their mattresses, there would be nothing, no cash for groceries or other necessities. He cleared his throat. "I think I've a ready-made casket for him back there. Another for the constable. I can donate those. Don't imagine I'll be staying here in Pony, anyway. Maybe you people'll help Mrs. Crane a little, find a preacher. I'll take care of the rest. Set a man to digging. No one to bury Elmer Dudley . . . but I'd be honored. Yes, indeed, I'll bury an honored friend, and say some things about him worth saying. . . ."

He had turned their minds to the practical details, and that was good.

"We'll bury them fitting and proper, yas, yas," said Pedersen. "And if the devils from New Yark come to the burying, I'll bury them, too, yas."

It was late in the day when they left. All except Mrs. Crane, who kept her vigil beside Philo in the back room. Pony was an empty place. Wind whipped through the streets, whistled around the corners of weathered clapboard buildings. A light flared in the Buffalo Hump saloon, but there were no customers. Another lamp filled the window of the hotel with a yellow glow. It was no longer Pyle's hotel. Doc didn't know the man who ran it now. From Butte, he'd heard.

The supper hour came and went. At last he slipped into the back room, darkened in the twilight, and slipped a hand over her shoulder. "The children will be wanting their supper," he said gently.

She looked up. "Yes, of course," she said. She stood up then, composed, glanced a last time at Philo, and walked out. "Thank you, Dr. Frede," she said as she stepped into the wind-scoured street. He watched the wind catch her green skirts and whip them around her figure as she trudged northward, alone.

He thought of leaving Pony. There'd be nothing left to stay for. He hadn't the faintest idea where he'd go. Another mining camp, no doubt. Another haven for a self-taught man, without degrees, without certificates on his walls. He lit a kerosene lamp in the back room. There'd be work tonight. He had a cottage on the north side of town, but also a tiny room at the rear of his office with a bunk in it. In his assorted professions, sometimes it was necessary to stay close at hand. He thought for a moment of eating over at Thornton's café, but he wasn't hungry. There were a few airtights in the back; he could heat some soup.

The front of his establishment was unlit, but that did not prevent Stop from entering. Doc heard the door and stuck his head into the front shop.

Sam Stop stood quietly, and even in the dusk Doc could see the strain and anger in his bronzed face. The banker wore his usual dark suit and cravat, which Doc had never seen disheveled.

"I hoped I'd find you here," Stop said. "Maybe you can tell me what happened."

Doc nodded, and Stop followed him into the lamplit rear room. And then his troubled brown eyes registered the terrible sight of Elmer Dudley and Philo Crane. The young banker took it in, saying nothing, and Doc wondered if the man was emotionless or just ground down to nothing after finding his house burned to ashes and his bank ransacked and empty.

"Tell me," said Stop quietly. "I can guess, but I want to hear it."

"Hardly know where to start. Where've you been? Back to Butte? You fetch any of Marcus Daley's riches to bail Ben out?"

"Word of my journeys gets around," Stop said wearily.

"Elmer told me," Doc said.

"No," said Sam Stop wearily. "No hope from Daley. He did send a confidential operator—a woman—by buckboard, but she met with a mysterious accident—runaway horse, or so they said. She never got here. Daley's gone East for a month."

"That mean no cash?"

"He's buying racehorses," Stop said bitterly. "That's what's important to him."

Doc stared at him. "You look all tuckered out, man. I have some coffee started here."

Stop smiled thinly. "What I need is your story."

Doc sighed. "I'm not guaranteeing I got it exactly right. Mostly bits and pieces from hysterical people, wounded men . . ."

He started with the bank, the maltreatment of Myrtle, the pillaging of every dime, and breaking into Louella's compartment in the safe and emptying it.

"Are they just keeping her gold?" Stop asked, his face hard.

"Looks like it. One of the uglies said maybe they'd give it back, if she turned over her business to the Waldorf boys, who no doubt would front for Kennedy and Widen."

"What happened at my house?" Stop asked abruptly.

Doc told him about Elmer's last stand, the posse he had quietly put together, arming miners.

"Those poor galoots from the pits hardly know how to shoot!" Stop exclaimed.

"Elmer knew that, but it was the only card he had left."

Stop shook his head, and Doc thought he caught self-recrimination in it. He went on with his story, told about the posse's march toward the Waldorf place—

"How's Ben and Jezebel?" Stop asked abruptly.

"No one knows. No one's even seen them. I was up there treating Kennedy, and the Waldorfs weren't visible."

"What'd you treat him for?"

"Knee in the groin. Twice."

Stop smiled faintly.

Doc told him the rest: the burning house, ransacked inside, the fire out of control, the barouche, the search for the Dowlings, and finally Elmer Dudley's assault on the glistening black carriage, and the shotguns that had picked off Crane and wounded Kraemer.

"They made a mistake," Stop said flatly. His eyes had gone hard.

"Not much you can do about it."

Stop seemed angry, but in the young banker it was barely visible, some harsh tension that suffused his tanned features and made his eyes glint. He walked over to the mortuary slab and peered down into the very still face of the constable. And stared a moment at Philo Crane, too.

"Elmer was a brave man," he said. "Braver than you can imagine. Do you know what it is to look into the bore of a gun pointed at you? And keep your head when it happens? Why did he do it? Do you know? Against all odds? Why did Crane, there, do it? Can you answer it? Our instincts are all the other way: Preserve ourselves, save our skins. What were they thinking—that they could whip the two most dangerous men I have ever seen? They're heroes, Dudley and Crane, and I hope every soul in Pony knows it. I don't know what makes heroes. Maybe they see a task that needs doing. Everyone is afraid to do it, and they just plunge ahead. Maybe it's fear—do the thing, or worse will happen. Maybe Philo, there, was thinking of his wife, his little ones, and what might come. . . . I think Elmer knew. It was evil. Sooner or later he had to deal with evil. Some folks don't think evil exists, don't like to put a name to it or call it sin. But Elmer knew. He shouldn't have done it. Someone else—left it to someone else . . ."

Stop paused. Doc stared. In that moment he had come closer

to penetrating the mystery of the young banker than ever before, and yet the man was as obscure as ever. It was a revelation that didn't reveal anything at all.

"I didn't want it to happen," Stop said, and Doc was puzzled by the enigmatic remark. "I waited too long," Stop added. "I hate it, hate doing it."

"Doing what?" Doc asked, profoundly curious.

Stop stared at him, saying nothing.

"Look, you haven't got a place to say. You haven't even got a change of clothes left. You can stay here if you want. Or Elmer's. Might have to share it with McDaniel if he's still there. But it's a roof. And we can rustle up some clothes—"

Stop shook his head. "I have other things. In a place."

"You got some other place?" asked Doc.

Stop just shook his head.

"What're you going to do?" Doc asked.

Stop stared through a window and into the night. "Go up there and try to get the money back. Louella's money, too."

Chapter Nineteen

Ben Waldorf had seen it from his bedroom window. Stop's house stood a quarter of a mile downslope, and a little south. When the smoke boiled up, he had trained his field glass on the place. He saw old Dudley and a band of armed miners hurry over there, then saw the Dowlings hunker down inside the barouche. He watched his lads from the mine try to douse the fire, fail, begin to search for the Dowlings. And he'd watched Elmer spring into the jaws of death, heard the heavy report of the shotguns, and then the crack of rifles, and saw lads fall. Moments later the black carriage rolled out, and the miners gathered their dead. He didn't know whether Elmer Dudley was alive or dead, and it gnawed at him.

There were too many things he didn't know, he thought. Such as whether Stop had been successful this time and if Daley would come through. Stop was due back any hour and probably would slip in after dark to avoid scrutiny.

He wasn't sure, either, whether he was a prisoner in his own house. He stayed mostly in his own bedroom, not because he had to—the door was not guarded—but because he detested his guests, which is what they politely called themselves. Jezebel usually stayed in her room as well.

His own room was solid and comfortable, with walnut wainscoting and a heavy four-poster bed that Jezebel had stuck in there. He had never gotten used to those four polished pillars of dark-hued wood and feared he would brain himself on them some night. There was a walk-in closet, a massive desk, a commode with a china washbasin and water pitcher, and a globe on a stand. The globe endlessly fascinated him. He could read well enough to make out nations and capitals, and could tell you in a trice where Afghanistan was. He wondered, though, why so many remote places had the same name, Terra Incognita.

Here he had whiled away hours while evil stalked the rest of his own house. Jezebel had swiftly grown bored and sometimes visited him. Whenever they were sure no Dowlings lurked outside doors, they talked endlessly of what they might do. Jezebel was sure that her arsenal of derringers would rescue them. Ben wasn't so sure. She had told Ben of Kennedy's amorous advances and Kennedy's fate, and they had chortled quietly.

Neither of them had tested their freedom. They had eaten in their rooms from trays supplied by Hip Hip. They had visited the necessary conveniences that lay in a separate brick structure behind the mansion. They had flatly turned down the financiers' occasional requests for meetings, meals, and parleys. Ben would not deal, and he would not even talk. Jezebel had given him several of her loaded derringers, and he had pocketed them absently. She had slipped two others to Hip Hip, who had grinned maniacally and slipped them into his cupboards. If it came to that, he'd rely on his old single-action Army-model Colt, battered and half rusted, which had been his constant companion during his prospecting days. If they came to kill him—he was aware of the possibility—he'd try to take at least one. Kennedy was his choice. The Dowlings were Kennedy's, and he suspected they might be the sort who needed masters and had all the weaknesses buried in them of masterless men.

If they did kill him, thinking they could easily control Jezebel and rid themselves of the young Waldorf pigs, they were in for a surprise. They would expect him to will his property to Jezebel, but he and Stop had drawn up something else altogether, a trust arrangement, incorporating the entire mining company, with Jezebel as beneficiary. Amos Galb would run things.

Ben Waldorf was an old man but not a toothless one. There had always been the lion in him, and more than once he had bared his fangs, especially in the months after he had struck gold and every sharper in the Northwest had tried to pry his holdings away from him. Now he chafed. He and Jezebel were being terrorized in their own home by the most ruthless and unprincipled men he had ever encountered. He didn't know what the future held, or whether he could hang on to his mine, but this house was his. And there hardened in him that afternoon a determination to drive out the alien presence there, again become the lord of his own manor. He wasn't afraid, at least not for himself. For Jezebel, perhaps, who had a life ahead, a life that could be fatally marred in moments. Still . . .

He slipped into Jezebel's room. She was irritable and full of scold.

"I'm going to do it, Tootsie. Tonight. Are you ready?"

She brightened. "I'll tell Hip Hip to be ready. I can't stand it cooped in here another minute."

"We might die," he said.

"So could they," she snapped. She was ready for them. She'd shoot, too, he knew. "Jasper's wandering around in his robe. Sort of bent over and gray." She giggled.

"If he's not in the den tonight, it's off," Ben warned. "I don't know where the Dowlings are, but I'll try to find out. You talk to Hip Hip."

"Do you think we can do it?"

"I don't know, Tootsie. But I'm ready to try anything."

He didn't tell her about what he had seen from his window, or about Elmer's probable fate. Now he didn't want to divert or upset her with other things. It'd be a small victory, this recovery of their own home, but at least one step forward.

"I'll have to prove something to them," she said.

That evening they dined in their rooms as usual but then drifted into the den at separate moments. Jasper Kennedy was present, in his robe, an expensive one with a chesterfield collar. He looked ashen but composed. Drago Widen slumped in Ben's wing chair, memorizing passages from St. Paul's First Letter to the Corinthians for his daily spiritual exercise.

Ben, if anything, looked less kempt than usual. He wore a loose canvas hunting jacket with baggy pockets, one of which contained his old revolver, and the other a double-barreled derringer.

"Well, Ben, are thee joining us?" asked Jasper. Not even the amber lamplight concealed the gray of his flesh.

"Thought I might."

Drago inserted the Bible's red ribbon at his page and set it aside. His gaze was brittle. "Are you ready to come to terms?" he demanded at once. "We plan to leave in the morning. The Dowlings are impatient."

"Nope, gents, we'll take what time we have, by contract, to get you evened up. Sam Stop's been out negotiating."

Drago flared visibly but then quieted himself with a crooked smile. "If the word from Marcus Daley is negative, I trust you'll not delay further, wasting valuable time."

Ben said nothing and eased into the remaining chair. Widen eyed him coldly, his mouth forming and discarding words. Then Jezebel swept in. She wore a scoop-necked summery pink dress, as much to torment Jasper Kennedy with the flash of creamy bosom as to conceal the burdens she carried in its large pockets.

Kennedy flinched visibly and turned away. It was their first encounter since the fateful one in her bedroom. Then Paddo appeared, a shadow just outside the entryway into the den, hovering protectively around his masters, visible and intimidating but not quite present.

Ben thought not to waste time. From the corner of his eye he saw Hip Hip in the dark hallway, a wraith behind Paddo Dowling, and knew the time had come to get on with it. Do or die, he thought, and in spite of his age and some serenity about death, his heart pounded.

Jezebel had slid around behind Jasper, her hands casually buried in the folds of the pink frock, where, Ben knew, they were

178

gripping a pair of over-and-under .44-caliber derringers. Ben stood, slipping his hands casually into the vast pockets of his duck-hunting jacket.

"Gents," he said. "You'll be leaving my house now." He let that sink in. No one said anything. Paddo's face, shadowed in the hallway, broke into a happy smirk.

"You'll be going to the hotel, or wherever you choose. It doesn't matter to me. But you'll leave at once and leave my wife and me in peace here in our own home."

There was dignity and authority in his words, and these reached Drago and Jasper, who reacted visibly. For an instant the two financiers didn't know how to reply.

"But your fine sons invited—" Drago said.

"They don't live here. I don't permit them in this house. And they are pigs. I won't permit you here anymore, either."

"Now, thee art upset, Ben. Why, it'll all be settled in the morning. Stop will have bad news for thee, and that'll be the end."

Outside, Ben heard the silky rattle of the barouche as it was drawn up. His yard and stable men, Gilberto and Alonzo, had harnessed the gray trotters and brought up the carriage right on schedule.

"Now," said Ben. "Right now."

"You are mistaken," said Paddo from the doorway.

Ben's deep blue eyes, full of ice, settled upon the smirking ugly. "I think not," he said. His hands, hidden from Paddo's view by Drago's chair, now held the old Colt and the little derringer in a line of fire that covered both Widen and the ugly. And in Jezebel's small, manicured hands a pair of deadly large-bore derringers had materialized.

"You had better be careful," Paddo rasped.

Jasper Kennedy had scarcely followed all this until he felt the cold, hard barrels of her weapons press into the back of his head and his shoulder.

Paddo leered at her. "You wouldn't shoot a popgun. Might hurt someone."

This was the moment she had prepared for. She had to be believed. "I will kill your employer instantly if you—or he—resist," she said evenly.

Kennedy reacted at once. "Now, now, my dear. Thee art reacting to unfortunate events—"

"I would kill you in an instant," she replied in a tone of voice that brooked no questioning.

"You might die, girlie."

"So will you."

The shot, which erupted like a cannon in the small room, seared inches from Paddo's chest, and the second crack sent a ball through Jasper Kennedy's upper arm, just as he bolted up from the chair. Acrid smoke hung in the room.

"I'm shot!" screamed Kennedy, grasping his reddening sleeve. "How could thee? How could thee?"

"Easy," she said, and tossed the empty derringer to the floor. She scooped another from her pockets.

Paddo reacted swiftly, slipping a hand back to his neck, where a throwing knife lay sheathed. But the press of hard metal into his back stopped him.

"Twitch one muscle and you go join ancestors," hissed Hip Hip.

"Wrap his wound," Ben snapped at Drago. The skinny financier leapt up and drew out his silk handkerchief.

"I'm dead, I'm dead." Jasper Kennedy moaned. "A man of peace. A Friend."

Widen wrestled the robe off the portly financier and bound the gouting wound with the kerchief.

Hip Hip's agile arm snaked around Paddo and plucked the revolver from his shoulder holster, slipped the boot knife and neck knives from their sheaths, found a derringer in his pocket, and removed his walking stick. The ugly turned beet-red.

"You are a dead man," he snapped at Hip Hip.

"Now get into that carriage out front," Ben commanded. "We'll bring your luggage to the hotel later. You'll be shot on sight if you come back."

"Thee will regret this," Jasper said. The bleeding had reddened Widen's kerchief and was barely slowed. "Get me to that quack doctor."

The financiers and Paddo Dowling were herded to the

barouche, and Paddo snaked it hastily down the slope to Pony.

"Keep an eye out for Lethbridge," Ben growled. "He's in town somewhere. The pair of them could come back."

"Next time I'll shoot to kill," said Jezebel fiercely. She opened windows, letting the night breeze pour through, purging the room not only of gunsmoke but also of toilet water and witch hazel.

Ben found Alonzo and Gilberto outside and set them to harnessing the buggy and hauling the financiers' things out of the bedrooms. In the empty maid's room where Paddo and Lethbridge had slept he found a small armory. Those things, dirks and sticks and long and short guns, and two new bullwhips, and an issue of the *Police Gazette*, he decided to keep for the time being.

In Widen's room was a feed sack full of currency and coin, and a carpetbag and two pigskin valises brimming with gold coins and bullion. Ben didn't know who that belonged to—he knew nothing of the ransacking of the bank and Louella's cache there—but he decided to keep it until he found out. Then, when everything had been loaded into the buggy, he pulled repeater rifles from his cabinet and gave one each to Hip Hip, Gilberto, and Alonzo, along with ample ammunition.

"Don't make mistakes," he said gruffly. "I'll be going in and out. Sam Stop may show up here."

Hip Hip squinted. "Maybe make big mistake," he said. "I make lots of mistake."

The brick mansion had brightened. Some oppressive pall had lifted from it.

"I'm going for a walk," Jezebel said. "I can't stand the thought of my room." She dropped the derringers into her pockets.

Ben nodded. "Don't wait up. I have things to do in town," he said. "Alonzo, you gather everything those uglies own and put it in your room. They may sneak back for it."

It was early, barely twilight, and he enjoyed the soft June air as he drove his buggy down the slope to Pony, keeping a sharp eye out for Lethbridge, who would still be armed. Paddo would rearm himself soon enough, he knew, from the small arsenal in the boot of the barouche. But he didn't really care. He parked at the hotel and told the clerk to haul everything upstairs. Lamps glowed in the two upstairs rooms overlooking the street, and he supposed Kennedy and Widen were there. Probably Doc Frede, too, looking after that flesh wound the hellcat had given Kennedy for a love token.

He left the buggy at the Goldstrike Hotel and trudged down the boardwalk to Frede's. He had to find out. A lamp illumined the front apothecary room. The door was not locked.

"Doc?" he said, but there was no response. He picked up the lamp and walked into the back room, holding it high. His heart sank. In the soft wavering light Elmer Dudley lay inert on the massive table. Frede had done nothing with him yet, and Ben saw the shredded shirt and the peppering of chest wounds. Then his eye caught another form over on the bunk, deep in shadow, and he recognized young Crane, good man, believer in things, as still as night. Young Crane, too, Ben thought. Destined for better things, for foreman and manager and maybe more. And a widow weeping and young mouths to feed. He sighed. Maybe he could help the girl, couldn't remember her name, but she was a spunky one. Yes, he'd do that even if he lost the mine. Get her on her feet.

He had the afternoon's story, then, or at least some of it, even if Frede wasn't around. He restored the lamp to its place on the counter and slipped out, staring up and down Pony's desolate street. Across the road, Spade's Mercantile hulked dark and forlorn. There was no pile of whittlings before the benches at Spade's; the wind had whipped them all away. Up a block, the brick bank sagged low in the dark and looked wrong. The night seemed chill, even though it was high summer. Down a way, he spotted lamplight at the Buffalo Hump, and faint glows below, at several of the saloons. He crossed over to the Buffalo Hump, where he'd whiled away much of his life in recent years.

It was empty, save for one familiar hulk at the bar, and a new man tended the bottles.

"Martin," he said.

Spade started. "Didn't expect you here, Ben. I thought you were all penned up in the brick pile."

"Booted 'em out," Ben said.

The bartender, a cadaverous man, approached, and Ben ordered a whiskey.

"This is Kennedy and Widen's place now. He works for them," Spade warned. "Ben, tell me quick. Are you going to make it? Meet that loan? I been holding out. Last one, I guess, thinking maybe you'll get on top. . . ."

The bartender laid the drink before Ben and waited silently for payment. Ben grumbled. Drinks had been on a tab before. Spade was silent.

"Don't know yet," said Ben. "I'm waiting for Stop."

"Saw him an hour ago, over in front of Frede's," Martin said. "Ben, I'll hang on as long as you do, fold if you do. These days I open afternoons and sit at the counter with a shotgun ready. Stubborn, I guess. Likely I'll get myself killed."

"You're doin' the right thing, Martin. Jist hang on, and we'll see how this here settles out."

Ben listened absently, wondering how he could contact Sam Stop, now that Stop's house was gone and Stop was no doubt a hunted man. That probably was where Lethbridge Dowling was that night, stalking the banker. One possibility, he thought. Elmer Dudley's house. Empty now. Stop might camp in it. . . .

The Buffalo Hump had gone gloomy. Just a few days ago there'd be a dozen or two men there on any night, and a dozen lamps shining. Now two lamps glowed, and the whole place looked sinister. It saddened Ben.

"Where's the rest?" Ben asked.

Martin shrugged. "You can guess. Bonack's left town. Pyle's here but fixing to leave. He's still got the apartment in the hotel but pays rent for it. Barteau . . . haven't seen him. Louella's still got her place, but it ain't makin' any money. Lost trade even before they hit the bank. Only business she's got is . . . uh, them two sons of yours."

"What happened to the bank?" Ben asked sharply.

Spade told him.

"Bank money. Louella's gold is up there," Ben muttered.

The door creaked, and Sam Stop slipped in, looking as kempt

as ever in his white shirt and cravat. Ben found himself faintly disappointed, as if Stop should be wearing something else.

"Found you," said Stop. He pointed to a table along the wall. "Let's sit over there. I'd prefer to watch the door."

It took only a few minutes to exchange news, with Spade filling them in about events in town.

Ben sighed. "It ain't good, Sam. No way to meet that loan."

"You wait," said Stop. "They made their last mistake."

"You want to come up and get the bank goods? Put it back in your safe?"

Stop thought a moment. "No. Not yet. What good would it do? They know the combination. You keep it. We'll get it in there later. Something I must do first."

Ben thought there was an odd, taut ring to Sam Stop's voice. "How do I get aholt of you now?"

Stop smiled. "You can't. But I'll be in touch."

With that he slipped out of the Buffalo Hump, choosing the rear door. The bartender stared.

Ben Waldorf downed his whiskey and stood. "I'll be seeing ya, Martin. Don't you go quittin' on me."

He stepped into the darkened street and walked toward his buggy at the hotel. It was splendid to be free of those pirates, if only for the moment, he thought. It was the last thought he had. The bullet caught him in the back of the head and felled him instantly.

Chapter Twenty

She didn't know she had loved him. It had never occurred to her until now. Even less had she known how she depended on him for anything. But now, in the humbling presence of death, she knew, and she desperately wished she had told him she loved him while he lived. Now it was too late. Perhaps he knew. Perhaps he had loved her, too.

She sat numbly, her pink frock askew, in Doc Frede's back room. The mortuary table could barely support its new burden, alongside Elmer Dudley. The single shot had entered the back of Ben's head and exited from the mouth. Doc had covered his head; he didn't want her to see that. But his arm hung from the table, and she stared at his big hand, with the massive, square fingers that had given direction and purpose to picks and shovels and mauls; a hand that had been as gentle upon her as it had been hard upon the unyielding rock.

"Epidemics," Doc muttered. "I cannot deal with epidemics. You shouldn't even be here."

He had a small British revolver in hand, eyeing his bolted front door with feist and fear.

She ignored him. There was a single lamp burning in the back room, making great black shadows. Still she didn't move. For the first time in her young life she felt small and crushed and afraid. The massive security of Ben's presence had vanished. The great red brick pile was nothing without his forceful presence. The derringers in her pockets were no comfort at all against the deadly force stalking the streets of Pony. She had walked here, seeing Ben Waldorf's fat sons leering and lounging against porch posts, seeing the smirk of a derbied Dowling at the hotel door. Seeing the silhouetted Drago Widen peering down into the darkened, dusty street from his lamplit window. They knew she was here, and she could only guess what her fate might be.

She heard the softest tap, not on the front door but on a rear window that was always curtained against the morbidly curious. The window opened out upon a small alleyway separating the next building, Hazel Folsom's dressmaking parlor. Jezebel froze. Doc Frede heard it, too, and stalked fiercely toward it but stayed to one side, casting no shadow on the curtain.

"Who's that?" he demanded.

"Stop."

"How do I know that?"

"You don't."

Doc considered. Then, "Lift the sash and come in. If you aren't Stop, you'll be dead." He stood to one side, his revolver ready.

The sash creaked upward slowly, and Stop's head emerged from the curtains, then the rest of him, until he stood in the lamplight. Doc and Jezebel stared. Something had transformed Sam Stop into an unfathomable stranger. He had indeed the same black hair and browned face and hands. But now he wore a midnight-blue flannel shirt that matched his dark jeans. And at his waist hung a dull black gun belt and two worn black leather holsters, with the grips of two large revolvers, also dull and worn, projecting up from them. It was not a belt with cartridge loops on it, or shells glinting in the night light; but just a worn black belt holding two deadly weapons.

Nor was that all. Something had changed in the man himself. The amiable banker had vanished, and the body hidden by the soft lines of business suits seemed edged and harsh and lean now. But it was his face that arrested them. Stop's familiar dark features were there, but his expression had changed. He was a different man, lean and taut and hard, with a cold deadliness in his eye that pulled Jezebel's breath away.

"Someone has to do it," he said harshly. "I waited too long. I could have stopped it before . . . this." He stared at the quiet form of Ben Waldorf. For the briefest moment something sad filled his eyes, and then they hardened again.

"Why did you wait? If you could have stopped them?" Doc asked quietly.

"Because . . . I hate this. I thought the world . . ." He left unsaid whatever he intended to say. His glinting eyes fixed on her. "You are in mortal danger."

"I know that," she said. "I'm armed." She had her parasol, too, the one with the weapon grip. "I'll take care of myself."

He shook his head impatiently. "I've no time to get you back up the hill. This'll have to do. Doc, can you shoot that?"

Havelock Frede looked annoyed. " I usually don't start epidemics," he said testily.

"Well, start one now," Stop said. He glared at them until they shrank from his gaze. "I'll be back," he said. With that he slipped through the window and into the black alley.

"Stop, be careful!" she cried.

He vanished as silently as he had come. Doc slid the sash down and fastened it—not that a fastened sash would stop anyone willing to break glass and enter.

"I guess we'd better blow out the lamp. I trust you'll manage, being here in pitch dark with the dead."

"I will watch from the front window," she said. "There's a little light in the street, and I can see who's coming."

Doc nodded and turned down the wick. Jezebel settled herself on the bench beneath the front window of the darkened apothecary shop, annoyed and frightened and despairing all at once. Doc hovered somewhere in the black bowels of the building.

The bench felt hard, but she settled down there, near the front door, listening to the relentless ticking of Doc Frede's wall clock.

When it chimed the quarter hour, she jumped. It made her think of time. She had never thought of time before.

Her eyes became accustomed to the dim light, and she studied the street intently. Well down the slope were a few pricks of light from the saloons. Up the street, a faint glow from the Goldstrike Hotel. And the rest was dark and starlit on a moonless night. Still, she made out shapes in the dirt road, human passage up and down; a dark bulk loitering under a porch pole. A heavy form which she supposed was one of Ben Waldorf's sons. If that fat hulk edged toward her window, she'd shoot him, kill him before his slimy hands pawed her. Then that hulk seemed to collapse like an accordion, and she heard the faint clatter of a weapon falling into the street.

Shots startled her, harsh racketing sounds. White muzzle flashes. One nearby, loud and violent. Sharp cracks and the low boom of a shotgun; she knew those sounds. She feared for Stop. Why was it? Stop was her salvation now—only Stop. God protect Stop! she thought, half mouthing the words. More shots, and the shatter of glass behind her. A bullet had struck the rear window, she thought.

"Doc?" she said softly. There was a soft thump in the rear. "Doc?"

Then an iron arm clasped her in a prison grip, and a rude hand pawed into her skirt pockets and yanked out one derringer, then the other.

She struggled, bit the vicious arm, and was slapped hard for it.

"You had better come quiet, missy. Mr. Kennedy wants you. He's taking you with him tonight after a bit o' business is done."

"I'm not going anywhere," she snapped.

Lethbridge Dowling chuckled. "You'll be living a soft life. Richer than any life old Waldorf gave you. Only, you got to enjoy it. If you fights it, you is dead or maimed up like an old hag—or maybe sold off to a fancy house. That's what you were, anyway, missy, Ben Waldorf's whore."

"Where's Doc Frede?" she demanded.

"Temporary put to sleep," he said, chortling. "He'll be busy in the morning. Have to plant Stop, along with the rest of the pile."

Jezebel's heart lurched. "Is Stop dead?" she asked softly.

"Good as dead," Lethbridge replied. "All duded up in six-guns. Banker wearing six-guns." He laughed. Then, harshly, "Are you coming peaceful, or do I drag you?"

"Let me get my parasol," she said. "It's pink," she added. "It goes with my frock."

He chortled. "Some hellcat," he said.

She walked meekly ahead of him, waving her pink parasol in the night, aware of his massive presence just behind her. The shooting had stopped. There was a hulk in the street.

"One of Waldorf's boys," Lethbridge said. It amused him. He didn't bother to pick up the rifle lying nearby.

She had one shot, she thought wildly. She didn't care about the Dowlings. When she pulled the shaft of the parasol off its deadly handle, her shot would be aimed at Jasper Kennedy's eyes.

She mounted the hotel steps and entered the lobby. There was a lamp wavering at the registration desk but no clerk. Another lamp softly illuminated the stairs and the corridor above. He prodded her up the stairs, then around to the front room on the left, and opened the door.

Jasper Kennedy was still in his chesterfield robe, but now there were a pair of holes in its sleeve, with white bandaging poking through. He looked drawn. Drago Widen sat easily in the other chair, amused by something.

Jasper's eyes raked her painfully. "Welcome, my dear Jezebel," he said. "Thee may sit there on the bed. We must wait a little bit, and then we'll be off."

"For what?" she demanded.

"Why, for that demented banker, Stop," he said. "I have decided to give thee one last chance. Thee are too beautiful and spirited to toss away meanly."

She laughed crazily, and the ring of it upset him. She glanced around. The door behind was closed, and Lethbridge Dowling had vanished. She thought to shoot him then and there, but Drago Widen watched her closely and with evident disgust. He had his Bible in hand.

"Thee are sole owner of a great mine," Jasper said.

"How do you know that?" she replied sharply.

"Come, come. He'd scarcely will it to those boys. I'm going to help thee manage it. But I'm afraid thou won't own it for long, since Drago and I have been forced to acquire it in payment of debt."

She wasn't listening. Her only thought was of Stop. She drifted to the window and stood where she could stare into the gloomy street.

"Thee shouldn't stand near the window," Jasper warned.

"I do what I choose."

The night was a ticking clock wound so tightly that it barely ticked at all. She made out a dark form edging along the far boardwalk. It was a bulky form, and the blackness at its head suggested a derby . . . or Stop? It was hard to tell. It made her heart thud. Then the form slipped into the inkiness under a storefront porch roof. On top of the roof, crouched at its far edge, was another dark form, leaner . . . Stop!

"Kill him," she whispered.

"Thee entertains unladylike thoughts," Jasper said reprovingly.

She didn't hear. The bulkier form slid out from under the far side of the roofed boardwalk, and the form on top sprang down, landing on the back of the other. There was a thud she could hear even from her window, and a flash of metal, and one form lay inert in the dust. Who? she wondered. Oh, God, who? A thinner, taller figure crouched, and then stood slowly.

"Stop!" she cried. She was sure one Dowling was dead or unconscious.

A rifle cracked from up the slope somewhere, and Stop spun and fell, and she could dimly see him writhing on the ground, just feet from the other hulk. Then he lay still.

"No!" she cried. "No!"

"Thee really shouldn't carry on so, my dear. Thee shall learn some manners soon, I imagine."

She glanced back toward Jasper, who sat easily in his armchair. The lamp had been dimmed to its lowest wick. Drago Widen had set aside his Bible and was whispering something that sounded like scripture.

It was all over, she thought. They'd shot him. Now they'd kill him if he wasn't already dead. Even as she thought it she saw the heavy bulk approach cautiously, the rifle pointed directly at Stop. A flash and a crack, and the bulky stalker folded up and thudded into the street. Stop struggled up, clutching his side, and careened off into a black alley. Alive! Wounded! But no match at all for the other Dowling, wherever he was—or the two financiers, for that matter.

Then the terrible silence settled, taut and cruel. Nothing happened. No shadowy passage through the street. The minutes stretched, and Jezebel peered desperately into the night, wanting to see something, anything. But the shadows brought no news. Then the heavy boom of a shotgun. But Stop didn't have a shotgun; he wore revolvers! They had finished him off, she thought desolately. Still, the brittle silence stretched on. Ten minutes, twenty. A half hour elapsed, and she thought it was a whole night.

"Well, Drago, shall we pack?" There was a delicious pleasure in Jasper's voice.

"Oh, we may as well wait until the Dowlings report," Drago said. "The Good Lord works his will slowly."

Jezebel thought about Ben, lying dead in Doc Frede's back room, the life snuffed from the great, rollicking bear of a man who had lived strong and was gentle. She thought about old, brave Elmer Dudley and about the young miner, Crane, and then about God. Or, rather, why God seemed to be on the side of these two men who invoked his name so often. What was God that he should let good people be slaughtered? She had never thought about God before.

Then at last a light tap. It startled them all.

"Who's there?" demanded Drago. A small, silvery revolver had materialized in his hand, and Jezebel noted another in Jasper's hand.

"Lethbridge," came the voice, and the door creaked open. Even in that low lamplight he looked wild and demented. His black derby had vanished. He peered around violently, glaring into shadows.

"Me brother . . . Paddo. Stop got him. Dead or injured, I don't know. And no help, with Frede out cold—"

"Calm thyself, my good man. Where's Stop?"

Lethbridge's lips curled back. "He's finished. Bleedin' to death. Slipped into some hideyhole, but he's done."

Jasper looked elated. "Why, then, it's done. Find him and finish him, just to be sure, and we'll be off."

"You isn't gonna wait for Paddo? If the lad lives?"

"Why, we'll make sure Frede gives him the best care," Jasper said.

"That ain't enough," said Lethbridge.

Something sagged in Jezebel. Stop had failed. She was a prisoner. Literally a prisoner. Born free, a citizen, but a prisoner here. She would be taken where she would not go. Mauled, disfigured, forced into a vile life if she resisted. It hit her then, what Ben had given, what Ben meant. If she had stayed with her increasingly drunken daddy, it might have been bad, in the end, almost like . . . this. Ben had rescued her. Oh, Ben . . .

In an hour or two she'd be bundled into a black coach, surrounded by three strong males, maybe four. And then—in the railroad coach, probably—made to submit. She felt the weakness of her sex, born smaller and lighter than the other. She had been aware of it for a long time, and her hellcatting was the defense she had raised out in the hard world of her daddy's shoe wagon.

The acrid smell reached her the same moment it caught the others. Smoke.

"What the hell?" Lethbridge snarled and yanked open the door to the corridor. Smoke billowed in, setting them to coughing. She peered out the window, and now the whole street danced and stuttered in an eerie orange light. There were three bulky forms illumined now in the dung and muck.

"The joint's burning!" Lethbridge exclaimed. "Stop done it."

He laughed carelessly. "You get packed up, gents, and we'll git on down. Stop's dead. This light'll shine in every hideyhole in town. What a dumb mistake!"

The back of the hotel was aflame, and crackling high now. Except for the smoke rolling through it, the front remained habitable. Two other guests and the Pyles poured out into the street, shouting. Leisurely the financiers stuffed clothing into valises, and Lethbridge shouldered them down to the small lobby, keeping a sharp eye out for Stop.

"You can have the hostler harness the trotters," Lethbridge said. "I'll finish Stop in ten minutes."

Jezebel coughed. The smoke grew thick and harsh and hurt her lungs, and she wanted to flee. At last, almost too late, she thought, they threaded down to the lobby, then out on to the porch. Lethbridge had vanished. Grumbling, Drago dragged the heavy valises and trunks out into the street while Jasper, still in his chesterfield robe, watched.

The whole rear of the hotel blazed now. Orange flame roared higher into the black night, thundering so loud that Jezebel could scarcely hear the cries of men. There were a few in the street now, braving the light. Only minutes before they had cowered in their homes, hearing shots in the dark and knowing one kind of life in Pony had died and another had started. Some formed a bucket brigade, pouring out pails on the roofs of nearby buildings. The Goldstrike Hotel was a loss, and no one tried to save it.

Even in the street the searing heat bit at Jezebel, flushing her face. She wished they would retreat farther from the collapsing hotel. She thought she heard shots, a shotgun booming again, but she could scarcely tell them from the boom and crack of the inferno.

Then something plucked at Drago Widen, standing a few feet from her. One moment he was standing; the next his knees folded, and he keeled face-first into the filth of the road and didn't move. She screamed. Jasper gasped. He grabbed her hand and dragged her into the shadow of an alleyway across the street and out of the weird orange light of the howling fire.

Then she saw Stop upslope, his arm clutched hard to his side, his shirt black and slick, limping horribly, gulping for air and not getting enough. Orange light flicked and darted off his tan face, making it grotesque. He was in the open now, not a shadow to protect him. He was alive, but for how long? She dreaded the final crack, the unseen blow that would smash him into the dung. And then, down the slope and across the street, she saw Lethbridge, lounging easily in shadow under a porched storefront, gliding with the catlike grace of a jaguar. He, too, was breathless, but grinning as he stalked. He had discarded his sawed-off shotgun, and a small deadly revolver glinted in his muscled hand.

It was the end, she knew. Stop didn't stand a chance.

"Stop," she cried. "He's there!"

Jasper's manicured hand caught her and yanked her back into the shadows.

"Thee must learn," he said sharply.

But Stop already knew where Lethbridge was, and he struggled ahead, straight toward the ugly, and even in the dancing orange light his bloodless face looked pale. He was on the brink of his own darkness.

Far up the street, in what had been Bonack's Livery, the black barouche stood harnessed and waiting. The hostler had finished his task and fled to the safety of his office. She stared at it, the conveyance that would carry her away forcibly.

Stop reached the center of the road at last and stood there in the amber light, panting visibly. He seemed not to have the strength to go farther. For long, heart-stopping moments nothing happened. Then she saw Lethbridge glide ahead again, deep in the shadows of the porch, edging ever closer. Within range now but wanting to get much closer. And still he stalked, his teeth gleaming yellow in trapped light. Then she saw he had two revolvers, one in each hand. What chance had Stop against a fusillade?

Stop stared. "You made a mistake," he said.

Lethbridge leapt forward the last fifty feet, a dark blur in the tricky light, and fired methodically, dancing sideways with each shot. Even Jezebel, who knew little of such things, could see some finely honed mastery of arms and war at work, terrible in its effect. The second shot caught Stop at the base of his neck and spun him. He staggered to one knee, and as he fell, he fired just once. Lethbridge dropped as if poleaxed, a blue hole in his forehead. Then Stop slowly sank.

"Stop!" she screamed, and raced toward him.

"Don't go, I say. Don't go," Jasper roared. He raced along behind her, his robe flapping, his heavy form puffing. He stopped and shot, a small, sharp crack. At her? At Stop? She didn't know. She whirled, yanked the shaft of her pink parasol off its handle, and whirled to face him. He stood just behind her, puffing, aiming not at Stop but at her. She lifted the derringer that had been the parasol handle, steadied her wavering hands as blood pulsed through her, peered down its short barrel into Jasper's face, and squeezed. A crack, a look of utter surprise.

"Jezebel," he gasped, astonished.

And fell heavily onto the earth.

Chapter Twenty-One

"Stop," she begged, "don't go. Please don't go."

He moved slowly. He was pale and fragile now, and his banker suits no longer fit him. Wearily he lifted the panniers and hitched them down on the packhorse.

She stood on Elmer Dudley's porch watching, hoping that her awning-striped dress, which caught the lavender of her eyes, would fetch his attention. But she knew it wouldn't.

"Why are you going?" she demanded.

He looked exhausted. Six weeks of Doc Frede's care and bed rest had scarcely brought him back.

He stared at her. There was a grayness still beneath the fading tan of his face. "Once they know, it isn't the same," he said. "It's never the same after."

"What's not the same?" she demanded. "You're a hero."

"That's it exactly," he said.

"I like you, Stop."

He put a foot in his stirrup and slowly drew himself onto his bay. Then he smiled, and for an instant there was the old flash of life in his eyes.

"Ben hid the gold in the bottom of my barn cistern. Have Amos Galb get it," he said, touching heels to his bay.

"I like you, Stop," she whispered desolately, and watched him trot down the lane.